GENESIS

Book 3 of the Shylmahn Trilogy

DAVID R. BESHEARS

Greybeard Publishing

GENESIS

Greybeard Publishing
P.O. Box 480
McCleary, WA 98557-0480

ISBN 978-1-947231-28-3
(hardcover edition)

Chapter One

The transport shuttle slowly descended onto the private landing pad. The side door opened a few moments later and EsJen started down the ramp. A sleek probe followed her out, hovering dutifully beside her, as two escort hurried ahead toward the modest building that served as the center of operations for the Northwest Province. They held the double doors open as EsJen climbed up the steps and entered the complex.

Several Shylmahn were in the foyer. All were dressed in traditional brown shirt and pants. EsJen acknowledged their greetings with a terse nod of the head and continued across the room, passing through another door that was being held open for her.

In addition to serving as the provincial command center, the facility also contained a set of offices that had been set aside for her use as leader of the Shylmahn. Her meeting room was at the far end of the hallway. She reached the doors before her escort could get to them, dismissed them with a wave of a hand as she walked across the room. She turned smoothly about and sat in the only chair, the probe moving into position to one side. She paused a moment, then placed a hand on a panel that was set into the right arm of the chair. A holo-table rose up from the floor in front of her. A holo-image flickered to life above the table.

Two Chehnon vehicles were visible, as seen from above, traveling across a meadow.

"Where are they now?" asked EsJen.

"Just leaving the eastern boundary of the province, entering open terrain," said ShahnTahr. The probe glided around to EsJen's left, moved around and hovered beside the holo-image.

"I don't like this," EsJen said sharply.

"That is understandable," said ShahnTahr. The artificial intelligence had been EsJen's constant companion and advisor for more than five years, since the day she had first taken on the task as leader of the Shylmahn; since the establishment of the truce between Shylmahn and Chehnon; since the day the TohPeht-ShahnTahr entity, that strange being that had once been TohPeht and had once been ShahnTahr, had become one; had then left on a personal quest for what it referred to as 'life experience'.

The ShahnTahr that had stayed behind, the pure intelligence that had guided Shylmahn society across thousands of years even as the entity evolved, read EsJen as it also continued to take in the readings coming from the probe they had left behind to follow the Chehnon vehicles.

"They are most likely from Carolyn's Keep and are now returning there," it said.

"Oh, they're Carolyn's all right." She watched as the vehicles came fully into the open and started across a wide plain. "Recall the probe," she stated flatly.

With that, the holo-image above the table spun about and went black. The holo-table lowered until the surface was again level with the floor.

The companion probe, the most sophisticated ever designed by Shahn-Tahr, eased nearer to EsJen until it was where he had long ago learned was the most comfortable distance for her.

"The occupants of those vehicles know that they have been observed," it said.

"Yes."

"You will respond?"

"I have to."

"Of course," said ShahnTahr. The synthetic voice was smooth and filled with nuance. Over the years, it had learned to use tone and gradation to greatest effect. "To not respond would in fact be interpreted as a response."

"I can't let it go," EsJen's words were almost a growl. "The violation of our borders is a serious breach of the truce."

"Carolyn Britton knows this," said ShahnTahr. "I must therefore wonder as to her true intent."

EsJen glanced up at the probe, almost as if she could read an expression on the plastic surface. "Something more than scavenging?" she asked.

"Perhaps."

"Assessing our defenses?"

"Perhaps," ShahnTahr repeated. "Or she could be attempting to determine the level of your resolve."

"In what way?" she asked. But she already knew. Carolyn Britton must have realized the possibility that those she sent into the province might be seen. She may have deemed it likely.

ShahnTahr asked what it considered to be obvious. "Might an underlying motive for entering restricted territory have been to observe your reaction?"

EsJen thought about that. "Carolyn is intelligent," she said finally, her voice measured. "More so than most Chehnon."

"Historical evidence would suggest that she is driven as much by emotion as by logic," said ShahnTahr.

"That works for her."

"Such a path is not recommended," ShahnTahr said hesitantly.

"Yes, yes." EsJen leaned back in her chair. "I understand only too well, my friend."

EsJen thought ShahnTahr's assessment was probably correct. Carolyn was pushing boundaries, testing her. To what end, she didn't know. It could mean trouble. It probably did mean trouble.

It shouldn't take NehLoc long to discover what the Chehnon were up to.

But Carolyn's reason for the blatant violation of the border was irrelevant to EsJen's immediate response. Short term, it didn't matter. The response would necessarily be the same.

This wasn't going to help matters with Michael. EsJen knew that the young leader of the Chehnon had been walking a fine line between keeping the human population content and maintaining a civil working relationship with the Shylmahn. It was for this reason that EsJen had on occasion made compromises with Michael; so long as it had been clear to her that he was trying to resolve a situation that was proving insoluble.

This would not be one of those occasions. She would not compromise. She could not appear to be giving ground.

Something had to be done.

§

Carolyn Britton stepped down from the wooden porch that fronted her office and started across the main yard. The quad was several hundred feet square, open to the sky and bordered by low buildings on three sides. Straight ahead was a high, heavy-timbered wall, and set into its center the front gate of the keep.

A small group had gathered around the two vehicles that had just arrived. Carolyn's assistant Steven, having met the team coming in, stepped away from them and smiled in her direction.

"Well, you have what you asked for," he said. *For what it's worth.*

Carolyn nodded absently and approached the team leader. "Mr. Jackson... any problems?"

"No ma'am," he said. "You are now the proud owner of the contents of two optometrist offices."

"Good work. Did you run into any of 'em?"

"No sign of Shillies while we were in the territory." Jackson was a brawny, middle-aged man, the leader of one of Carolyn's special units. "Coming out, we spotted one of their shuttles just as we crossed the border. It cut loose a probe that followed us for a bit. That was it."

"All right," said Carolyn. "See the equipment gets over to building 6." With that, Jackson was dismissed. Carolyn turned her attention back to Steven. "Our other matter," she stated flatly.

"A couple of minutes out," said Steven.

Carolyn started again toward the gate. The two guards opened it as she approached. A yellow, grassy plain spread away from the keep, with a narrow dirt road cutting across the landscape from the gate out to the horizon.

Carolyn stopped after ten paces and looked up at the sky. It was pale blue, and but for a few scattered clouds was empty.

"Any minute," said Steven.

"So you said."

"So I did." Steven surveyed the sky another moment, then glanced back at the gate. "I'm not sure what we're going to do with all that eye doctor equipment. We don't have an eye doctor that knows how to use it."

"So keep looking for one," said Carolyn. "They can't all be dead."

Steven frowned. "And if they are? All dead, I mean?"

"Then start studying." Carolyn reached into a pocket and pulled out a pair of reading glasses. She handed them to Steven. "Get me something stronger out of stores. These aren't doing it for me. I can hardly read a damn thing."

Steven put the glasses into his pocket and said nothing. Carolyn was in a real mood.

The two waited in silence.

Steven was closing in on thirty years old. He had never known a world without the Shylmahn; without supply shortages. He had never known a world that had eye doctors in every mall; never knew a time with grocery stores on every corner.

But Carolyn had. She was in her fifties now, with aches and pains and failing eyes. She remembered the *before time*. She remembered convenience stores and cable television and movie theaters... and eye doctors.

She heard the experimental aircraft before she saw it. It was a sound like nothing she had ever heard before; a hollow humming noise with the hint of a breezy sound.

"There it is," said Steven, pointing.

Carolyn saw it then. It looked small and fragile. It was tubular in shape, about thirty feet long, the fuselage not more than six or seven feet wide. It had stubby wings, probably not designed to help much with lift; not that she knew anything about aerodynamics; about as much as she knew about optometry. Maybe they helped that weird looking tail with guidance...

"I don't know how that thing can stay in the air," she said.

"Shillie technology."

She gave him a withering look. "I know that, Steven." The aircraft was a hybrid of human and Shillie technology. Humans couldn't rely on Shillie energy pods for power, so the Phoenix Labs had come up with their own version of the generators.

This was the flyer's first long distance flight, following months of shorter test runs down south.

"Sure is an odd looking thing," said Steven.

"About what I would expect them to come up with."

The aircraft flew overhead, swung around and came back. It slowed and finally stopped, hung in midair about fifty feet up and a hundred feet ahead of Carolyn. After a handful of seconds, it began to descend. When it was still a dozen feet or so up, the tall grass beneath it started to flutter and twist. The flyer continued downward and settled on the ground.

Carolyn grumbled. "Let's greet our guests."

They were halfway to the craft when a narrow side door opened midway along the fuselage. Jason Britton stepped out, a big grin wrinkling up his weathered face.

"Hello, Sis," he called out. He stepped quickly toward her and gave her a hug.

"Hey, Jase," Carolyn droned.

Joseph climbed down out of the aircraft next. His smile wasn't as broad and bright, but it was just as genuine. He approached Carolyn without saying a word and wrapped his arms around her.

"Hello, Joey," she sighed, once they had pulled apart.

"Good to see you, Carolyn." Joseph held a hand out to Steven. "Steven... it's been a long time."

"Yes, sir." Steven shook Joseph's hand. "A couple of years, I think."

Carolyn was looking beyond her brothers at the strange flyer that had brought them.

"Interesting toy," she said.

"Quite," said Jason.

Carolyn took a couple of steps toward the craft. "What do you plan on doing with it?"

"This one's a prototype, one of a kind. We've been using it to work out the kinks."

"You flew a test prototype with kinks a thousand miles?"

A slow, deliberate grin. "We have most of the bugs sorted out."

Carolyn grumbled under her breath, turned away shaking her head. "Couple of crazy old farts." She called out over her shoulder, "Come on then, now that you're here."

"This way, please," Steven urged, following Carolyn but looking back at Jason and Joseph. He sounded as though he was trying to soften the edge to his boss's tone.

"Right behind you, my man," said Jason, still wearing his weathered grin.

Up ahead, Carolyn continued to grumble. "You made it here alive, after all. I guess I can listen to what ya' got to say."

Jason winked at Steven, spoke past him to his sister. "Much appreciated, Sis."

"Yeah, yeah," Carolyn droned. "It'll no doubt cost me as much as every other time I let you through my gates."

Jason leaned toward Joseph, who was following silently beside his brother. "And such fine gates they are," he mumbled. "Wouldn't you say?"

"No comment on them one way or the other, brother."

With that they passed through the threshold and entered the keep. It was more of a fort than a keep. The perimeter walls were twenty feet high, constructed of rough timbers leaning slightly outward. The open plaza was bordered with low structures, and behind the structures directly opposite was a neighborhood of squat buildings. These lined a single dirt roadway that opened to the plaza just to the right of Carolyn's office, wound around the back of the keep, and emptied back into the plaza just to thc left of her office.

They followed Carolyn up onto the porch and through the narrow door. Inside, a desk took up a third of the small front room, a table and chairs took up the rest. A pair of windows let in outside light and a closed door led to the back of the building.

A large map covered much of one wall. Joseph noted that it was a detailed diagram of the northwest, including the Shylmahn's Northwest Province, within which were flagged numerous long-abandoned human cities and towns.

"Have a seat," said Carolyn. She sat behind her desk and leaned back, watching her brothers' movements. Once Jason and Joseph had taken their seats at the table, she looked up at Steven. "Would you mind putting on some tea?"

"Of course," said Steven.

"It's not bad," she told her brothers. "Not great, but not bad."

"I'm sure it will be amazing, as always," said Jason.

Carolyn sighed noisily. "What do you want, Jason?"

"Same thing we always want when we come knocking, Sis."

"My help. Yeah. I got that from the message. What form might this assistance take?"

Jason looked over at Joseph. Joseph motioned over his shoulder at the map on the wall behind him.

"We need you to get us to one of those little flags," he said.

The old train consisted of two passenger cars and an engine with its tender car loaded with cords of seasoned wood. The train wasn't much really, but was still a beautiful sight as it sat there in the Freetown train station, ready to take on passengers.

Miriam Foster stood on the wooden station platform, keeping far enough back that she could take in the full view, leaning forward on her cane. There was a small travel bag at her feet.

She watched an old man dressed in a faded, striped cap climb down from the engine. He scratched at his scruffy gray beard as he spoke to a young man barely out of his teens. Miriam couldn't hear what the old engineer was saying, but by his movements she could see that he was instructing the boy in the ways of the steam locomotive.

The engineer and his apprentice; the old guy wouldn't be around forever, and there were very few people left who knew how to run and maintain a locomotive.

She turned at the sound of a group gathering on the platform outside the passenger cars. Some were already climbing up into the train, most didn't appear to be in that much of a hurry. For the moment they were content to simply take it all in.

Miriam heard a pair of feet shuffling behind her, recognized the sound as belonging to Craig Warren, long-time mayor of Freetown.

"The place won't be the same without you, Miriam." Craig stepped up beside her. Now in his early forties, he wasn't much younger than Miriam, but young enough that he had very little memory of the time before the Shylmahn.

"I shouldn't be gone that long," she said.

"Long enough. And you never know. We can't afford to lose you." Freetown had changed a lot in the last five years. With the truce had come the ability for the citizens of the town to live out in the open. Freetown was the capital of the North American Province, and Craig also served as the governor of the province. After a bumpy beginning, he had taken to the position. "Besides, we'll all miss you."

"I appreciate the sentiment, Craig, though I have to wonder where it's coming from."

"Quite genuine, I assure you." Craig looked around them, nodded appreciatively. "The station came together quite well, don't you think?"

"They did a wonderful job." The train station had only been completed for a few weeks, and it still had the smell of freshly cut lumber. The construction crew had moved on to the next stop along the northwest train route. The team was a small town all to itself, bringing with it all the equipment, materials, tents and wagons and supplies they needed.

Craig and Miriam watched in silence as the group of passengers continued to file onto the train. Those seeing them off searched the windows of the passenger cars for where their family and friends were settling in.

The engineer moved back to the step jutting out from the side of the engine and waited to catch Craig's attention.

"Looks like he's about ready," said Craig.

Miriam picked up her bag, pushed off on her cane and started toward the nearest passenger car. Craig followed beside her, leaned near as she climbed up onto the step.

"You be sure that Michael... you know..."

"I know," she said softly.

She disappeared inside the passenger car and Craig took three slow steps back to the center of the wooden platform. He saw her settle in beside one of the windows just as the train lurched forward. There was a loud clattering as each of the cars settled into position.

Annie Gomez hurried out onto the platform and came to a shuffling stop next to Craig.

"Damn," she grumbled. "I wanted to say goodbye."

Craig turned about and started away. "If it's any consolation, I don't think her mind is anywhere near here." He glanced once in Annie's direction as she followed him out of the train station and down the steps to the main walkway leading to the outer village. "How's the boy?"

Freetown's medical facility had moved from the one room in Annie's house to a six room center in the heart of the Inner Village. She now had two assistants working with her, but Annie was still the community doctor.

"He'll pull through," she said. Willie McKinney had taken an unplanned nose dive off the third level terrace while repairing the railing.

"Good to hear." Craig stopped and turned toward the outer perimeter. The sound of the train's whistle rolled across the open terrain and over the high walls that still bordered the Outer Village.

"Hey," said Annie. "Miriam will be all right."

Craig sighed. "I suppose so."

Annie smiled knowingly. "It's the rest of us you're really worried about."

Craig returned Annie's smile with a warm smile of his own. "No, no," he said. "We'll be fine. I'm sure we'll be fine."

"Michael does know what he's doing."

With that, Craig's warm smile turned to more of a lighthearted grin. "Does he?"

"All right," said Annie. "Maybe *know* is too strong a word."

Craig's grin eased to a frown. "Do any of us?"

Miriam was lulled to sleep by the gentle rocking of the train car and the dull vibration of the heavy wheels rolling along the tracks; this in spite of the excited chatter of her fellow travelers. It all became background noise to her, a muffled, hollow roar of white noise pushing against her ears.

Some of the passengers would be getting off at New Beginning, the community that Ethan Perry had established soon after the truce with the Shylmahn. It had prospered, as Freetown had prospered, and Miriam was glad of it. The last thing she wanted was for Ethan and his followers to return to Freetown and start stirring up trouble all over again.

Most of the other passengers would be leaving the train at the growing administrative community of Garden City, home of the governing council representing humans and where Michael was headquartered, though a few would be continuing further on, some going as far as Phoenix, southern-most destination for the train.

Travel had become increasingly common since the truce, but it remained a difficult proposition. Train travel was slowly changing all that. The north-south route was almost complete, connecting Metcalf in the north to Phoenix in the south, and all points in between. A few short east-west legs had also already been laid down, with workable engines pulling flatbeds to transport supplies from the main line, with an occasional passenger car.

Miriam was jostled awake at the first stop after Freetown, little more than a crossroads out on the open prairie about an hour out. The construction team had put up a small wooden building so that passengers could wait for their train protected from the weather.

A man and woman waited now on the open deck, walked to the forward car as soon as the train stopped. No one got off, and the train pulled away as soon as the couple was aboard.

Miriam heard the man in the seat in front of her comment to his companion that there seemed to be a lot more vegetation at the station than when they had last passed through.

"It looks like they're making a real effort; landscaping, even way out here. Times are certainly changing."

Oh, yes, thought Miriam. *Changing... most definitely changing.*

She dozed off again, and slept until a young woman came through the car handing out sandwiches.

Joseph stepped out the door of the small cabin that he and Jason had been provided during their stay at Carolyn's Keep. He sat down on the small wooden stoop. It was early evening, the sun had set and a cool breeze was working its down the narrow, shack-lined street.

Jason followed him out and had to step around him.

"No worries, Joey," he said. "She'll analyze and then analyze some more, and then she'll join us."

"We should have told her."

Jason's expression tightened slightly. "No, no, no... I don't think so."

"She doesn't take being lied to very well."

"Omission. Not the same thing."

"Exactly the same thing." Joseph rested his forearms on his knees, stared down at the ground beneath his feet. "You know damn well it is."

Jason stared thoughtfully at his brother. Joseph's shoulders were slumped forward, the weight of his upper body bearing heavily on his knees, his wavy hair falling in front of his face.

Joseph had never handled this sort of thing well. It wasn't in his nature.

It was, however, in Jason's.

"You let me deal with this," he said. "I can handle Carolyn."

"I don't like it."

"I know." Jason grinned. "Hey... weird, isn't it? She trusts me, and you're the one on her shit list."

They both knew that it wasn't that she trusted Jason. Hell, she didn't trust him one bit; but she *understood* him. She knew what to expect with him.

But Joseph... she had never forgiven Joseph for the way he had manipulated her, and everyone else, in his backdoor dealings with the Shillies in coming up with this truce.

Now this. It was the same damn thing all over again. They were using her. And she knew it.

"She has a right to know."

"That may be true," agreed Jason. "But we would risk losing her help. We can't have that."

Joseph rose slowly to his feet, stepped beside Jason and leaned back against the wall of the shack. "Jason, you both have a better chance of surviving this if she knows that we're playing the Shillies."

Jason's expression turned hard. "We've been working for months to make her their focus. If she's not in, we risk losing it all. That is unacceptable. I'll tell her whatever it takes to get her on that flyer."

Carolyn stood before the map hanging in her office. She was staring sharply at one of the tiny flags.

Some... *thing*, some artifact, that Joseph had stashed away years ago was hidden under that pin; something so important that it was worth risking all their lives to bring out of the province.

At least, that's what they said.

What a load of crap.

What the hell are they up to?

The pin with the little flag on it wasn't talking.

"Carolyn?" Steven stood in the doorway leading to the back room.

"What?" Carolyn grumbled. She glared at the little flag. *Talk to me, damn you.*

"Can you trust them?" he asked.

"No," she sighed. "I can't."

"But you're going anyway," he stated calmly.

"Whatever they're up to, it's important."

"I don't doubt that."

Carolyn turned away from the map. She looked side-glance at Steven as she returned to her desk. "I'll bitch about it, and I'll bitch about it some more, but in the end..."

"You'll give in to them."

"Yeah... but they'll have to give me more than they have so far," she said, matter-of-factly. "Jason knows that."

"How about they give you the truth?"

"Fat chance of that."

Chapter Two

EsJen sat in her chair and watched in silence as NehLoc circled the holo-table, calmly studying the recording of the Chehnon vehicle leaving the province.

A matter such as this would under normal circumstances be the responsibility of someone well below that of her director of security. But this was an extraordinary situation. The Chehnon that had violated the truce were Carolyn Britton's people, not simple scavengers.

The holo-image went dark, the table lowered into the floor. NehLoc turned to EsJen.

"I see," he stated simply.

"Our response must be measured, but it must be resolute."

"This Chehnon has been troublesome from the very beginning, and her actions since the establishment of the truce have grown increasingly antagonistic."

EsJen nodded solemnly. She noted that NehLoc made no attempt to push it further. He would wait, let her come to the same conclusion as he regarding Carolyn. They each knew exactly where the other stood when it came to all matters Chehnon; the Britton family in particular.

But EsJen would have to bear the political consequences of wherever they took this matter. Not that NehLoc himself considered the relationship between Shylmahn and Chehnon to be political. For him, the Chehnon were little more than a natural resource of this new world, albeit a troublesome one.

"I do not want this to weaken Michael's position with the Chehnon," EsJen said at last.

"That may prove difficult." Any forceful action they took would undoubtedly generate howls of indignation from the disgruntled. NehLoc knew the Chehnon mind better than most, perhaps better than did EsJen. He could see where this might lead. He, unlike EsJen, would not mind at all if it did take them down that path.

But he knew that EsJen wanted to make this coexistence with these creatures work, and he had come to respect both her intelligence and her judgment. He would do what he could to support her in her efforts, so long as those efforts did not threaten the Shylmahn.

"A quarantine of the Keep," he suggested. "No vehicles in or out. Appropriate, considering their offense."

EsJen considered this. "A measured response," she acceded.

"Quite reasonable."

"But no violence, NehLoc, unless there is no other option."

"As you wish." If he could do this for EsJen, it would show the Chehnon that the Shylmahn were sincere in their efforts to maintain the peace, while at the same time demonstrating that EsJen could prove a formidable enemy, should it come to that.

"Make your plans," she said. "But do not move forward on them until I have advised Michael as to what is to come."

"EsJen—"

She stopped him with a raised hand. "Not to worry, NehLoc. Just enough time that he is not taken by surprise."

Jenny Britton stood on the planked deck in front of the small, wood-framed building. Two saddled horses were tied at the ring post set at the corner of the building. Low-growing vegetation bordered the deck and the one-room structure, with the railroad tracks running north to south directly in front of the platform.

Several miles distant, a purplish blur on the western horizon, the foothills rose up from the plain. Jenny's cabin was there; her way station for the underground that had helped smuggle hundreds out of the occupied territory, back before the truce with the Shylmahn.

She missed it already.

Many had thought that she would leave her isolated cabin once the truce had been established.

Not yet.

Her work wasn't quite finished.

The door behind her opened and Monroe stepped out onto the platform holding two mugs in one hand. He set a small travel bag down on the wooden bench beside the door. The big, burly mountain man had remained her friend and frequent companion through the ensuing years since the truce. And though she would deny it and it had never been spoken aloud, he had remained her protector as well.

He held out the mugs and she took one of them.

"Really, Monroe, you don't have to stay. I'll be fine."

"I take your horse, and the train doesn't come?" He shook his head. "I'll wait."

She took a sip from the mug, spoke then over the rim. "Thank you."

"No bother." Monroe wasn't happy with the turn of events. It had been coming for some time, and he understood the necessity, but he didn't like it.

He wished that he was going with her, but that was not the way it was to be.

He frowned, an expression not very different from his normal countenance, and glanced up the tracks to the north. No sign of the train.

"Don't worry about me," Jenny said sharply.

"I'm not worried."

"Of course you are. You always worry."

"You'll be fine," Monroe stated flatly. "You know how to take care of yourself."

Jenny grinned. "Yes I do."

"And Miriam will be with you."

Jenny gave another grin. Monroe liked Miriam. They were both tough, sharp, and neither of them took any crap from anyone. Both remembered the *before time*, Monroe being a few years older than Miriam. Miriam had been a young teenager surviving on her own when Jenny's parents had taken her in. She had been as an older sister to Jenny and Michael, and later had been their strongest ally.

"There it is," Monroe said softly.

Looking up the tracks to the vanishing point in the distance, Jenny could just make out a shadow sitting on the horizon. It was another minute or more before it was finally recognizable as the front of the locomotive, and several minutes more before the train came to a steamy, calamitous stop directly in front of them.

Jenny picked up her bag and turned to face Monroe.

"I'll see you soon," she said, and placed her mug into his hand.

Monroe stood stiffly and gave her a silent, unreadable nod.

Jenny shook her head in disbelief and gave him a hug. When they pulled apart, he gave a second sharp, grave nod. Jenny turned and started to toward the nearest passenger car. When she looked back to Monroe a final time, she could see that there was something more he wanted to say. "Yes?" she asked.

"It is nothing," he said at last. "Say hello to Michael for me."

"I will." Once aboard, she found the rack to stow her bag. The train lurched forward and pulled away from the station as she went looking for Miriam.

She passed a number of people that she recognized, if not by name then at least by face. Most acknowledged her with a smile and a brief hello. Several stood and gave her a hug before letting her pass.

She found Miriam sitting alone, staring out the window at the passing terrain. When she sat down beside her, Miriam reached across and grasped Jenny's hand, her attention still focused beyond the glass.

"How are you, Jenny?"

"Well. How are you?"

Miriam gave a thin smile, but didn't answer.

Jenny glanced casually around them, though she had already scanned her surroundings when she came into the car. Most of the seats within hearing distance were occupied. They couldn't talk freely here.

"Are you excited about the trip?" she asked.

"I already miss home," said Miriam.

"Me, too."

"I suppose it's good to get away now and then."

"Always been a bit of a homebody myself," said Jenny.

"I have been accused of that on more than one occasion." Miriam turned away from the window and faced Jenny for the first time. "I could use some air."

The two of them stood and walked to the end of the car, stepped out onto the narrow platform. Miriam rested her elbows on the railing and Jenny moved in beside her. The wheels were clanking noisily and they could hear the working of the locomotive at the head of the train.

"Now that it's finally happening, I can hardly believe it," said Jenny.

"It's been a long time coming," said Miriam. She gave Jenny a comforting smile. "Are you nervous?"

"I'm all right. A bit worried about Michael."

"What he does is completely his decision." Miriam turned back to the scene before them, passing by them. She took in a long breath, let out a satisfied sigh. "We'll give him what facts we can, those he doesn't already know, and he'll have to take it from there."

"You don't really have any doubts about his staying with us, do you?"

"No."

"Then what?"

"We have misled him," said Miriam. "Or at the very least, we've kept him in the dark."

"We had no choice. We all agreed that we had no choice."

"Absolutely. And now our day of reckoning has come."

They fell silent, both looking out at the tall yellow grass of the plain. There was a lot of seeming emptiness here. Misleading... how symbolic.

Immediately following the establishing of the truce between human and Shylmahn, Joseph Britton had initiated the next phase of his multi-year plan, a scheme that would hopefully one day see humanity regaining their world. Only a handful of people knew the full extent of it. A slightly larger circle knew elements of it but not the full picture, nor how it would all eventually come together. Others still, while being a part of it, knew nothing of the plan at all.

Michael was of the small group of insiders, or so he thought. Because of his vital role as the official leader of the humans, and the relationship with the Shylmahn that such a position required, Joseph and Jason had decided that he had to be kept in the dark on a number of things, and that he needed to be purposely misled on still others.

Very different from the way they had dealt with Carolyn, and for very different reasons; but just as distasteful.

Jenny had been strongly opposed to Michael being used, and misused, in this way. However, as time went by and Michael settled into his role, she began to see subtle changes in him and in his relationship with the Shylmahn. Perhaps out of necessity due to the responsibilities of his position, he had grown much more—*accommodating*—in his dealings with the Shylmahn, and with EsJen in particular.

Jenny slowly came to realize that her father had known this would happen. He placed no blame, made no accusations. He had simply understood that if Michael was to be an effective representative of the humans that he was going to have to make choices and decisions that, while they might be unpopular, would be necessary, and that as he struggled to make the coexistence of Human and Shylmahn work, he would need to make conciliations.

Knowing too much of Joseph's true intentions would have compromised his effectiveness in the role that he had accepted, and to do less than his best as leader would have compromised Joseph's plans.

It had to be this way.

Miriam had understood this from the beginning. This had surprised Jenny, considering the loyalty Miriam had always shown Michael. But then, Miriam had always held herself to an even higher and more absolute loyalty... that to Joseph.

Joseph had proven himself deserving of that loyalty again and again. Nonetheless, for Jenny it had been difficult to have to make a choice between her brother Michael and her father Joseph. She and Michael had been close their entire lives. Her father, while a legendary figure and a constant shadow over their lives, had been absent for years at a time.

And then somewhere along the way it came to her that Miriam hadn't really made the choice of one over the other. Rather, her choice had been to abide by Joseph's decision, having agreed with the logic. It was the right choice to make. She hadn't decided against Michael, and she thought no less of him. She no doubt respected him all the more for the sacrifice he was making and those he would yet make.

Jenny looked over at Miriam now; a strong woman, determined and confident, a cane her life-long companion following that disastrous mission that had killed Jenny and Michael's mother. She was looking out at the landscape passing by them, wind blowing at her hair, already showing signs of gray though she was still in her forties.

Yes, Jenny could stand by this woman. It made possible all the decisions that would otherwise be impossible.

Carolyn leaned over the small table and looked down at the map that Jason had spread out before them. Joseph reached out and pointed at a spot that had been highlighted.

"There," he said. "Little town called John's Park. It's hidden in an old movie house that I used as a message drop."

"How can you be sure it's still there?"

"It's there. Cover was blown as a drop; made it the perfect place to stash it."

Carolyn straightened, put her hands on her hips. "Component from a Shillie energy pod." She sounded skeptical.

"That's right," said Jason.

"I got my hands on it three years ago," said Joseph. "Didn't have a need for it at the time, but knew it was important."

Carolyn looked at Jason. "Phoenix couldn't use it?"

"No way to integrate it into what we were working on. Not worth the risk to bring it out."

"So what's changed?"

Jason glanced once at Joseph before looking back to Carolyn. "We've been working on something."

"What?"

"Something that will give us a big bang."

"You mean like those disrupters you guys came up with?" The disrupters were able to cancel out the Shillie shields, which consisted of hundreds of concentrated energy blasts. They weren't really explosive themselves.

"More bang."

"How much more?"

"A lot more. *Major* more."

Carolyn studied Jason's face for telltale signs that he might be hiding something. He was. The guy was smooth. But not smooth enough. She looked then to Joseph. He gave her a thin smile.

Okay, that one was easy. Definitely hiding something.

But... a big bang. She liked the sound of that.

"And you need this piece of an energy pod in order to finish your... whatever it is."

"We can't do it without it," said Joseph.

"This is part of your big plan, then."

"That's right."

"And this gets us our planet back..."

"That's right."

Carolyn frowned. She had thought they were getting their planet back the last time Joseph's plan came together. That had been bullshit. After that, it was several years before she so much as said hello her brother.

But Jason had finally convinced her that Joseph had been thinking long range, and that the truce had been but a necessary step in his grander scheme.

Carolyn's frown turned into a hard glare as she focused her attention on Joseph.

"Are you f—"

"This gets us our planet back."

Carolyn turned back to the map. Her frown slowly returned. "That doesn't really answer my question, does it?"

Neither Joseph nor Jason answered.

Oh great, thought Carolyn. *Bastards...*

"So what do you need me for?" she finally asked.

Jason let out a breath he hadn't known he had been holding. "Joseph is going south, meeting up with Miriam to set things in motion. Meanwhile, you and I go into the province and retrieve the component."

"And you're afraid to go in by yourself?"

"You know that area a lot better than I do."

"That's crap."

"And... with two of us going in, better odds that at least one of us makes it out with the device. And someone has to get the device to Phoenix."

EsJen was alone in the command center, nervously shifting position in her chair, anxiously watching the double doors on the other side of the room.

She had sent the ShahnTahr probe to escort TohPeht-ShahnTahr in.

After all this time... TohPeht-ShahnTahr.

She had also sent for BehLahk. Her science advisor had once been close to TohPeht, even as TohPeht had been slowly merging with ShahnTahr. She wanted his perspective.

The doors opened and ShahnTahr—her ShahnTahr—glided into the room, hovering four feet above the floor.

TohPeht-ShahnTahr, the merged entities of the one-time Shylmahn leader and the artificial intelligence, then walked calmly into the room, two paces behind the probe.

EsJen stepped down from her seat of command and stood to one side, giving it over to TohPeht-ShahnTahr.

He would have nothing of it. "No, no, EsJen. That is not me. Please... sit down." His smile was bright and genuine. He had a comfortable, relaxed air about him. He looked around the room, taking in everything, as he waited for EsJen to return to her chair.

"It is good to see you, EsJen," said TohPeht-ShahnTahr, though he hadn't yet returned his attention to her.

"And you." EsJen slid back and rested her hands on the arms of the chair. "It has been a very long time."

"I have been away, yes... but my location was always known."

Yes, thought EsJen. *And still inaccessible.* She had kept track of his whereabouts, made certain that he was safe. There was always someone available to him if he needed anything.

"Your experiences... were they of value to you?"

"I have grown much in so very many ways."

"And now?"

"And now," TohPeht-ShahnTahr sighed. "I come to serve."

I serve, thought EsJen. The most solemn credo of the Shylmahn. It lay within the very soul of every individual. It bound one to all.

"Of course," said EsJen.

"Though I would not presume to take the place of ShahnTahr," he said, indicating the probe that hovered at EsJen's shoulder. The device that was but one extension of the ShahnTahr AI.

EsJen nodded in silent acknowledgement. She did not look to Shahn-Tahr, she did not need to. And ShahnTahr, for his part, made no comment. None was necessary.

BehLahk entered the room, stepped up beside TohPeht-ShahnTahr.

"I came as soon as I received your request," he said to EsJen.

EsJen gave another silent nod, and BehLahk turned to the new arrival. "It is good to see you, TohPeht-ShahnTahr. I have followed your travels with keen interest and, if I might be perfectly honest, with some envy."

"I would have welcomed your company, BehLahk. And please, call me TohPeht. The full name is so unwieldy. There is no reason to be so exacting."

"As you wish," said BehLahk. Interesting. Prior to his departure on this five year journey of exploration and self-discovery, it had been TohPeht-ShahnTahr's own wish to be referred to by his conjoined name.

"The gears in your brain turn, my friend," said TohPeht. "I can almost hear them."

"I apologize. I suppose I do tend to overanalyze." *Is such a thing possible? I do not think so.*

"BehLahk," said EsJen. "TohPeht has asked to serve."

"The desire of all Shylmahn," said BehLahk with a slight bow.

"And I would accept his request," said EsJen. "His perspective should serve well in counsel."

"Of that I have no doubt," said BehLahk.

EsJen noted the guardedness in BehLahk's observation. So he did not feel quite as at ease as he let on.

The probe hovering two feet to EsJen's left shifted position slightly.

"I welcome you home, TohPeht," it said calmly. "My brother."

EsJen looked with some surprise at ShahnTahr. It took her a moment to replay the previous few seconds in her mind and realize that, yes, it had said that.

BehLahk too was taken unawares at the statement, but had spent decades cultivating his ability to keep emotions and feelings in check. He let be seen only what he wanted seen. He gave now a generous, well thought-out smile.

TohPeht took a half step toward the probe and bowed his head ceremoniously. "I thank you, ShahnTahr. There is much I would share with you."

"I look forward to it."

BehLahk followed the winding path up the hillside outside the center. TohPeht-ShahnTahr, *TohPeht*, stood on the ridge top, his back to the center, looking out across the landscape and the setting sun in the distance.

"Good evening, BehLahk," he said, not taking his gaze from the horizon, seemingly unwilling to miss one moment of the sunset.

"Hello, TohPeht." BehLahk took a moment to admire the scene. Yes, it did generate some emotion within him, but then he had always been open to such things of this world. In this he had something in common with TohPeht. Not the TohPeht he once knew, but this new individual most certainly.

BehLahk had received regular reports on the activities and observations of TohPeht over the previous five years, so he felt that he should have known what to expect. But this being that stood beside him could not be represented with words. The changes, *the evolution*, could not be adequately reflected in a report.

TohPeht was correct in his request not to be labeled as TohPeht-ShahnTahr. That name implied that both were in there somewhere, and the fact was that neither was there. He had indeed become one; that *one* was something very different from either of the original two entities.

"Are you finished with your analysis, BehLahk?" said TohPeht.

"Watching the gears again, TohPeht?"

"Watching the sunset... but the sound of wheels grinding is distracting."

"I apologize... again."

TohPeht shrugged. *Very human,* thought BehLahk.

"Are you here to stay, TohPeht? With us?"

"For a brief time only."

"Then why did you return?"

"To serve."

"There are many ways to serve."

Before them, the sun finished its descent below the horizon. The purples and oranges and reds streaked out from the vanishing point, swept across the landscape and painted the sky like the inside of a shell. TohPeht smiled softly, closed his eyes and let the experience seep into his being.

He opened his eyes then, slowly, turned his head and looked directly at BehLahk for the first time.

"Something is going to happen," he said. "I need to be here."

BehLahk knew that Joseph Britton was planning something, was working on something, had been since the declaration of the truce, but he did not believe the Chehnon was in any way a serious threat. At least not yet. BehLahk was always prepared for any eventuality; and his own plans were progressing nicely.

Is that what brought TohPeht halfway around the world? wondered BehLahk. *My activities?* He did not see how. He had been very careful. As always.

"What is it you believe is going to happen, TohPeht?"

TohPeht smiled unsettlingly before turning back to the scene laid out in front of them. "You have nothing to fear from me, BehLahk."

He knows, thought BehLahk. *How can he know?* And then, *how much does he know?*

"Surely you are not suggesting that—"

"I trust your heart, my friend."

"Then what brings you here?"

"The world speaks to me. In so many ways."

Human philosophy now...

"In what way?" he asked. "Not literarily, surely."

Again TohPeht smiled. "That, too."

Victoria found Michael in the small garden outside his office. It looked as though he had been doing some weeding, but now he sat on the wooden bench, lost in thought.

Her husband had aged considerably over the last five years. He was barely thirty, but he looked older. The struggle to balance his role as head of the governing council with that of covert member of his father's underground had taken its toll. Either would have been difficult, but both taken together, with their frequently conflicting agendas, was a nearly impossible task for one person.

And yet somehow Michael Britton had managed that task for five years. He had forged a working, if inelegant, relationship with EsJen. He had managed to keep the peace between Human and Shylmahn despite the frequent violations of the truce by both sides.

And all the while he and Victoria had continued to work with Joseph and the others of the underground as they slowly advanced some little-understood plan of Joseph's, the ultimate goal of which seemed less and less achievable, less and less real: to force the Shylmahn to leave Earth.

Michael's main contribution to the cause had been to provide the administrative cover that allowed facilities to become established, and to operate unseen by humans and Shylmahn alike, and for supply lines to those facilities to operate undocumented.

Other than Michael, none on the governing council knew of these hidden facilities within facilities or of the research that went on within them.

Victoria had a feeling that Michael wished that he didn't know, either.

He had doubts. She didn't know how deeply these underlying doubts went, but she knew they were there.

She sat down on the bench beside him. "Gardening?"

"Not so much," he said. He folded his arms across his chest and tilted his head back so that he was staring up at the sky. "Just taking a break from the paperwork."

"Preparing for the meeting tomorrow?"

"If you can call it that."

"The preparations, or the meeting?"

"Yeah..."

"Mayors are coming in for this, aren't they?"

"Trade agreements. Ugh."

"Sorry," she said, giving him a sympathetic smile. She had noticed an influx of people coming in from outlying districts the last few days. She had recognized some of the faces. "I know this is your least favorite thing in all the world."

"We all make sacrifices, I suppose."

"Some of us more than others, but okay."

"I'll get through it," he groaned. "Somehow."

"Is Craig coming?" Victoria hadn't seen Craig for some time; mayor of Freetown, governor of the province. And their friend.

"He's sending Miriam."

"Oh," Victoria said softly. Probably some resistance business, then.

The door she had come through a few minutes earlier opened. A woman appeared in the doorway, and a moment later a three year old boy maneuvered his way around her and ran into the garden.

Victoria smiled broadly and called out to the woman. "Thank you, Anna."

"Don't be so quick with the thanks, Victoria. He's a wild one today." Anna gave a pleasant grin and closed the door.

Nate ran up to Victoria and pushed himself up against her legs.

Victoria reached down and wrapped her arms around him, gave him a tight squeeze.

"And how was your morning, Nate?"

"Mark got in trouble. His mom had to come get him."

"Ah. And how about you?"

"I behaved," Nate managed in a long, sad sigh.

Poor ole' Nate, thought Michael. *He behaved. How tedious.*

"Not as bad as all that, was it?"

Nate shrugged. "Okay."

Three years old and already a thrill seeker.

Chapter Three

Joseph had already packed the Jeep, which was parked in front of the row of garages set along the north wall of the keep. He finished the inspection under the hood, closed it and started around toward the driver's door.

It was just past dawn, the sun's rays had yet to reach down into the keep, but the sky was already brightening.

"You about ready?" Jason came around the corner, Carolyn close behind him.

"Just about."

It was going to be a long trip, and Joseph wanted to be sure he got there well ahead of the train. It wouldn't do to park himself along the tracks, only to find out later the train had long since gone by.

"Safe journey," said Jason. He held out his hand.

"I'll be fine." Joseph pointed sternly at his brother. "You be careful, Jase."

"No problem."

"We've got 'em worked up. There's no telling—"

"No problem."

"Uh, huh." They shook hands, then hugged. Joseph turned to Carolyn, who had been standing silent to one side. "Thank you, Sis. For everything."

"Yeah, well," Carolyn grumbled. She reached out and grudgingly hugged her brother.

"Be careful." He nodded then in Jason's direction. "Keep a close eye on this guy."

"Of course."

"We'll see you in ten days," said Jason.

"If everything goes to plan."

"It'll go to plan. You be there."

"Do my best."

"Let's do it." Jason backed away with a sharp nod. He followed Carolyn as they headed toward the front of the keep. They stepped up onto the porch of her office just as the Jeep came around the corner and headed toward the main gate. The guards were expecting him, and pulled the gates open as the Jeep drew near.

"Jason," Carolyn started, watching the gates close again. "Are you ready to tell me what's going on?"

"I don't know what you mean."

"Bullshit."

"Carolyn."

"Joey could have taken you right to that message drop in John's Park. It was his goddamned drop, for Christ's sake. You don't need me for this."

"Joey has a job. He can't do both. Besides, you're more familiar with the way the Shillies are doing things in there than Joey or me."

"That's weak, Jason; especially for you."

Jason let out a long, sorrowful sigh. "All right," he said finally.

"Yes?" Cautiously.

"All right," he said again, more forcefully. "We need you, specifically. You."

"Uh, huh."

"We need you to do this because you are who you are."

She thought about that for a long moment. "You want the Shillies to see Carolyn Britton go into their precious province and come out with whatever the hell this thing is we're going in there for."

"That's right."

"And what Joey said about them being 'worked up'. You guys have been digging at 'em. Crap. You've been poking their brains with a stick, haven't you?"

"Our dear brother has," said Jason, a hint of pride in his voice. "For the last five years he's been... poking their brains with a stick."

"Now you've got 'em thinking a whole bunch a' scary shit's going down, and—"

"Joey's been puttin' your face smack on the front of the cereal box every chance he got."

"That son of a bitch."

"Yeah," Jason grinned. "Pretty cool, huh?"

Steven came rushing up before she could respond. He caught his breath and was just about to say something when an alarm began to sound. A moment later, two Shillie fighters roared overhead and were gone just as fast.

"Shillie fighters," said Steven.

*No shit...*Carolyn frowned.

"I wonder what they want," said Jason.

"I have a pretty good idea," said Carolyn. She grimaced at the sound of the alarm, turned to Steven. "Turn that damn thing off."

Ten minutes later, Jason was leaning against the wall just outside the gate, watching Carolyn and Steven finish up a heated discussion with the Shillies. The Shylmahn shuttle that the fighters had escorted in had landed a few hundred feet from the keep. Three Shylmahn had stepped out. They had said nothing, waited for Carolyn to come out to meet with them. It was the routine.

Jason recognized NehLoc. Since he seldom used advisers or assistants, the other two were no doubt his security.

Carolyn didn't look too pleased with the way the conversation was going. She finally raised her hands up in frustration and stalked off in the direction of the keep, leaving Steven to say their goodbyes to the Shylmahn.

She stopped in front of Jason, body trembling in anger, jaw clenched. Behind her, the shuttle lifted off, Steven still near enough to feel the blast of air.

"Quarantine," Carolyn stated.

"Something you said?"

"They saw my team come out of the province. Apparently they took offense."

"As you knew they would. You can't be that surprised. And this quarantine?"

"He said it was EsJen's measured response. Which is his way of saying that it would have been worse, had it been his decision."

Steven stood beside them. "It's not permanent."

Jason looked to Carolyn for an explanation.

"Three months," she said. "No vehicles in or out."

"What about food and supplies?"

"We can come and go on foot," said Steven. "We can tend to fields, walk to and from other settlements, that sort of thing. But no vehicles, no wagons or carts."

"Wow," said Jason. "She grounded you; and took away your car keys."

Carolyn sent Steven back into the keep with a nod of her head. He would explain the situation to her staff, and she would meet with them later to determine strategy.

Now though, she and Jason had strategies of their own to sort out.

Carolyn had stowed Jason's flyer outside the keep. She had an underground complex beneath the grove of trees several hundred yards south; the only trees Carolyn had left standing for a thousand feet in any direction. Jason now knew why.

An underground passageway ran from the keep to the hidden complex. That would get them to the flyer unseen, but then what?

Three Shillie surveillance probes appeared suddenly, dropping out of the sky. They hovered directly in front of Carolyn and Jason. After a few moments, two moved off in opposite directions along the wall of the keep. The third moved into position to one side of the gate.

The structural design of the probes had changed little over the last few years, not since the major advances just prior to the truce, but the sensors they contained continued to improve. This both Carolyn and Jason had found time and again.

"Well, sister," said Jason, turning about and stepping before the front gate probe. "It appears that I've dropped in for a visit at exactly the wrong time."

"You can hang out here for three months, or you can start walking."

They both knew neither of those options was going to happen.

"I guess that depends on your cooking."

Joseph unfolded the old pre-invasion map and spread it across the hood of the Jeep. He opened his compass and set it on the map. He had been driving for seven hours and had a good idea where he was, but he had expected to come across the old highway by now. His plan was to follow it down as far as he could before cutting cross-country to the railroad tracks south of where the train with Miriam and Jenny would be.

Back in the Jeep, he started out again and continued southwest. Another half hour and he spotted what he was looking for.

A large, rectangular road sign stood alone in the distance, mounted on a pair of four by six posts. As he drew nearer, he could see smaller, shorter roadside markers and signs running north to south away from the sign. He slowed and turned the vehicle up onto a wide band of smooth surface.

It was an old county highway, covered in a thin layer of dirt, dry grass and weeds; a thirty foot wide, straight band cutting across the landscape. The yellow center line was no longer visible, but the highway was bordered with markers and the occasional sign, making it easy to follow and making the drive much smoother.

He drove south until near dusk, stopping briefly several times to verify his location; once when he came to a sign listing the distances in miles to long-dead towns, twice at intersections of crossroads.

He turned in at an abandoned general store that sat alone on the highway, drove the Jeep around back. He covered the vehicle with a faded, well-worn tarp that had been brought along for just this purpose.

Walking amongst the shoulder-high shelves in the front of the store, Joseph didn't see anything that he could use. Not that he had been looking for anything in particular. He had brought most of what he needed with him. He worked his way to the back and into a private office. There was a couch in the office that had held up well enough over the decades that he could use as his bed. He cleared the top of the desk and set his canvas sack on it. He took out a small portable stove, a sealed package containing the dehydrated ingredients for a stew, and a water bottle and spoon.

Once his dinner was heating, he sat at the desk and brought out his map. He calculated that he was four hours from the tracks and where he calculated best to meet up with the train. According to the train's schedule, such as it was, it should reach that point in eight and a half hours.

Four and half hours to spare.

So, half an hour for dinner, and say three hours of sleep. That would still give him an hour buffer.

He reached again into his canvas sack and brought out a beat up old clock with a scratched plastic cover over the face. He set the time to 12:00, set the alarm for 3:30. He wound up the clock, flipped the alarm switch to on and set it on the desk.

The stew was beginning to bubble.

Jason followed Carolyn along a narrow side street and into a small shack that was set against the south wall of the keep. The room they entered was empty but for an opening in the center of the floor. A steep stairwell led down to a wood-paneled underground tunnel; dim lights were set high on the wall every seven steps.

The tunnel opened into a room with several tables and workbenches, hardwood floors, paneling on the walls, and a ceiling that had been painted a dull white. An open door on the left opened to a large room with a number of tables and chairs.

They continued straight ahead to another door and down another narrow hall, coming out at last into a vehicle bay. There were four stalls along one wall, all occupied. A rectangular platform set into the floor, ten feet wide by thirty feet long, took up much of the usually empty space in front of the stalls.

It wasn't empty at the moment. Jason's flyer sat on the platform, looking much larger than its actual size in the confined space.

Steven came up to them as they came in. "You're all set."

Jason nodded in thank you. "Interesting place you have here," he said.

"It serves us well enough," said Carolyn. She stepped around him and walked toward the shuttle.

"Yes," Jason spoke after her. "So you said."

Carolyn had told him that while they normally came and went through the keep's front gate, there were times when it was best the Shillies not know what they were about. This facility offered a less conspicuous way to and from the keep, by either foot or vehicle.

Jason noted the ladder mounted on the left wall leading up to a small hatch in the ceiling. The hatch was beside a much larger access panel. This larger panel was directly above the platform on which the flyer now sat.

As Jason and Steven approached the shuttle, two men stepped over to an apparatus of cogged wooden wheels and a two-handled crank. The machinery was connected to a larger collection of gears set beneath the floor. Slow, easy turns of the two-person crank device could raise and lower the platform with very little exertion.

Jason held out a hand to Steven. "Thank you for everything, sir."

"My pleasure." With that, Steven stepped back, looked to the front of the flyer and the pair of windows. He offered a wave to Carolyn, who was settling into the cockpit. She gave a two-fingered wave in return.

Jason stepped up into the shuttle, pressed a button that closed the side door behind him.

The interior of the craft was even smaller than the exterior would suggest. The bulk of the flyer was taken up with the engine, hidden behind an interior wall. The cabin offered just enough room for two people and their gear.

The platform on which the shuttle rested began to lift from the floor even before Jason had a chance to climb into the seat beside Carolyn. Above them, the access panel was sliding slowly aside.

"So, Sis... what do you think of our chances on getting away unseen?"

Carolyn gave her brother a bored look, pulled an old pair of reading glasses out of her pocket and put them on. She studied the panel in front of her.

"We don't usually have guardian probes watching our comings and goings," she said, continuing to focus on the handful of gauges. "And I don't know what their monitoring parameters are."

"The way they've positioned themselves, I would guess they're functioning much like guards posted on a prison wall."

"If that's true, they may have their sensors pulled in tight, within say... fifty feet or so beyond the keep walls. They may not reach out this far."

They both knew their odds of getting away unseen were slim; but then that would just feed into the Carolyn Britton persona that Joseph had been creating.

They rose up into the open, continued to rise until the platform locked into position at ground level. Camouflage netting was hung in place forty feet above them, still well below the top of the tree canopy. Not normally an issue, as up until now everything that came up out of the ground was either on wheels or on foot. Not so this time. This was the first flyer.

Carolyn's people had attached the flyer to the back of a pickup to get it here, but Jason had assured her that he could get it out under its own power.

He flipped a simple switch to power it on. The sound that came from the back was little more than a low hum. He touched a small panel in front of him and it illuminated. He gave it three more taps and the shuttle lifted. One foot, two feet, two and a half feet.

It hovered.

He pushed a touchpad and a four inch square section of panel lifted from the board. He slowly slid a fingertip in a smooth arc across the clear plastic face. The ship turned about, mirroring the movement of the fingertip, without leaving its position above the platform.

He moved his other hand above a thin strip of panel set into the console beside him. He rested the pad of a fingertip on the surface. As he moved it slowly forward, the ship moved slowly and silently forward.

"Not bad," Carolyn conceded.

"Thanks."

He guided the ship through the grove of trees away from the keep. Within a few moments they were out in the open.

"You ready?" he asked.

"Do I look ready?"

"Of course you do."

He made a few adjustments and the flyer rose up into the sky at a steep angle.

The young Shylmahn watch officer stood silently before the holo-table, above which hovered a wild array of moving images. Each of the three probes assigned to the Chehnon community sent its incoming sensor data to this station, as well as feeding it to the central security system for processing and storage.

The visual sensor feed displays were each accompanied by additional sensor data, most of which was shown in the holo display as text or simple graphics. All of this information was presented together with the other probe feeds.

A fourth set of data was also being displayed. This came from a mid-altitude probe hovering thousands of feet above the community. It was one of fourteen probes of a new design recently completed and brought on line over the previous few months. From synchronous low-altitude positions around the world, these probes were able to monitor the state of affairs on the ground from a completely new and unique perspective.

The sensor data coming in from the probes that were monitoring the keep showed all to be quiet. Dusk had come to the Chehnon community. The creatures would probably be settling into their nests for the evening.

Of course, the officer knew that night was also when Chehnon were most likely to attempt clandestine activity; an opportunity for them to scurry about in the dark.

And this particular Chehnon, this Carolyn of the Britton, was the most irksome and problematic of all the creatures.

The young officer had been hearing stories of the Britton family throughout his entire life. From what he knew of it, it would have been best if they had been eliminated at the very start.

Something in the cloud of images above the holo-table caught his attention.

He lifted a hand and brushed away extraneous images.

The one remaining image showed an object moving out of a grove of trees some short distance south of the community.

He rested a hand on one of the service panels of the holo-table. A few deft movements of his fingers and the low-altitude probe locked sensors onto the object, maintained surveillance as it moved out onto the plain.

He moved his hand to the communications panel, touched a pad, then stood at rest, continued to monitor what was clearly a shuttle, albeit of unfamiliar design.

It was several minutes before NehLoc came into the room.

"What is it?" asked NehLoc.

"You asked to be alerted if there was—"

"What is it?" he asked again, more sharply.

"A small shuttle, sir. Unknown configuration. It was monitored coming out of a small forest a short distance from the Chehnon community."

"Shuttle?" NehLoc stepped up to the holo-table. The young watch officer stepped to one side, awaited instructions. "I see," NehLoc mumbled to himself.

Not one of Shylmahn design, but it definitely had some Shylmahn in its ancestry. Quite likely something Carolyn Britton's brother brought up from their *Phoenix Labs*.

We should have dealt with that facility long ago.

NehLoc moved his hand over a panel. A flick of a finger and the holo-image of the flyer expanded thirty percent.

"Should I send fighters, sir?" asked the officer.

"Of course not," NehLoc said absently. *What an odd little craft*, he thought.

The watch officer stood unmoving, uncertain.

NehLoc reset the holo-display. "Monitor only. I want to know where that aircraft goes."

"Yes, sir."

NehLoc started toward the door, hesitated, looked back at the holo-display. He knew that all the data was being fed to the central security system, and therefore to ShahnTahr, but...

"Send that feed on a separate channel directly to ShahnTahr," he told the officer. "Flag it with my name." He turned about and was gone, leaving the watch officer to mumble out a feeble, trailing *yes sir* in the direction of NehLoc's retreating figure.

Jason brought the flyer down to an altitude of two hundred feet just as they crossed the eastern boundary of the Shylmahn's Northwest Province, leaving the flat, open plain behind. Below were the grassy foothills ahead of the Cascades.

Carolyn returned from the back of the cabin and settled back into her seat. Other than voicing a grudging compliment about the shuttle, she spoke very little. For the most part she watched in silence as Jason maneuvered the craft through the rising mountains, keeping it just below the highest ridges on either side of them.

They came out above what had once been a major highway crossing the Cascades, and Jason steered them toward it, then directly above it. He followed it for some time before finally having to leave it and head north.

En route they passed over several long-dead towns. After so many years of neglect, even the wide, main thoroughfares had mostly overgrown, with tall grass and weeds sprouting up through cracks in asphalt and concrete. Many store roofs had collapsed, gutters hung loose, broken windows let rainy weather in and let torn, faded curtains hang limply outside.

They came out above a wide valley and Jason steered the flyer up the center of it, barely twelve feet above the remains of a narrow county highway. Faded stripes of yellow paint occasionally shown through the tall grass.

Carolyn spotted a sign directly up ahead.

"Head west once you get past the sign."

"Got it," said Jason. He knew this was the crossroads of the narrow road that wound its way through those hills and on into John's Park. "Waddya think? Park it outside and hoof it in?"

"Why?" shrugged Carolyn. "They know we're here or they don't. I'd just as soon get in quick and get out quicker."

"Sounds good to me."

Ten minutes later Jason landed the little shuttle in the middle of Main Street right outside the old movie house.

"Joseph's message drop was downstairs," said Carolyn. "Storage room, hole in the far wall behind the shelves."

Jason smiled and settled back with a low sigh, gave no sign of going in to get the artifact. "Joey built up one heck of an operation, back in the day. Didn't he? And he did it all by his lonesome."

"Sure. I'll give him that."

"Think about it, Sis. The guy goes from working at a mill to running a major underground insurgence operation with a bunch of rookie spies; all in a matter of months."

"I know," droned Carolyn. "I was there."

"I mean, I was trained for it, but Joey—"

"Are we doin' this, or what?"

"Yeah," said Jason. "Yeah, we're doin' it."

Jason remained settled in. No hurry. It took a few seconds. Carolyn frowned then, leaned back heavily in her seat.

He wants to make damn sure they see we're here.

"Shit," she said.

"Hmm?"

"We hang out a few, just in case they somehow missed us flying in?"

"Hmm?"

"They're not stupid, Jase. They know we're here."

"Do you want to go get it, or shall I?"

"Hell." She shifted her seat around and stood up. "God knows I can use the fresh air."

And I expect they gotta make sure they see that it's me. Eh, brother?

She went to the back of the cabin and opened the door. The front doors of the old theater were directly opposite.

Inside, the lobby smelled of old, wet carpet. What light there was streamed in through the set of windows spanning the front wall on either side of the double doors. She walked over to a side hallway and down to the last door on the right. She pulled out her flashlight and took the stairs down to a second hallway. This one had three doors along one wall. She stepped through the third door and into a long, narrow room lined with shelves. She pulled the shelf away from the far wall, lifted aside a thin board that was hanging on a hook on the wall.

There was a small cubbyhole set into the wall, about a foot square. Carolyn pulled out a metal box and set it on a nearby table. Opening the lid, she found a plastic cylinder about nine inches long, four inches in diameter, with a number of slides and levers set into the side.

Definitely Shillie design and it looked very much like a component that might fit into one of their energy pods.

She placed the artifact carefully back into the box and headed back upstairs. Reaching the lobby, she found Jason standing near the door, leaning against the jamb with his arms folded.

"I see you found it," he said. He pushed himself away from the wall.

"That much of what you said was true," she answered.

"It's what I don't say that you gotta watch out for." He stepped to the door and held it open for her. "Shall we go?"

"I'm for that."

EsJen crossed the room and returned to her seat. Her fingertips tapped absently on the chair's arm, and when she turned her head, her hair fell in front of one golden-flecked eye. She brushed the gold strands aside.

"Well?" she asked.

There was no one else in the room.

"The craft has just lifted off." ShahnTahr's voice came as if from the walls, from the ceiling; soft, warm, pleasant.

"Give me a live image."

The holo-table rose from the floor. A holo-image burst into life above the surface even before the table was fully in position.

The shuttle, seen from above. It was out over the trees and still rising.

"Carolyn Britton was carrying a small box when she left the structure," ShahnTahr stated.

"Show me."

A static image of Carolyn overlay the live image of the shuttle. She had a metal box tucked under her arm, the length about that of the Chehnon's forearm.

"All right," she said. "ShahnTahr, where are you?"

"South hall, outside laboratory six. I'm on my way."

"Ideas on where she's headed?" she asked. The static image was gone.

"The craft has yet to settle into a course."

"I doubt she goes back to her Keep."

"There has been no indication that they will be turning in that direction," said ShahnTahr. The doors at the opposite end of the room opened and the ShahnTahr probe glided in. "Should we eliminate the craft?"

"No," she stated firmly.

"They may pose an inordinate risk."

"I would know what that risk is."

"Yes, EsJen."

"And what is in that box."

The ship leveled at nine hundred feet. Carolyn leaned near the window, watched the forested landscape pass beneath them. It was beautiful. She didn't make it into the province nearly as often as she'd like... the Cascades, the Sound, the peninsula. She spent most of her days out on a grassy plain, huddled behind the high walls of the keep.

But once they had their planet back...

Carolyn settled back. Beside her, Jason made a final adjustment with a flurry of his fingers.

"Done and done," he said.

Carolyn said nothing. Her gaze returned to the scene beyond the window. Tree-blanketed mountains spread out to the horizon.

"What's on your mind, Carolyn?"

She gave a shrug, a half smile. "Nothing."

"I doubt that. Your mind would crack under the vacuum of *nothing*."

"Whatever that means."

"It means you would never allow for the presence of nothing. You wouldn't know what to do with it."

She let her head drop back against the seat. "Whatever you say, Jason."

She missed home. She really, really missed home. Pre-invasion home. Somehow, seeing their world from this altitude did something, pulled at something inside her. There was an ache. Deep. Emotional.

She drew a picture in her mind. A map. She put Bril's island there. Joseph's house was over there. The plant where he worked over there. Liz, not far from Joey. The bank where Liz worked; Robert's store. Daryl and Susan's house was over there, a couple of towns over. There was Seattle, the skyline intact and spectacular. And all of it, the whole northwest, all in the shadow of Mt. Rainier.

There was a sudden, blinding flash of light. It filled the world outside the flyer and then burst into the cabin. The craft shuddered, bolted forward and jarred back.

Jason was immediately over the control panel, hands and fingers dancing across pads and knobs and levers.

"Crap, crap, and crap."

"What the hell, Jase?"

"Just a guess, Carolyn... but I'd say we've been shot."

Carolyn shifted forward. "What can I do?"

Jason shook his head sharply, continued to work the controls. Lighted pads on the panel were blinking out, one by one.

"Strap in, Sis. I got nothin' here."

"Shit." Carolyn slid back, pulled the harness across her chest.

Jason watched the rest of the panel go dark, then he too slid back into his seat and strapped in.

Carolyn watched the horizon slide up until all she could see was the blanket of green. The image of forest canopy quickly lost its gentle swathe and became thousands of individual treetops.

Her last thought before the world in front of her turned into a thick mass of tree trunks was that Jason's experimental flyer was handling this uncontrolled descent rather well.

NehLoc looked dispassionately at the holo-display. He could just make out the wreckage of the hybrid shuttle half-hidden in the trees. The fuselage was twisted, one side torn open. He could see little else.

Beside him, the young watch officer stood at one of the holo-table panels. He made a few adjustments. The image didn't improve very much.

"We'll have probes on site in a few minutes," he said.

"Thank you," said NehLoc. "I want people on the ground. I want the Chehnon bodies recovered, and I want whatever they came into the province to retrieve in my hands. Now.

Chapter Four

Miriam was dozing in her aisle seat. Jenny sat beside her, staring absently into the darkness beyond the window. Most of those in the passenger car sat in silence, many with eyes closed, heads bobbing, having long since run out of things to say to one another. There was the rumbling vibration of wheels on track, the faint sound of the train's engine, and little else.

Jenny felt herself being gently tugged forward. The train was coming to a stop.

She knew they were a long way from the next station. Apparently, so did many of her fellow passengers. A number of them began grumbling that the next scheduled stop wasn't for some hours, that there was no train station outside; that they were out in the middle of nowhere.

Miriam opened her eyes, stretched stiffened muscles.

"Must be your father," she said quietly.

Jenny slid the window open and poked her head outside.

There, up ahead, near the front of the train, a Jeep was parked beside the tracks. Joseph Britton lifted his canvas sack off the hood of the vehicle and started walking along the train toward the passenger cars.

Jenny waved, and her father waved back. He picked up the pace, knowing now which car to climb onto. Jenny pulled her head back in and nodded to Miriam. They slid out of their seats and walked down the aisle, Miriam using her cane. Unsettled whispers and questions continued from those they passed on their way to the front of the car.

They met Joseph outside as he climbed up the steps, the train already starting forward again. Miriam took his bag and tossed it inside, onto a shelf just inside the door. They remained outside.

"Good to see you, Joseph," she said, and gave her adopted father a hug.

"Good to see you, Miriam. How are you?" He turned then to Jenny and they hugged. "Hey, Jen."

"Hey, Dad." They pulled apart, then hugged again. "Missed you."

Joseph had missed so much of her life. It had only been these last years since the truce that they had managed to reconnect. "I was beginning to think the train had already gone by. Another few minutes and I'd have gone chasing after you."

Miriam smiled at that. "You being here must mean Jason's flyer is a success."

"It flies like a dream."

"And they got off all right?" asked Jenny.

"They were all set to go when I left. By now, I figure they've already gone into the province. We'll play it like they did."

Miriam hooked her cane onto the wrought iron rails enclosing the platform, gazed out at the darkness, at the shadows passing by. "The vine is taking hold," she said calmly.

"I saw signs of it on the way here."

"Stuff gives me the willies," said Jenny.

"That's the idea," said Joseph.

"Hopefully it'll scare the hell outta the Shillies," said Miriam.

A plant, a very alien plant, so very much like the Veltahk, the vine that had dominated half the world of Shylmah, now growing here on Earth. The initial Earth strain was developed in the Phoenix Labs at Joseph's direction, after which variations were created to thrive in every major ecosystem on Earth. It had then been planted simultaneously all over the world.

A wonderfully terrifying gift comes a-haunting from the Shylmahn past. The stuff was growing like mad. It should be up in their faces before they ever figured out something was wrong.

"Oh, they will not be happy," said Joseph.

The plant was the first component in Joseph's plan. The second, and much less obvious, had been in the works for several years. He wouldn't know for certain how well that was coming along until all of it came together. He did have some evidence that it was progressing during his rare meetings with BehLahk, and hoped to find out more very soon.

The third and final element had also been progressing for some time, and Jason was working on bringing that one to fruition right now.

Each component was important in its own way, but he doubted any one of them could do the job on its own. If all three were successful, and if Joseph could get all three to come together at the same time, the humans might just get their planet back.

"Are you all right?" asked Miriam.

"What?" Joseph realized that he had been lost in thought. Over the decades, he had spent way too much time by himself. "Sorry," he said finally. "Wandering off by myself again."

Jenny knew that feeling. She had spent years living alone in the cabin, serving as the stationmaster. There had been Monroe, dropping in occasionally as he travelled from wherever he had been to wherever he was going, ostensibly to visit but more likely to make sure she was all right; and of course her brother Michael, coming through every few months, back before the truce. He always spent a few days there while on his way into the province, and then a day or two on his way out with a group of refugees.

For the most part she had been on her own; much as her father had. After her mother had been killed, Joseph had gone back into the province, had spent years building and expanding his silent revolution; a secret war of which no one knew.

Everyone would know of it soon enough.

"Not long now." Jenny said dully, nodded to the dark shadows in the night.

"The vine?"

"All of it."

The world Jenny knew was about to change forever. It had been a conscious decision; the actions leading up to the birth of this new world, for good or bad, driven mostly by the Britton family, and for the most part unbeknownst to most of humanity.

God, I hope we know what the hell we're doing.

Jason lay on the ground beneath the canopy of evergreen, a huge blackberry bush forming a great wall behind him. His head was propped up on a seat cushion taken from the flyer. He could see the wreckage off to his left. Carolyn was sitting a few yards in front of him, her back to a tree trunk. Her forearms rested on her knees and she stared down at the ground between her feet.

She had a cut on her cheek, and the front of her shirt was dark with blood.

Not hers... Jason's.

Carolyn had bandaged him as best she could. His torso was wrapped and his left leg was in a tourniquet that she loosened and retightened every few minutes. The gash on his forehead had been cleaned and the bleeding stopped.

None of that really mattered. They both knew it. Jason had minutes, and not many of those.

Carolyn coughed and spit. It was red.

She was worse than she looked, and she didn't look all that great.

"Damn," she mumbled.

"Yeah," Jason managed.

Carolyn lifted her head, looked at Jason. She appeared about to say something, finally decided against it and lowered her head again. She spit out another mouthful of blood, took in a weak breath.

"You need to get out of here, Sis," said Jason.

"I'll go when I'm ready. I'm not ready."

"What are you waiting for?"

"Fuck you."

"Carolyn... you have get to Phoenix."

"No I don't."

"Shit," Jason grumbled. "Pissed at me right to the end, eh Sis?"

"I'm pissed at the situation."

Jason managed a thin smile. He had to rest. He really, really needed to rest. He just didn't have the time to rest. "I said it from the start. One of us has to make it out of here. Now... well, it looks like it's going to be you."

Carolyn lifted her gaze and gave him a withering glare.

Jason returned the glare with a smirk. "Hey, you're not my first choice, either."

That got a bit of a chuckle from her. She laid her head back, bumped it softly against the tree trunk. "I can't believe this family. The whole freakin' family. Sacrificing everything, year after fucking year, decade after decade; shit, like anyone will ever know."

"Go," Jason sighed softly. He no longer had the energy for more than that single word.

She had to get away. If this was going to work, one of them had to get away. It didn't really matter if she made it to Phoenix or not, but she had to get out of the province. They had to know she escaped with the pod component. Everything depended on it.

Carolyn studied her brother's face. She could read something there. Life fading, and some pain... but mostly... *desperation*.

"All right," she said. Shit, this was really important to him. "I'll go."

"Thank you."

Carolyn struggled to her feet. "You owe me, you bastard."

Jason barely managed a move of the head in reply. Even the faint smile was almost too much.

Carolyn went over to what remained of the fusclage and searched for the box containing the energy pod component. She found it, and also found a plastic bottle of water. She returned to her brother and knelt beside him.

She placed the bottle in his hand, but he weakly pushed it away. The look in his eyes said that she would need it more than he.

He wouldn't be taking another drink in this lifetime.

She stuffed the water bottle into her jacket pocket.

"I'll be seein' ya, Jase," she whispered.

One corner of Jason's mouth curled slightly.

Carolyn reached out, put an arm around her brother's head and gently pulled him toward her. She laid him back again, stood and left without another word.

He watched her disappear into the shadows of the forest. The world grew quiet. Jason was finally able to relax. He felt better. He realized that he had been expending valuable energy in his attempt to conserve enough energy to urge Carolyn to get the hell out of here. Now that he had nothing to do but wait, that he could let go, he found himself able to kick back and take stock, to mentally check off each of the items remaining on his to-do list.

And to wait for the inevitable arrival of the Shillies...

It was so quiet. And yet, there were sounds. A small animal scurrying about in the blackberry bush behind him; what he took for a squirrel scrambling up a nearby tree trunk in fits and starts. A bird chirping nearby.

The world was dark, but that was because his eyes were closed. It was easier that way.

A cool breeze was brushing across his face.

A new sound, then. This one was artificial.

He knew that sound, but it was difficult to recall what it was. And then it came to him.

A shuttle...

Of course. A shuttle. A Shillie shuttle. It was landing. Very near.

Some time passed. He didn't know how much, but some. A little.

He sensed a presence nearby. Someone, some *thing*, was standing over him.

He opened his eyes.

It took a few seconds; more than a few. He struggled to focus. Then he struggled to process what he saw.

A Shylmahn... leaning a bit forward, looking down at him, studying him.

Jason drew what little energy he had left from wherever it might be in his system. He smiled. He licked his lips, drew in a thin thread of breath, marshaled that energy in one last push.

"Hey man," he said. "How's it goin'?"

EsJen pushed the metal door open and stepped outside. The door closed behind her with a soft hush as she started down the wide walkway.

Few of her fellow Shylmahn truly appreciated gardens such as this, but the number was growing. As much as they were adapting the Chehnon environment to their own needs, the Shylmahn were adapting to Chehno;

and not just the environment and its myriad ecosystems, but the variety of foods as well. Many had begun dabbling in the native Chehnon ways in diet, social customs and mannerisms.

Are we losing what makes us Shylmahn?

How often had that question come into her thoughts these last few years? And what would that really mean?

This is our home now, she told herself. We are as much of this world as we are of Shylmah. More so. That other world is forever lost to us. Should we not adapt, to truly become one with this new world, even as we adapt this new world to us?

But what of our culture, what of our social fabric? What of our history? What of all that makes us... *us*?

If we lose that, what really was the purpose in reaching out to the stars to survive? Will we truly have survived if we are no longer Shylmahn?

I'm talking myself in circles.

The walkway emptied onto a small patio of paving stones, benches, a low wall covered in ivy. Beyond the wall was an open, treeless plain, and beyond that the horizon. The sun was just coming up, splashing dawn colors across the landscape.

As she stood taking in the peace of the morning, she heard the door she had come through at the other end of the walkway open, a moment later hush closed.

That would be BehLahk.

EsJen had hoped for more alone time.

Ah, well. Let the day begin.

She spoke to the sound of the approaching footsteps behind her without turning from the sight of the coming dawn.

"BehLahk. How are you this morning?"

"I am quite fine, EsJen." He stood beside her. "Perhaps as fine as the arrival of this wonderful new day."

It is extraordinary, to be sure, she thought to herself. The sun had finished its climb up from the horizon and was now in full bloom. The sky was clear. It was going to be a warm, sunny day.

She indicated they should walk and started down a narrow path that ran along the back of the garden. BehLahk strolled along beside her.

"You wish to discuss TohPeht?" he asked. BehLahk and TohPeht-ShahnTahr had met again and had talked several times since TohPeht's return.

"As much as you feel comfortable relating to me," said EsJen. She would never ask BehLahk to violate the trust he had managed to establish with this entity born of the joining of TohPeht and the intelligence that had been ShahnTahr. Yet she would know the true motive behind TohPeht's return.

"Nothing has passed between us that I cannot share, EsJen."

"That is good." She had no way of knowing whether or not BehLahk was being fully truthful. The Shylmahn scientist had become quite adept at deception, an art that he had picked up from the Chehnon. "First and foremost then, my friend... has TohPeht spoken to you of his reasons for returning from his quest for life experiences?"

"I am afraid that he has not," BehLahk said smoothly. "However, I would say that whatever it is that has drawn TohPeht home, the reason may be insignificant, and may in fact be nothing more than another aspect of his journey."

"I would not be comfortable relying on such an assumption."

"I simply postulate a possibility," he shrugged. "I myself would not assume it to be so without something more than an untested hypothesis. Still, the fact that he has said or done nothing to suggest there is anything untoward afoot is in itself evidence of a sort."

Unless the purpose of his return is to bear witness to this "untoward" event as part of his gathering of life experiences, thought EsJen. She couldn't bring herself to say such a thing aloud.

"EsJen, whatever his reason for returning, he continues to hold the well-being of the Shylmahn close to his heart." BehLahk smiled then. "And on that assumption, I do most comfortably rely."

The walkway spilled into a small square. EsJen stopped and faced BehLahk directly.

"Very well," she stated. "I will be patient; as patient as I am able. But I ask that the moment you know something, the moment you suspect something, that you let me know."

"Of course." BehLahk gave a half nod. "But I am confident that once he chooses to impart his purpose, he will do so first to you, and not to me."

"Then under the one circumstance, I will be the first to know; under the other, the second."

"Of course." BehLahk gave another half nod. "You may rest assured."

I do not, she thought, and she started walking again. BehLahk's increasing use of Chehnon idioms sometimes irritated her. He seemed to find it clever. She found it unsettling, all the more so as she occasionally found herself doing the same thing.

They started along another walkway, continued in silence as they worked their way around the perimeter of the garden and eventually back to the door. Once there, she dismissed him with a nod.

Alone again, EsJen returned to the courtyard at the far end of the garden. She sat at one of the benches, closed her eyes to the warming rays of the sun.

The ShahnTahr companion probe eased down silently beside and behind her. It would wait. EsJen would communicate when ready.

As it waited, ShahnTahr carried on with its many other duties; processing information, assigning and directing tasks as requested and required by EsJen.

And it continued to assimilate the information regarding the recent incident concerning the Chehnon Carolyn Britton and Jason Britton. Data was processed and a standalone summary was being created that would no doubt be a primary element of discussion once EsJen was ready. The processed data was also being integrated into and associations established with a number of existing ongoing narratives.

NehLoc had been well within his sphere of authority when he had directed the Chehnon flyer to be brought down. And since EsJen had not given specific instructions that it not be, there was little she could do at this point in the way of direct disciplinary action.

For ShahnTahr, the real concern with NehLoc was that he had taken such action knowing full well that EsJen would not have approved. She would most certainly have used her position to insist that the craft be brought down in such a way as to ensure the occupants were unharmed and then taken into custody.

The fact that NehLoc had taken the action he had, in the way that he had, was an indicator to ShahnTahr that NehLoc likely had underlying secondary motivations. Perhaps it had been a declaration to other Chehnon. Such was the preferred of the possibilities that came to ShahnTahr's mind. Anything else portended unprecedented issues lay ahead involving NehLoc.

Observation for now. ShahnTahr would make recommendations as further data warranted.

The matter requiring immediate resolution was the departure from the crash site of the surviving Chehnon and that she had taken the object with her.

"All right, ShahnTahr. Let's talk." EsJen straightened, though she remained seated on the bench. ShahnTahr moved into the position customary for exchange with her.

The ensuing conversation went much as he had believed it would.

EsJen quickly set aside the issue of NehLoc and entered into a discussion of the potential repercussions resulting from the actions that had been taken.

First, as ShahnTahr anticipated, was the matter of Carolyn Britton's departure from the crash site with the object. It was most likely an energy pod component. Importance had obviously been placed on recovering the artifact, and had involved considerable risk. Whatever their need for the component at this time, it was essential to Shylmahn interests that this Chehnon be taken into custody and the Shylmahn object reclaimed.

Second was the matter of the death of the other Chehnon. EsJen was concerned as to how the native population would respond to the elimination of Jason Britton. From the general populace there was the potential of a martyrdom response, a reaction perhaps even encouraged by individuals looking for just such an opportunity.

While this was a very real possibility, EsJen was even more concerned by the possible reaction of individuals more closely tied to the subject, specifically the other members of the Britton family and those with whom they had surrounded themselves.

The Britton family was an enduring risk smoldering just under the surface of the truce between Shylmahn and Chehnon, but they had also played a key role in that very truce and were largely responsible for its continuing existence, and for the continuing peace.

This made for a very tenuous and complex relationship, one that to now EsJen had managed to maintain despite numerous impediments. ShahnTahr agreed that the elimination of Jason Britton did create the potential for the disruption of that relationship and the re-ignition of the conflict between Shylmahn and the Chehnon that the truce had to now quelled.

A return to open conflict would be a distraction from the ongoing advancement of the Shylmahn society, and the security and progress of the society was and always would be ShahnTahr's primary purpose, whatever his current role. As such, while discord with the Chehnon was not a serious calculable long-term threat, at least not one that ShahnTahr could at present identify, open conflict would not be beneficial to the purpose. The continuing existence of a compliant Chehnon population had value.

And so EsJen would focus her efforts first on maintaining the relationship with the Chehnon Michael Britton, and second in doing whatever she could to support him in his efforts to keep his population calm in the face of the impending crisis.

Michael would certainly be displeased over the death of his uncle and the inevitable detainment of his aunt. But EsJen was hopeful that he would be able to set aside his personal feelings, and acting in his role as leader of the Chehnon would focus on the greater good.

EsJen frequently used Michael's sense of duty to his position to gently guide him. She would do so now.

And so back to the issue of Carolyn Britton and the energy pod component that she most likely had in her possession. She would be detained and questioned, and the reason behind reacquiring the artifact discovered. Until the purpose was identified, it had to be assumed the threat was real and imminent.

Several items of data had come to ShahnTahr's attention over the previous few years that alluded to a surreptitious project the Chehnon were working on, the development of some grand device. While nothing definitive had been noted, the implication was that it was either a device that could impart significant yet precisely targeted destruction, or an enhanced version of the energy disruption device the Chehnon had developed and used prior to the truce five years earlier.

If there was such a project, which was as yet far from certain, then the attempt to reacquire the long-hidden stolen piece of equipment might be related to that project. And any device they developed that utilized a component of a Shylmahn energy pod could well prove to be a very real and significant threat.

The effort recently expended and the risks taken to recover the component would suggest the completion of the project to be close at hand.

The apprehension of the Chehnon Carolyn Britton was imperative.

BehLahk came into the cafeteria, walked around the eight tables and smiled at the food server standing behind the counter. She smiled back and began preparing a plate for him. She made a few suggestions and he obligingly went along. She knew that he enjoyed trying new things and always pointed out when there was something different on the lunch menu.

He had only taken a few bites of his meal when TohPeht-ShahnTahr sat down opposite him, a glass of water in one hand and a piece of fruit in the other.

"Hello, BehLahk," said TohPeht.

"Good afternoon, TohPeht," said BehLahk. "How are you today?"

"Quite well. Thank you for asking." TohPeht took a bite of his fruit, chewed a moment and swallowed, studying BehLahk as he did so. "How goes your research?"

"Well." They had discussed his research on a number of occasions these past days, most recently just the evening before. There was nothing to add.

BehLahk took a drink from his glass of juice, looked over the rim of the glass at the unique being sitting across from him.

He could not take the credit, nor the blame, for what had happened to TohPeht, but BehLahk had from the beginning done what he could to fashion circumstances, to nudge and maneuver, to create situations that would make the Shylmahn race and their new home as one, as they had once been with their birth world. He could not have known that the course he had set down would have led to the creation of the TohPeht-ShahnTahr hybrid sitting before him, but considering the guiding hand he had used with them both, perhaps this being was just what was needed to complete the task he had set for himself.

The Shylmahn must become an integral part of the ecosystem of this new world. There must be some adaptation on their part, both physical and cultural. Physical would come by necessity and by exposure, the guiding influence of a millennia of evolution. Cultural, on the other hand, would require a change in society, in thinking, in the way the Shylmahn interacted with the other elements of the ecosystem into which they were trying to integrate.

But the new home must also adapt. There must be, by necessity, changes to the ecosystem, adjustments and a shifting of the norm as niches struggled to adapt and push into neighboring niches.

Caution must be taken, however, to ensure that the entire ecosystem did not collapse.

BehLahk watched as a thin, veiled smile slowly appeared within TohPeht's tranquil expression.

"What is it?" he asked.

"Nothing, really," said TohPeht. "Just a passing thought. A whisper of words."

"Hmm. There's a lot of that going around."

"Is there?"

"I don't know, really," said BehLahk. *It's just something the Chehnon say...*

"Oh." TohPeht smiled again. This one was more out in the open. "How was your meeting with EsJen this morning? It went well, I trust?"

"She is dealing with a lot of issues right now."

"Did she discuss them with you?"

BehLahk gave TohPeht a knowing look. "You know that she didn't."

"Do I?" TohPeht shrugged the human shrug he had become familiar with. "Perhaps so. The subject of the downed Chehnon flyer didn't come up?"

"Our conversation was primarily about you."

"Was it?"

BehLahk used two fingers to push his plate aside. He drank the last of his juice and set the empty glass carefully beside the plate.

"What does ShahnTahr think will come of it?" he asked.

"The shooting down of the flyer?" TohPeht thought about that a moment, gave another of his shrugs. "Much depends on how EsJen can guide Michael."

That's about how BehLahk figured it. At least, insofar as anything could be done.

This could actually work in favor of BehLahk's plans, if things went just right. The problem was that there was very little that BehLahk could do to push things along.

He would continue as planned and hope that EsJen was successful.

Just not too successful.

BehLahk placed his hands on the table and laced his fingers together.

"Do you have alternative options, should EsJen—"

"I believe so," said TohPeht. His humor was gone. "I have some influence with ShahnTahr."

Unsettling if true, thought BehLahk. But an important tool, should it be needed. He wasn't always able to guide ShahnTahr as much he would like. To use TohPeht as intermediary to ShahnTahr offered new possibilities.

BehLahk had to rein in a sudden rush of thoughts. He would explore this later. Now, he and TohPeht had other concerns.

"Have you made arrangements?" he asked.

"I have," said TohPeht. "It is to be a simple field trip. I have requested that you accompany me."

Chapter Five

Victoria rounded the corner of the narrow hall just as Michael stepped out of his office. He had a folder tucked under his arm, overstuffed with pages of notes and talking points; on his way to the meeting of the governing council. He dreaded it. The idea of being trapped in a room filled with city and regional administrators for hours on end chilled him.

Victoria came to a sharp, stiff stop directly in front of him, took a deep breath and a dramatic pause.

Uh oh, he thought.

"Miriam didn't come alone," she stated.

"Craig's with her?" Michael liked Craig. The mayor of Freetown could usually be counted on to stand with him.

Victoria shook her head ominously. "Jenny," she said. "And your father."

Okay, now that was odd. He could see Jenny showing up; they hadn't seen each other in a while. And she would know of the meeting, so it would be an opportunity to meet up with some of her other friends, as well.

But his father? Now?

The three of them? Jenny, Miriam and his father, at the same time?

"They came together?" he asked.

"It looks that way."

This was serious, then. With Miriam coming in Craig's place, Michael had expected resistance business, but this must be big.

Damn. He couldn't just blow off the council meeting.

"They'll have to wait. I can't miss the meeting." He raised a brow. "Can I?"

Victoria smiled consolingly. "Sorry. No. But take comfort. Miriam will be with you."

"There is that, I suppose."

"Nate will keep Jenny and your father busy." Joseph hadn't seen his grandson in a long time.

Michael lifted up the folder and started away, grumbling. "They could be in for a long wait."

He wasn't yet half way to the meeting hall when a young woman came rushing up, blocking his path. She had an anxious, almost frightened look on her face. She fumbled with her words, but did finally manage to get it out.

"EsJen is here."

EsJen stood waiting at the far end of a short, narrow table. The wall on her right was all windows, beyond which was a small courtyard. Light shone through the glass and into the little conference room, splashing sunshine across the floor, the table, and the opposite wall.

The door opened. Michael Britton came into the room. He set a folder down on the table, looked curiously at the leader of the Shylmahn.

EsJen thought he appeared nervous; more nervous than she would have expected. She and Michael had a cordial enough relationship. They actually got along fairly well.

Arriving here unannounced and unexpected might make him a bit anxious, but this was more. A lot more.

Something was going on.

"Michael," she nodded in greeting. "Is everything all right?"

"Hello, EsJen. I was about to ask you the same thing."

"Have I come at a bad time?"

Oh, no, not at all... thought Michael. *Just the biggest governing council meeting ever, and my father and Jenny show up with Miriam, with who-knows-what going on... and now you?*

"No. Not at all." Michael indicated the chair beside EsJen. "Please, have a seat."

They sat facing one another. Michael clasped his hands and placed them on the folder in front of him. EsJen held her hands in her lap.

"I'm sorry to have arrived unannounced," she said. "I am afraid this could not wait for the established channels."

Now Michael really was worried. This couldn't be coincidence, EsJen and Joseph Britton arriving at virtually the same time.

"That's all right, EsJen. You are welcome here anytime."

"Thank you, Michael. I appreciate that. I really do."

"So, what is it?"

"I'm afraid I have bad news. I thought you should hear it from me."

"All right." Michael did his best not to squirm in his chair. His interlaced fingers tensed.

"It's about Jason Britton. He is your uncle, is he not?"

"Jason?" *resistance business...* "Is something wrong?"

"I'm very sorry. He was in the Province, traveling in a small flyer. Covert activity, I regret to say. The craft was brought down."

"Is he all right?"

"The action was taken without my authorization; but it was with justification."

"EsJen?"

"He did not survive."

"Oh, geez." Michael leaned forward, pushing the folder, his hands pressing down. "Oh, EsJen."

"I am sorry, Michael," said EsJen. "He should not have been in the Province. Bringing down the flyer was fully within protocol. They did not need further authorization."

"Flyer?" he asked numbly. "What sort of flyer?"

"NehLoc referred to it as a hybrid. A small craft, mix of Chehnon and Shylmahn technology. We have not seen anything like it before."

So, thought Michael. *Another little secret out of Phoenix Labs. I always seem to be out of the loop, and yet they are always so quick to tell me different.*

They no doubt thought it best, considering his role as head of the council, and the relationship this necessarily created with EsJen.

Perhaps they were right, but he sometimes felt manipulated. Hell, he always felt manipulated; by his father, by Phoenix, by everyone.

"EsJen..."

"Yes, I know."

"This isn't going to go down well."

"I know," said EsJen.

Michael leaned back in his chair. He wanted to kick at something, hit something, lash out at something; at someone; at anyone.

Jason... gone...

"Damn it, EsJen. Setting aside my own feelings, Jason was important. He wasn't just an old fossil out of the past. He was really, really important."

"I understand."

This isn't going to go away, thought Michael. *This is going to stir up a lot of trouble. Damn, what the hell am I supposed to do?*

"There can be no ignoring this."

"You are the leader of the Chehnon, Michael. Your actions must be dictated by that, and not by personal feelings."

"Don't give me that crap, EsJen." Everyone might look for him to respond as the head of the governing council, but they would in fact expect him to respond as the nephew of Jason Britton.

EsJen sighed. She had to tread carefully here. "Let us not forget that Jason Britton was working against the greater good, and had been doing so for many years."

"You don't get it, EsJen. After all these years, how can you not get it? You still only see it from your side. Can't you at least glimpse what we see?"

"Michael, I—"

"Jason Britton was one of a handful of bright lights shining against a bloodthirsty invasion. That is what people see. Many of us weren't even born yet, have no memories of the invasion, have no idea what Earth was like before the Shylmahn, but we do know that a few selfless humans, like Jason, and Carolyn, and my father, led the fight against invaders who murdered hundreds of millions of people. That is how most humans see him. All the more so now that you have made him a martyr."

§

Michael met Joseph in the small courtyard outside the meeting room where he and EsJen had met only minutes before. Michael told him that his brother had been killed by the Shylmahn while he had been piloting a flyer inside the province. He watched his father take two steps over to the concrete bench and sit down, lean forward and rest his arms on his knees, clasp his hands together. He took a deep breath. It came out slow and shaky.

"Are you okay?" Michael sat down beside him.

"No."

For a long time then, neither said anything. Joseph had lost a lot of family over the years, especially during those first years of the invasion. He had lost brothers and sisters, nephews and nieces. He had lost his wife, Michael's mother.

Michael saw it all coming back now on his father's face. There was a lot of pain there. And anger.

There was rage there.

The fight wasn't yet over.

"Dad," Michael prompted finally.

"Yeah," Joseph managed. He let out a smooth, calming sigh.

"We need to be careful," said Michael. "We can't let this get out of control."

Joseph didn't respond to that.

That made Michael nervous.

"Dad," he started again. "Dad, what was Jason doing in the Province?"

"He was getting something for me; something that I left in there a long time ago."

Well, that sounded awfully damned rehearsed.

"And?"

"And... and we need it."

"I get that," said Michael. "What is it? What's so important that it's worth—"

"Shillie tech."

This was frustrating.

"That's it? That's all you're gonna tell me?"

Joseph shrugged. "I'm sorry, Michael. There's nothing else to tell."

Oh, come on, thought Michael. *Something big is coming down, and I'm being shut out. Completely shut out. Damn it, I'm a leader in the resistance.*

Wasn't he?

Maybe not... not if he was being spoon-fed only what they wanted him to know.

Damn it.

And what about this flyer that Jason had been piloting? How had he been left out of that? Set aside his role in the resistance, such as it was, shouldn't the head of the council have been aware of an experimental flyer being developed in Phoenix? Since the establishment of the treaty five years earlier, humans were permitted to fly, but there hadn't been much of it. Hardly any at all, in fact. There were a few small planes using vegetable-based bio-fuel, but practically speaking, humans were grounded.

So this was damned important.

Joseph sighed tiredly. "No hidden agenda, Michael; at least not one that I'm aware of. When I got to Phoenix, I was as surprised as you when Jason suggested we fly back."

"You two flew up here together?"

"Like I said, I sent him into the Province."

You went to Phoenix Labs, you and Jason flew back in an experimental flyer, and you sent him into the Shylmahn Province to retrieve some Shillie tech that you just had to have.

And there's nothing more to tell me? Really?

Michael wanted more, wanted answers, needed answers, but it was clear he wasn't going to get anything that Joseph didn't think he should know. Yes, his father may have been an everyman before the coming of the Shylmahn, but that was a long, long time ago. These days, Joseph Britton seldom did or said anything without first carefully calculating exactly how it would impact his plan to return the planet to humanity.

And just where do I fit into it? Michael wondered. *Apparently not where I thought...*

A door on the opposite side of the courtyard opened. Miriam and Jenny entered from a small side hall. Michael watched them follow a walkway around the edge of the courtyard and wind their way toward him. It appeared to Michael that Miriam was relying more on her cane than the last time he had seen her. The years were telling on her.

He welcomed them somberly, hugged them, held their hands, promised them that they would get together after the meeting. He was already late.

"I'll join you there in a minute," said Miriam.

It was left to Joseph to break the news to Miriam and Jenny.

Outwardly, Jenny took it the hardest. She had always been particularly close to her uncle, going back to her days as stationmaster. For the moment, however, she managed to steel herself, as did Miriam, and they all tried to assess what this might mean to the mission, to their plans.

"EsJen didn't tell Michael anything about Carolyn being involved," said Joseph.

"But she was definitely there. With Jason," Miriam stated. "Wasn't she?"

"Yes."

"Then..."

"It means that Carolyn is alive," said Joseph. "Or she was."

"Was she captured?" asked Jenny.

"I don't know. Probably not."

"No?" asked Miriam.

"If she had been, I think they would have said something. But if she's still out there, then EsJen isn't sure what might happen next; too many unknowns. She'd as soon track her down and capture her, and then tell us about it after the fact."

"I suppose you're right."

"And the artifact?" asked Jenny.

"My guess is that Carolyn has it, and she's trying to get it out of the province."

Miriam spoke softly. "Then everything is still on."

"It looks that way."

"How much did you tell Michael?" asked Jenny.

Joseph shook his head slowly, tiredly, sadly.

Jenny nodded.

Miriam pointed her cane in the direction of the door. "I should get to the meeting." She didn't sound very enthusiastic about the prospect of spending the afternoon with a bunch of people she didn't really like, arguing politics and bickering over meaningless crap.

All right, so there was probably some important crap, too; but sorting through the one to get to the other was really unpleasant.

Carolyn stood silent, unmoving, her back against the wall of the front showroom of the pre-invasion car dealership. The large plate glass window spanned the wall thirty feet in front of her, revealing the street beyond. The sun shone through the glass, illuminating and warming the entire showroom floor, reflecting off three once-shiny new cars that sat waiting for prospective buyers. A blur of heat rose up from the metal.

Carolyn watched the movement in the street beyond.

Four Shylmahn walked slowly, methodically down the center of the avenue, carefully taking in the scene around them, ever alert for any movement, two hunter probes traveling with them.

One of the Shillies glanced in the direction of the large glass wall of the car dealership. The reflection of the glass and Carolyn's blending into the wall behind her made her almost invisible.

But one of the primary sensors of hunter probes was thermal.

Carolyn hoped the heat in the room and the heat rising up from the metal of the vehicles between her and the probes would mask her body heat.

The hunting party continued on past.

She waited. She gave it a slow thirty count, then moved to the open hallway on her right and followed it to the six-bay garage in the back of the building. She was careful to keep her steps soft and not make any unnecessary noise. She wasn't in the clear yet. Those probes could pick up the sound of a human clearing her throat from a very long way away.

She walked to the car that was parked in the second bay. A small SUV, all wheel drive. The hood was up and a toolkit was unrolled and laid out on the fender. Her half-eaten biscuit was sitting next to the box of new spark plugs. She picked up the biscuit and took a bite. She set the remainder back down, leaned in under the hood and got back to work.

EsJen stepped into her private shuttle's passenger section and settled into her seat, one of only four in the spacious compartment. One of her two escort continued to the forward section, the other took his position in the seat at the back of the shuttle.

The ShahnTahr probe hovered near the small table near EsJen.

EsJen eased into her seat. She took long, slow breaths and rested her head back against the headrest. Looking out the portal, she saw the Chehnon's administration complex, and beyond that the little community they called Garden City.

"Well?" she asked ShahnTahr, without looking at the probe.

"Michael Britton knows nothing of the device the Chehnon are developing." ShahnTahr had of course followed the conversation between EsJen and Michael, monitoring the meeting through the sensor that was clipped inside EsJen's collar.

"It would seem they have kept their leader in the dark."

"We suspected as much."

"His involvement with the resistance is minimal. I wonder if he realizes how minimal."

"Designed misdirection, perhaps."

"Likely."

"Interesting," said ShahnTahr. "And... what of Michael's concern regarding a possible uprising over the Jason Britton incident?"

"I believe it best that we stay out of it for now. Let him deal with it."

There was a low rumble, the shuttle shook slightly and began to rise. EsJen turned from the portal, looked forward and lifted a hand, then a finger. A few moments later, a petite Shylmahn came into the passenger compartment with a glass of water.

"Thank you," said EsJen, taking the glass. The staff person returned forward.

EsJen took a sip and set the glass into a holder on the table. She let her hands drop into her lap, again laid her head back against the headrest.

ShahnTahr moved the probe around in front of her, just beyond the table.

"What of the device, EsJen?" asked ShahnTahr. Everything ShahnTahr knew, all the information that he had gathered over the previous five years, independently and collectively, told him the device was almost complete. "Its development cannot be allowed to continue."

"Therefore, Carolyn Britton cannot take the component from the province," said EsJen. "She must be stopped."

"Agreed," ShahnTahr stated.

EsJen let her gaze drift back to the portal, to the clouds beyond the glass. "I will not let the Chehnon do to this world what we did to Shylmah," she said.

"Of course not."

"Madness," she said quietly. "Unforgivable madness."

Chapter Six

There were four tables pushed together in the middle of the conference room, creating one large table for the twenty council members and guests. Michael sat at one end with three others.

Miriam sat at the opposite end, and for most of the meeting had remained silent. She had spoken only rarely and had raised her voice only once, when that jerk from Newtown, who was there representing that even bigger jerk Ethan Perry, had suggested they slow down the expansion of the train routes. He was concerned that it might be making the Shylmahn nervous.

What a moron.

Fortunately this particular discussion came near the end of the meeting. The guy gave her a cool glare as he marched past on his way out with the others, leaving only Miriam and Michael in the room.

Michael leaned back in his chair. He managed a cheerless smile.

"It went better than I thought it would," he said.

"No one pulled a weapon."

"I thought for a moment that you might."

"Nah. Everyone knows Harlan's an idiot. If he suggests something, you can almost guarantee it's not going anywhere." She shrugged then. "I just can't stand the man."

"Evidently."

Another shrug. "I never claimed to be a politician."

"And yet here we are."

"I blame your father."

"Yes. Strange how that worked out." He stood then, walked the length of the tables and sat down near Miriam. He leaned forward and placed his arms on the table, clasped his hands together.

Miriam waited. Michael didn't say anything for a long time.

"Miriam," he started at last. He took a deep breath, stared at his hands. "I need to know what's going on."

"The plan goes on. Jason's death doesn't change that."

"Yes, the plan. The grand plan. Joseph Britton's great, multi-year plan."

"Your father's plan."

Michael sat back with force, waved his hands out in front of him. "And just what is that plan, Miriam? What is my role in it? Is any of what I've been told the truth? Am I a part of this thing, or just a tool of it?"

"Michael—"

"The truth, Miriam."

"We each have our part. Our... role." Miriam spoke softly; so softly that Michael had no choice but to lean closer.

"There was a time when I thought I knew what that meant," he answered. "But I don't. Not really. I never did."

"It means that we each know what we need to know. No more; certainly no less. You know exactly what it is necessary for you to know. It doesn't matter that you are Joseph's son. It doesn't matter that you are the head of the council."

"I'm guessing that my being the head of the council has meant that—"

"You know what you need to know," Miriam stated firmly. "No more, no less."

"All right," he said after a long pause. He leaned back again, took a moment to sort out his thoughts. He had said what he intended to say, asked what he had intended to ask, hadn't really expected to get any answers. "So, what is it that I need to know now? What brings you here now? Certainly not this meeting."

"Most certainly not this meeting." To business then. "Something is going to happen, and you need to be ready when it does. You had to be kept out of the loop on this until now. It was important. Only a few people knew of it, and fewer still know the full story."

"Okay, Miriam. So what is it?"

"The world is about to change, and we are the ones changing it." A deep breath, then... "You know of the plant on the Shillie home world?"

"Some gigantic plant covering a whole continent."

"The Veltahk."

Michael felt himself going slightly numb. Not for the first time this day. "What about it?"

"There're three ways to work the Shillies."

"Okay..." he shifted forward.

"One, show 'em they're losing who they are, losing their culture. Losing their... Shylmahn. It's like their soul. Just the thought of losing it freaks 'em out."

Yeah, we're doing that, thought Michael.

"Two, threaten worldwide destruction, like what they did to their own planet."

Oh, god... is that what Jason was involved in?

"And three?"

"Yes. And three. Bring the Veltahk here. The thing that eventually drove them from their world. Bring 'em face to face with it all over again."

"Are you telling me... but... how?"

"Designed and developed by Phoenix Labs, at your father's direction."

We're hitting the Shylmahn with all three, all at once...

"Miriam... Are you saying we're going to cover the world with this plant?"

"It's already done. There are different variations growing in every climate on Earth. And it's spreading like wildfire."

"Are you insane?"

"Probably," said Miriam. "Let's hope the Shillies think so."

The moon and stars were hidden behind a thick blanket of heavy clouds, leaving the night very dark. Jenny found her father sitting at a wooden picnic table on a narrow greenbelt that ran along a row of small, clean, well-built cabins. He had been given the use of one of the cabins while they were in Garden City.

"Can't sleep?" she asked, and she sat down beside him.

"I'll go in a minute," he said.

"Hmm. Me neither."

"How's Michael?'

He knew how Michael was. Jenny knew that he knew how Michael was.

"Dad, you can't go in after Carolyn."

"No?" Joseph grinned sheepishly. "No, I suppose not."

"You don't know where she is. Even if you did, you would only be calling attention to her."

"That was part of the plan."

"You know what I mean."

"I know," he said. "I just... feel responsible."

"You are responsible. You sent her in there. That doesn't change anything."

"So," Joseph sighed again. "How's Michael?"

Now Jenny grinned. "He's fine. I'll keep an eye on him."

"Sorry to put that on you."

"I understand." Jenny glanced at a nearby shrub. A young azalea. Would it survive in the new world they were creating? "Are you and Miriam leaving tomorrow?" she asked.

"Day after."

"I thought—"

"No southbound train tomorrow. There's work on the tracks up north."

"It's not because of, *you know*... is it?"

"I don't think so. Not yet."

"Good," said Jenny. "That would certainly push up the schedule, wouldn't it?"

"I think we're all right," said Joseph. "So long as Carolyn can get out of the province."

"If anyone can, she can."

Carolyn brought the small SUV to a slow stop. Up ahead, the county highway was covered in fallen trees and branches for a stretch of fifty or sixty feet. She got out of the car. After checking either side of the road for a passable route around the debris, she set about to clear the road.

Tossing aside the smaller branches and pulling aside the smallest tree, she was left with a larger tree that was too heavy to move out of the way on her own. The top of the tree was only about six feet beyond the pavement, but she saw no way around it, not even with all wheel drive. She returned to her car and brought out a length of rope. She tied one end to the tree-top, the other to the undercarriage of her car just under the front bumper. Climbing in behind the wheel, she started up the engine and put the vehicle in reverse. She pulled the tree back enough to bring the top of the tree onto the pavement and dragged it a few more feet for good measure.

She got out and untied the rope from the tree and the undercarriage, not easy now that she'd managed to pull the knots tight.

She heard it then as she was tossing the rope back into the car. The sound was unmistakable. It was a Shillie shuttle, coming from the south.

Carolyn thought about making a run for the trees, didn't think she had time. She dropped to the pavement instead and rolled under the car.

The shuttle was overhead seconds later, about a hundred feet or so up, and following the highway. It was traveling slow for a shuttle, maybe fifty or sixty miles an hour. Passing over the scene, it never slowed. Still, Carolyn waited for the sound to fade before sliding out again into the open.

Perhaps they thought the car was abandoned.

Would they come back and check?

She would, if she were them.

If this was a regular route for them, the car parked on the highway would be a new sight. It hadn't been here before. If abandoned, it had to be recent. If not abandoned, it would soon be on the move.

Damn... If she continued in the car, she'd be following after the shuttle. If they don't see her right off, once they made it back here and found the vehicle gone, it wouldn't take much to track her down.

If she left the car, feigning abandoned, and continued on foot, while it's true she could have gone in any direction, weren't they likely to follow the highway south? As that was where the car had been traveling?

Shit, she grumbled, and climbed in behind the wheel. She would follow the highway to the next side road, take that for a ways and then leave it hidden under the canopy of trees.

No. Not the next side road... the one after that.

Yeah, sure... that'll confuse 'em... she sneered.

Still, it was better than nothing.

She only hoped to make this mad dash before the Shillies returned.

And then I'm back on foot... crap.

Joseph and Miriam boarded the train, finding only four others in the passenger car. It was a family; mom and dad, two kids no more than eight or nine years old.

Choosing a pair of seats furthest from the family, Joseph sat down next to the window, Miriam in the aisle seat beside him.

Jenny was standing on the platform outside. She waved when she saw her father settling in.

Joseph opened the window and poked his head out. "You sure you're going to be all right?" he asked.

"I'll be fine, Dad."

"Jenny, I'm really sorry. If there was any other way..."

"It's all right."

"No, it's not, but..." he sighed. He felt really uncomfortable about putting this on her. Her only reason for staying behind was to keep an eye on her brother. If he showed any indication that he was about to do or say something that would conflict with their plans, she was to gently dissuade him.

Just how he might threaten their plans, or how she might deter or redirect him if he did, were gray areas.

The train lurched forward. Jenny gave another slight wave and Joseph raised a hand in good-bye. He slid the window closed and settled back in his seat.

"She'll be fine," said Miriam.

"Yeah," he mumbled. "And I'm still a bastard."

"Because a' that?" Miriam made a face and gave him a raspberry. "You're a bastard, but that ain't why."

Up near the front of the car, the older of the two children was kneeling in his seat, arms dangling over the seatback. The boy was staring unflinchingly at Joseph and Miriam.

Miriam lifted her hand and wiggled her fingers. The boy started to smile, chose instead not to. He maintained his hard frown, his steady gaze. His focus moved from Miriam to Joseph and then back to Miriam.

The mom tapped the boy on the shoulder, whispered harshly. When the boy refused to budge, she grabbed him by the shirt and pulled him down into his seat.

"It's gonna be a long trip," Miriam grumbled. She wasn't really what one would call a kid person.

And with the scheduled stops, it really would be a long trip; at least two full days to Phoenix Labs, Miriam's eventual destination. They were set to meet someone at each of those scheduled stops, or so was the plan. Beginning several weeks earlier, the embedded team at each location was to have someone waiting at the station during the time of their scheduled stop, this in the event a courier was on board with a message.

On this run, that courier was Joseph Britton, and the message was a biggie.

The depot was small, even by current standards. The building itself was little more than a shed, eight feet by ten. A wooden porch fronted the building, spanning corner to corner. Eddie Blythe sat on the roughhewn bench next to the door.

He leaned forward, glanced up the tracks.

Nothing.

He leaned back again and rested an elbow on the back of the bench. There was no rush. He had all day; all week, for that matter.

The little village he had finally chosen to call home was quiet and isolated, which suited him just fine. After the war with the Shillies, and that bizarre final scuffle that had led to the truce, quiet and isolated was absolutely okay by Eddie Blythe.

He was still part of the resistance, such as it was, though this was mostly due to Miguel. He and Miguel had found themselves back in Freetown immediately after the truce, and had worked out of there for almost two years before volunteering to help set up this outpost. The outpost eventually became a village.

Eddie would just as soon have gotten lost out here, never more to have to deal with the Shillies. But Miguel had other ideas. He had never wavered in his loyalty to Jason Britton, and Jason Britton wasn't about to let the whole resistance thing go. So long as Jason was alive and there was a Shillie walking around on the planet, there would be a resistance.

And if it made Miguel happy, Eddie was okay with it. Besides, the work was easy. There was little to do these past few years but for the occasional recon mission. Even now, all he had to do was make the half mile walk out here to the train depot once a week on the off chance the courier had a message for his four person team.

For the most part, life was good for Eddie Blythe.

He heard the train whistle.

Ah well... time to go to work. He stood up and took a step across the deck. After half a minute he saw the nose of the engine as a smear of shadow up where the tracks met to a vanishing point. A half minute more and it had taken full shape, approaching quickly, and before long the depot was enveloped in noise; the engine, tender car and a pair of passenger cars filled the empty space before him.

It wasn't the regular courier that stepped out to meet him, but Joseph Britton himself; Jason's brother, and from what he had personally observed arguably even more crazy than Jason when it came to the Shillies. Eddie didn't know him all that well, but he knew that these days it was Joseph who was behind most of what was going on when it came to stirring up trouble with the Shillies.

"Joseph," he said with a nod and a thin smile. He held out his hand and Joseph shook it.

Joseph briefly turned his attention to the front of the train. The engineer gave a sharp nod, set about making ready for whenever Joseph was ready.

Joseph turned back and gave a friendly smile. "Eddie, isn't it?" he asked.

"That's right," said Eddie. "This must be important, to bring you out here."

"Oh, just thought I'd take the opportunity to stretch my legs." He looked again to the engineer, who was busily fussing about his locomotive. He held up a hand, showed five fingers. The engineer waved acknowledgement and returned to his work.

Eddie looked at the windows of the nearest passenger car. A kid had his face plastered against the glass of one window, staring unflinching. It was unsettling.

Joseph looked back at what seemed to be making Eddie uncomfortable. He smiled at the boy, waved. The boy couldn't help himself. He grinned.

Joseph rested a hand on Eddie's shoulder. "Can we walk?" he asked, and with that they stepped down from the platform. They walked around behind the station and started along the trail that led back to the village. Eddie grew increasingly anxious the longer Joseph held his silence, and Joseph didn't seem in any rush to let him in on this important news. They were a good distance from the station before Joseph glanced casually back behind them and came to a stop. He turned and looked at Eddie.

"We're about to make this place extremely uncomfortable for the Shillies," he said.

Oh... is my life about to get complicated? Eddie wondered. He asked aloud, "Is that right?"

"Yes. That's right. There are going to be some major changes, and people need to know that the changes are our doing."

"And are we going to like these changes?" asked Eddie. From Joseph's tone, he suspected not.

"I wouldn't think so."

Eddie sighed softly. *Oh, yes...* he thought. *This man is about to make my life a whole helluva lot more complicated.*

He saw Joseph look over at the vegetation bordering the trail. What was that odd expression on his face?

Joseph turned to face Eddie. "And the Shillies are not going to be happy at all."

Chapter Seven

There was just enough room between the trees for the pilot to maneuver NehLoc's command shuttle to a safe landing, leaving a few yards to spare on any side. A wall of fir and alder encircled the forest clearing. The ship was twice the size of the standard Shylmahn shuttle craft, necessary so that NehLoc could bring his center of operations with him whenever he went into the wild.

In addition to the cockpit, passenger compartment and the power room, this shuttle had an operations room with three console stations and a holo station, all continually staffed. In the rear of the craft was NehLoc's small private office.

The narrow door opened and NehLoc came out of his office and entered operations. He said nothing to those at the consoles as he continued on into passenger compartment.

Two others of his team stood at the outer door, which was slowly opening outward and downward, forming a ramp. A hunter probe hovered beside them, moved out ahead of them before the ramp had locked into place.

"Ready to go," stated the taller of the two, looking back at NehLoc.

"Proceed," said NehLoc. He followed them out of the craft and down the ramp. They stepped out onto a spongy forest floor of thick mulch. The landing pads of the shuttle were buried deep in it. The air was cool and moist, and the clearing had a pungent, acrid smell.

The probe, hovering four feet in the air, had waited for the team to leave the craft. It started now to their right, reached the clearing perimeter and continued into the shadow of the trees without slowing. They followed, with NehLoc's escort carrying Shylmahn hand weapons at the ready.

NehLoc, while he had a weapon, kept it holstered. He already knew what they would find, and there wasn't any real danger expected.

They stepped out into a much smaller clearing. An old Chehnon-made vehicle was parked there, a few branches thrown over it as camouflage. It was also somewhat hidden from above by the canopy of trees that reached out over the clearing from the perimeter.

NehLoc's escort took up positions on either side of the clearing as NehLoc walked slowly around the car, absently pulling the branches off the vehicle that Carolyn had thrown haphazardly onto the hood, the roof, the windows. Coming around the back of the vehicle, he could see the road through an opening in the trees; the road by which the vehicle had traveled to get here. The Chehnon Carolyn Britton had driven several miles along that road from the main highway before abandoning it here.

Once she had been seen on the highway, her options had been limited; for her, none of them good. NehLoc believed she had made the best choice among those available to her. It had just been her bad luck that the vehicle had been found so quickly. The original sighting had been reported immediately, and rather than simply sending another shuttle back to investigate, a set of search probes had been brought in and dispatched in all directions from the location of the sighting on the main highway. It hadn't taken long.

The Chehnon was still deep inside the province, and now she was on foot. Being on foot, she was going to be all the more difficult to find, but now it was only a matter of time.

She was traveling light, NehLoc could see that by the amount of gear she had left behind, but he had eight probes out there looking for her, and they would find her.

His hunter probe had finished an investigation of the perimeter and had apparently found no signs of the possible path she had taken. She must have hidden her tracks well. NehLoc suspected she had returned to the nearby road, with the hard surface and a quick track out of here. She would take it as long as she felt comfortable, would then look for a trail that would leave minimal signs of her passing.

NehLoc followed the vehicle's tire tracks the twenty feet back to the road, stepped from the thick, spongy mulch and out onto the hardpan of the narrow forest service road. She might have gone back toward the main highway, but NehLoc suspected not. Still, he wouldn't leave it to chance. Probes had been sent in both directions, and from those then outward.

That was a lot of ground to cover.

NehLoc pushed back the doubt that tried to creep in. Doubt would solve nothing. This Chehnon must be found, and therefore would be found.

He turned about and looked back into the small clearing. Most of it was in shadow, but one thin ray of sunlight managed to streak in through the treetops, striking the vehicle at the back window.

He studied the scene.

Something was bothering him.

He didn't know it right off; didn't know at first that there was in fact something bothering him. But he was uncomfortable. It was an underlying sense of anxiety.

Something wasn't right.

Dread rose slowly up to his consciousness.

Something is wrong.

It wasn't the car. It wasn't the tire tracks. Something else. Something else. What?

The vegetation.

Oh no, oh no, oh no...

There it was; in the brush on the side of the road.

Mixed in with the natural vegetation, already beginning to choke it out.

It didn't really look the same, but... the leaves, the vines. Somehow, it was. It didn't really look like Veltahk, but it was the Veltahk. It wasn't, but it was.

Veltahk. But how? How could it be?

NehLoc stumbled forward, one step, two... slowly knelt down before the vegetation growing along the roadside. The leaves weren't exactly the same, nor the vines, but he was not mistaken. At this stage in the development, the leaves were much smaller, as were the vines. But it was the Veltahk.

NehLoc stood, stepped back. He was numb. He was confused.

How could this be?

Somebody did this. Who would do this?

Carolyn Britton?

He doubted that. He knew this Chehnon's heart. He knew Carolyn Britton more than he knew, or could know, any other Chehnon. She would never do something like this.

And in any event, she couldn't.

A Shylmahn? No... no, that was not possible.

He dropped to his knees, reached in and began pulling. He gripped the vines and pulled, ripping the vines from within the natural Chehnon vegetation.

"Here!" he called out, almost a scream. "Here! Now! Come here! Help me!" NehLoc continued ripping at the vines, found himself buried now chest deep in the leaves and vines and branches. It was a lost cause. He knew it to be a lost cause even as he continued tearing at the vegetation, native blackberry vines scratching at his Shylmahn flesh; blackberry vines that were already being overwhelmed by this strange, bizarre variation of the Veltahk.

His two escort rushed up beside him, stopped suddenly, terrified at the sight of their leader down on his hands and knees apparently gone insane.

And then first one, then the other somehow managed to see beyond the inexplicable...

"Veltahk," said one in a trembling whisper.

BehLahk came into EsJen's garden, started down the winding walkway toward the tiny courtyard near the far end. He found EsJen sitting on one of the stone benches, the ShahnTahr probe hovering nearby, as always. Here the surrounding garden wall was half-height, revealing the horizon beyond. It was cool out, the sky overhead a pale gray.

EsJen appeared lost in thought, her expression as blank as ShahnTahr's smooth metal surface. Neither acknowledged BehLahk's arrival. Misleading, he knew. They both knew that he was here. He sat down on the bench beside her, clasped his hands together and waited.

Bad things were coming. Very bad; far worse than what BehLahk had expected, and he had expected a lot. For years he had worked tirelessly to ensure the Shylmahn maintained their identity as a people, as Shylmahn, while at the same time pushing to integrate them into this new world; changes they would need to make in order to deal with and interact with the Chehnon, integrate with the ecosystem of this world. They would need to accept subtle changes in culture and society in order to better become one with this world that was now their home.

He had tread carefully in these efforts, as EsJen took a progressively harder line on such matters. She hadn't started that way; her present severe stance was a direct result of her experiences. That stance only grew more acute with time, and she more cynical and distrustful. It was therefore often more prudent that BehLahk work behind the scenes to create situations that would lead ShahnTahr to recommend to EsJen those paths or actions that would further advance BehLahk's goals and not try to come at her directly. One time it may be a confrontation with the Chehnon, another he might find a circumstance where Chehnon and Shylmahn should work together, or at least appear to do so. One day the Shylmahn would seem to suffer at the hands of a Chehnon action, whether or not that action ever really took place at all. Another day, it would be better that Shylmahn were the beneficiaries of a Chehnon kindness, more often than not that kindness manufactured by BehLahk himself.

And it wasn't just the relationship with the Chehnon. For BehLahk, this wasn't even the most important factor in the Shylmahn assimilation. Where might their culture benefit by adapting to this world? Where might their people benefit by a new way of doing or thinking?

This was more difficult, and often required that BehLahk covertly guide fellow Shylmahn unseen, and then make certain a positive light was shone upon the action.

Of recent concern to BehLahk had been the return of the much evolved TohPeht-ShahnTahr entity and what impact this might have on his gentle guidance. What he found, through cautious exchange, was that TohPeht felt very much as he. Carefully done, this genuinely new entity could be an ally; unless it turned out that his goals conflicted with TohPeht's own ultimate ambitions. He had come back for a reason.

And there was of course BehLahk's ever-present uncertainty: Joseph Britton. BehLahk and this Chehnon had abided by an uneasy alliance for years. Each knew just enough of the other's plans to know that for the present their interests converged. Each knew the other's mind and way of thinking just well enough to know that they would dance this dance only so long as there was benefit and that the other's gain did not outweigh his own.

But this?

The Veltahk...

No, BehLahk had most definitely not seen this. No one had seen this. No Shylmahn could possibly have anticipated this.

And it must have been a very closely held secret among the humans as well, for BehLahk's Chehnon spies had not known of it.

EsJen shifted position, straightened. ShahnTahr moved slightly to one side.

"Joseph has done this," said EsJen, a harsh whisper.

No one else is capable, thought BehLahk. Certainly not a Shylmahn. And no Chehnon other than Joseph Britton had enough knowledge of the Shylmahn home world, or of the impact this would have on the Shylmahn psyche.

"Yes," BehLahk stated simply.

"Almost certainly," said ShahnTahr.

"I would not have believed he would do such a thing," said EsJen.

"Joseph Britton is quite focused in his purpose," said BehLahk. "And his singular goal is to remove us from this world."

"But this will destroy it."

"The ecosystem of this world will change significantly," said Shahn-Tahr.

Quite brilliant, in its way, thought BehLahk. So, my dear friend... from the shoulders of the two-headed monster that is your grand scheme has sprouted a third, this one by far the most diabolical. I am impressed. Horrified, but impressed.

"If I might observe," BehLahk began. "First Joseph Britton holds a mirror up before the Shylmahn, attempts to shed a negative light on how this world has changed us, how it continues to change who we are; change our culture, our society, knowing how so very deeply we feel the Shylmahn within us.

"Second... we have managed to gather from several sources evidence of a mysterious weapon they are quietly developing."

"Joseph knew very well that we would figure out what they were doing," said EsJen. "He wanted us to know."

"Yes," agreed BehLahk. "It is important that we know they have it, and we must believe they are prepared to unleash it upon the world."

"I now believe them capable of anything."

"Quite," BehLahk said crisply.

EsJen trembled, breathed an audible shudder. "And now... now this."

"The final element," said BehLahk. "The key to it all; Joseph Britton transforms his world into the very thing we left behind. The very reason we left Shylmah."

"A most extreme action," ShahnTahr stated.

"I gave him that key," EsJen said sourly. "I told him of our world, of our culture. I told him of the Veltahk. I gave him everything that he needed."

"A most devious creature, yes," BehLahk sighed. "But if not this, EsJen, he would have born something else."

"And so?"

"And so? And so, how could we choose not to leave of our own accord?"

"Are you suggesting we abandon Chehno?"

"I suggest nothing. Joseph Britton is most certainly encouraging our departure."

EsJen's facial expression went icy. "We will not leave."

"Of course not," said BehLahk, betraying little emotion.

EsJen looked from BehLahk to the probe hovering nearby. "ShahnTahr. You have been curiously quiet."

"There has been little for me to contribute."

"I would know your thoughts."

"My thoughts," stated ShahnTahr. "As regards the Chehnon variation of the Veltahk, my thoughts include that it is not yet fully rooted within the ecosystem. While it is very unlikely that we will be able to eradicate it, it may yet be possible."

"BehLahk?" asked EsJen.

"We of course began research the moment NehLoc sent news of the discovery." BehLahk doubted very much they would have any answers in time, if ever. Still, as ShahnTahr said, the Veltahk was not yet fully entrenched. All available staff were investigating.

"My thoughts as they regard the Chehnon weapon," ShahnTahr continued, "must include the observation that it is likewise not yet fully realized. All available data suggests that it is unlikely to become so without incorporating the component currently in the possession of the Chehnon Carolyn Britton."

"NehLoc is close to apprehending Carolyn Britton," said EsJen.

Assuming they found an answer to the Veltahk, and that they were able to prevent the Chehnon from completing their weapon, BehLahk felt they could deal with the rest of it. But that was assuming a lot. He wasn't as confident as EsJen of NehLoc's imminent success, and was even less confident that the Veltahk could be stopped before swallowing up the world.

Would their failure in preventing either or both compel EsJen to abandon this, their second home? BehLahk had doubts. This emotion of EsJen's, more Chehnon than Shylmahn he realized, was rooted in her extraordinary relationship with Joseph Britton, and could very well compel her to take a stand when logic would suggest they consider leaving.

EsJen leaned forward and stood up. Holding her elbows in cupped hands, she turned slowly about and looked beyond the garden, beyond the half-wall, toward the horizon. The gray skies had brightened, but the sun had yet to burn through the thick clouds. She said nothing.

"EsJen, we need to keep all of our options open," said BehLahk.

"Sixty percent of our transport ships are still in orbit," said ShahnTahr. "But it will take time to make them ready for departure."

"You assume we have some place to go," said EsJen. "We do not."

That was true. Unlike their last migration, they wouldn't have centuries to search for a new home. This time, they would probably have to pick a direction and go.

"Sending a few shuttles up to our mothballed ships wouldn't take resources from our other endeavors," said BehLahk. He stood and stepped up beside her. "ShahnTahr could dispatch a few teams to investigate their status and outline the steps necessary to prepare the ships, should we choose to leave."

"That would seem a reasonable action that would in no way obligate us," ShahnTahr agreed.

EsJen's tense facial muscles suggested to BehLahk that she wanted very much to say no. *No. We are not leaving, so there is no reason to return to the ships that brought us here.*

Oh, why did we leave any ships up there?

Her duty required that she give her people the best possible chance of success should they in fact have no choice but to leave this world.

"Very well." She looked to ShahnTahr. "Send your teams."

"Very well."

"And if it turns out that we have no choice but to go, we'll want to send probes out ahead of the convoy. Design one."

"Of course," said ShahnTahr.

EsJen turned and looked sharply at BehLahk. "You will see to it that we never have to use that option, BehLahk. I want that disgusting Veltahk mutation gone. Eliminate it."

"I will do my best."

"You will do it."

"I serve." BehLahk took a step back, gave a slight bow and turned away, leaving EsJen alone, looking out beyond her garden, across the landscape of this, her home for more than a quarter of century.

Carolyn followed the creek bed, dry but for a few muddy puddles, up the gently sloping hillside. Steeper terrain rose up seventy feet to either side of the creek, covered in brush and scrubby alder, the vegetation beginning to choke out the creek itself. The narrow sliver of sky just visible overhead was a light gray, appeared distant and apart from this isolated ravine.

Carolyn had a pack strapped to her back and wore a utility belt with canteen, knife and a holstered pistol. She had a rifle slung over one shoulder, and used a tall hiking staff that looked like it would make a mean weapon should the need present itself.

She reached the opening to a storm drain midway up the hillside. She had planned to follow the creek up as far as it took her and then blaze a trail the rest of the way up. Discovering the storm drains, she realized that she may have found a safer route. The Shillie probes wouldn't find her in there unless they actually went in looking for her, and she doubted they would do that.

This underground passageway should take her all way into the nearby city. Rain runoff no doubt emptied into these drains, which in turn emptied into this creek, creating it. The rainfall had been light the last few weeks, which would explain the dry creek bed.

She passed through an entrance framed in concrete blocks and entered the tunnel. Safely inside, she slithered from her pack and brought out a flashlight. The interior was a six foot diameter pipe of corrugated metal. The floor was covered in wet debris and shallow puddles. She could stand straight without hunching over, but just barely.

Other than the occasional air vent and the even more rare small side tunnel, the way ahead was fairly straight, and half an hour later she reached a metal ladder bolted to the wall; overhead she could make out the underside of a storm drain lid. She thought about it a moment, decided to continue on. The next one should be further into whatever city she was now traveling beneath.

She came to an intersection in the storm drain system twenty minutes later. The tunnels to the left and right had several feet less headroom than the main drain, which continued straight ahead.

The ladder took her up to the heavy lid. She had to rest her staff against the rungs in order to position herself to get better leverage and shoulder her way up, pushing the lid aside as she forced her way into the daylight.

Carolyn knew that she was in one of the communities south of Seattle and Tacoma, but didn't know which. Looking around her now, she certainly didn't recognize it. After satisfying herself that she wasn't being observed, at least overtly, she knelt down and reached back into the drain, brought out her wooden hiking stick. She pushed the lid back into place, no reason to make this underground route obvious, and then made a more careful assessment of her surroundings.

There were no tall buildings visible nearby or in the distance. This street and the side streets that she could see were lined with warehouses, commercial buildings, service industry offices. Weeds grew from cracks in the weathered street, the wide sidewalks, and from the seams in the walls of the building. The rain gutters running along roof edges now served as narrow planters, the thin, stalk-like weeds two feet tall.

She sensed movement up the street, a shifting shadow or reflected light, and stepped quickly into the recess of the front entrance of the nearest building. The door was locked. She considered breaking the window that was set next to the door, decided against it. She stepped back out and hurried down the sidewalk, turned into the alley. Finding a side door that was unlocked, she slipped inside. A narrow hallway opened into an office that fronted the warehouse. Dull light streamed in from the front windows. She moved quickly through a cluster of metal desks and toward the front of the room. She recalled her and Joseph hiding out in a small store some years earlier, with the street beyond, the whole town in fact, crawling with Shillies.

Leaning against the wall and looking out the window now, Carolyn saw nothing. The street outside was quiet.

She went numb then at a noise behind her. A faint scraping sound, as of shoes sliding on wooden floor.

"All right, then," she said softly, and turned around.

A figure sat on a step midway up the staircase leading to a second floor above the office. He was human.

"Hey lady," he said calmly. "Somebody's been looking for you."

Carolyn had to smile at that. She wriggled out of her backpack, took the several steps to the nearest desk and set it on the desktop.

"Hell, man, just about everybody's been looking for me."

"Yeah," he chuckled. "That's kinda the way I hear it." He went quiet then. After a couple of awkward seconds, Carolyn dropped into the chair behind the desk.

And so I guess we wait, she thought. She leaned back and put her feet up.

Thirty minutes later Kenneth came through the side door.

He had changed a lot the last few years, and Carolyn didn't recognize him at first. Long gone was her little brother's lost little boy look. His face had weathered and he sported a short beard. His hair was much longer than his military cut of years past, and there was gray salted through it. He had filled out some, as well.

Beyond the physical changes, there was a confidence about him; in his manner, his walk, and behind his sharp, clear eyes.

"Kenneth?" Carolyn stood. They met in the middle of the room.

"Hey, Sis."

They hugged, tentatively at first, then more worthy of a brother and sister who have been apart a very long time.

"Wow," she said as she finally pulled back. "What the hell are you doing here?"

"We just thought, you know, maybe you could use a lift. We live a couple of towns over. You may have heard of the place. Seattle."

"No shit?"

"I didn't say that." Kenneth looked around the room, chose a nearby chair and spun it about, sat down. "So. Ya' got every Shillie and Shillie probe in the province out trying to find you. What makes you so damned popular?"

"Other than my looks and my amazing personality?" She stepped back to the desk and opened her backpack. "No, dear brother. 'tis not I they seek. 'tis what I carry they find so fascinating. I have a most interesting toy... or, so I am told."

By every indication, Seattle was now just a big, empty corpse of a city, a relic from humanity's long dead past.

Considering there were only a few hundred people living in it, it was.

Sitting in the back seat beside her brother, Carolyn watched the building fronts drift slowly past as they drove through the narrow thoroughfares of downtown. Dark windows were dull, gray-black eyes. Facades had fallen away and lay on the sidewalks, some strewn in the streets so that the driver had to steer around them. Many of the doors stood open, who knew for how many years? Who was the last person to step through that door, she wondered. Or that door? Why? What had been happening that this forgotten soul hadn't taken the few seconds to close it?

"We're just up ahead," said Kenneth. Carolyn nodded silently, continued to take it all in. She hadn't been in a big city in a very long time. These days she and her teams focused mostly on the smaller communities, both inside and outside the Shylmahn province. Easier to get in, get things done, and get out again.

Kenneth had told her that his was one of four groups in Seattle. The smallest had fourteen people, give or take, the largest almost a hundred.

And his group?

Somewhere in between, he had said.

For the most part, the Shillies left them alone. The Seattle groups stuck mostly to Seattle, and were seldom a threat to the Shillies. For their part, the Shillies didn't have an interest in Seattle. So, despite being deep inside the Shylmahn province, smack dab in the middle of it, they were only very rarely bothered.

And the four groups living within the city generally left each other alone, as well. One exception was that they all monitored for any sign of Shillie probes entering the city and let each other know whenever they were around. It wasn't a perfect system, the city was a very big placc, but for the most part it worked.

It was one of the other groups that had alerted Kenneth to Carolyn having popped up out onto the street of a nearby town a few hours earlier. Kenneth had people all over looking for her, hoping to get to her before the Shillies did, and yet it was one of Victor's people that spotted her.

The only reason Kenneth had shown up as quickly as he had was because he had already been in that very same town at the time. He hadn't been in Seattle for several days; had been out looking for his sister.

The way back here had been very roundabout. Carolyn could see that they had very specific, very precise requirements when traveling from one location to another. They would enter one location under one mode of travel, exit in another direction under another mode of travel and only after a scheduled time frame had passed.

Once actually within Seattle's city limits, they had taken several underground routes and driven a long, narrow gauntlet of a street that Kenneth had told her was "intensely monitored" by his team before finally coming out here onto one of downtown's major thoroughfares.

"We're right here," he said to her as the driver turned left and took a steep driveway down into an underground garage beneath one of the major hotels from the past.

The driver turned on the headlights as they drove across the garage level, which was empty until they reached the far corner. They parked in an empty stall among a collection of other vehicles, at least a dozen by Carolyn's count, probably a bit more.

Kenneth led her to a nearby door and up a dark stairwell. They came out on the fifth floor. Overhead lighting offered a warm, comfortable glow to the hallway, powered by an unseen, unheard generator, with power lines running in the ceiling.

He let her get settled into a room, hers while she was here, and asked her to join him in the "commons" later. His group had turned several suites at the far end of the floor into a large gathering area where the members of the group spent much of their time together.

Her room was bright and airy, almost cheery. It had hot and cold running water, a light in the main room and another in the bathroom. The bed was clean and comfortable.

She felt guilty at the extravagance, and yet didn't want to leave. A hot shower, clean clothes and few minutes relaxing on the bed... she was ready to doze off.

There was a knock at the door and she bolted upright. For a moment she didn't know where she was, where that sound was coming from, or what threat it might pose.

She had fallen asleep.

"Yeah, coming," she called out.

A middle-aged woman stood in the hall, ready to take Carolyn to the commons, if she wanted.

Wow, she thought. *How long was I out?*

Long enough to have Kenneth send someone down for her, apparently.

As roomy as the commons might be, it was cluttered with couches and chairs, tables pushed against walls, a couple of card tables with folding chairs.

Carolyn went straight for the table with the coffee pots and collection of white ceramic coffee cups that had originally come from the hotel restaurant. She settled into one of the folding chairs, in direct line of sight to the canister holding the artifact that sat on a table.

Kenneth settled into the chair opposite hers. They spoke again about family, a little about Bril's island. Kenneth had been out there a few times. It was showing signs of coming back to life.

"Who knows?" He shrugged. "I may move back there someday."

Too much had happened there. Carolyn couldn't see herself ever going back, even if it was possible at some point.

She nodded in the direction of the canister. "I have to get that to Phoenix," she said. "As quickly as I can." She had already told him of the cost already paid for that damned thing; about Jason.

"We get you out of the province, we can get you to Phoenix. It's getting you out of the province."

"The Shillies do seem determined to prevent that."

Kenneth looked side-glance at Carolyn. "You do know you were heading north when we picked you up."

Of course she knew that. But going north had been her only option. The Shillies had been closing in on her whatever direction she went.

"I was heading for the Sound," she said. "Thought maybe I'd find a boat."

Kenneth grumbled. "You'll never get out that way. Shillies watch the water real close, these days."

Carolyn gave a shoulder shrug in silent response.

"We'll get you out," said Kenneth. "Don't you worry."

Chapter Eight

NehLoc turned away from the communications console and returned to his workstation. He spoke to the assistant as he sat down.

"Tell the pilot to make ready," he said. "And alert the field teams. They must return as quickly as possible."

"Yes, NehLoc." The assistant stepped through the narrow door and into the shuttle's main cabin. NehLoc turned slowly about in his chair until he was facing the window. His shuttle was parked in the center of the main street of the long-deserted Chehnon community; yet another Chehnon community.

They had lost Carolyn Britton's trail. She could be anywhere. The probes didn't have a clue.

How can that be?

As disquieting as that was, it wasn't the reason EsJen had just asked to meet with him, to meet with all the key staff.

No, this meeting was to address the other impending disaster. The Veltahk.

It was impossible. Yet it was true. He himself had spotted it several times since his own initial discovery of the plant. Others working in the wild were coming across it as well; worse yet, there were variations cropping up in different ecosystems all over the planet.

Joseph Britton... it had to be...

NehLoc had never been one to underestimate the ingenuity of these creatures, and he had no doubt they were unbalanced enough to unleash such a horror onto a world for which they professed their undying adoration. But he had to admit... he had not thought them bright enough. Yet somehow they had managed to replicate the Veltahk... here on Chehno.

Joseph Britton. Carolyn Britton. He should have eliminated them years ago. He should have eliminated all of them. Michael as well.

The whole nest of Brittons.

Now... a fine mess we're in, now...

At least they had finally dealt with Jason Britton.

The assistant returned, stood just inside the door.

"Yes?" asked NehLoc. He kept his gaze on the scene beyond the window. A dilapidated building just a few yards distant blocked his view.

"Both teams are on their way back to the shuttle. The pilot is preparing to lift off immediately upon their return."

NehLoc nodded in response, said nothing. The assistant waited a few moments, in case there was more, finally backed out and closed the door.

NehLoc let out a long, disgusted sigh.

He silently wondered ... which of the creatures had given him greater grief over the years? Carolyn Britton or Joseph Britton?

Oh, to be rid of that family...

Michael sat on one of the wooden benches that lined the enclosed playground, Victoria standing beside him. They watched young Nate playing with several other children. Moms and dads and nannies and babysitters sat on other benches or strolled along the surrounding walkway.

"You weren't supposed to tell me this," Victoria stated. Her arms were folded across her chest. She kept her eyes on Nate.

"The word is already out. Besides, from what Miriam said, once it officially goes public they want everyone to know that it's our doing."

"They've all gone insane."

"That's what I said." Michael looked sadly at their son. "What kind of freakish world is he going to grow up in?"

"To be perfectly honest, Michael, what kind of freakish world is he growing up in now?"

"You're not defending them?"

"Hell no. To save us from the Shylmahn, they destroy our world? My god, it's demented."

"It's no wonder they couldn't tell me." Michael shifted and stood up.

Victoria gave a dark sigh. "And it just might work."

"What?"

"You said it yourself. Joseph is throwing everything at 'em, all at once. With this as the kicker? It could work."

"I can't believe—"

"It's still insane, and it probably *won't* work—"

"It won't," Michael insisted. "I know EsJen. She'll push back, and she'll push back hard."

"You're probably right."

"And here we all are, together, Shylmahn and Human, on a planet made uninhabitable by our own hand." Michael eased himself back onto the bench. "My father's great plan."

And it is a great plan, thought Victoria. Multifaceted, all encompassing, and completely, totally, outrageously insane.

Jenny stood at the window, beyond which was a children's playground. There were swings and merry-go-rounds, sandboxes and climbing bars. Eight or nine children were playing in the yard, including her nephew Nate.

Wooden benches bordered the playground, and behind these a wide concrete walkway ran the perimeter.

Jenny watched her brother Michael and Victoria in some pretty deep discussion.

"I feel so sorry for him," she said.

Monroe stood beside her. He had arrived just that morning. "I've always felt sorry for him."

"I know." She smiled a sad smile. Monroe was even less a political animal than Michael, and that was saying a lot. Monroe liked Michael, and had always pitied Michael the life he had been forced to live.

"This doesn't feel right," said Monroe.

"I know." She turned from the window, gave a side-glance up at Monroe. He was still looking out the window at Michael and Victoria. His expression was unreadable; as always.

In the days since she had last seen him, Monroe had travelled by horse to three outlying communities on his way here, leaving word with local leaders of the underground as to what was coming. He himself wasn't comfortable with it, probably felt much as Michael felt, but he was loyal to the cause.

It nonetheless gripped at his heart.

He had journeyed two separate paths these past five years. Along one path there had been the truce with the Shylmahn, a fragile peace in which surviving Human and Shylmahn lived side by side, many of the human communities growing despite the sometimes oppressive rules set down by that truce.

Most humans were content with that first path. After so much horror and bloodshed, so much sorrow, the quiet of this path was a welcome relief. They were willing to live out their lives in the shadow of the new masters of the planet.

Some were not content.

The Britton Family, legends from an all-but-forgotten war long since lost, fought a war no one knew was being waged. For them, and for those standing with them, the first path was a facade, behind which lay the true path upon which their world travelled.

Along this path, forbidding times lay ahead.

Kenneth steered the strange-looking vehicle off the main highway and started down the much narrower, much more heavily overgrown side road. It was often difficult to see what was paved road and what was not.

Carolyn sat in the other seat, one hand on the support bar. To her, the rig she found herself in looked like it may have at one time been a Jeep, but it had been heavily modified. Two seats in a small cabin beneath a removable top; a plastic box behind them the width of the vehicle held supplies. Metal straps held four fuel tanks under the frame, two carrying gasoline, the other two homebrewed biofuel. The multi-fuel engine was capable of running on either.

Kenneth had calculated they probably had enough fuel to reach Phoenix, but it would be close. If they could find old-world gas along the way, so much the better. And it was likely. Even after so many years, there was still a considerable amount of gasoline waiting in underground tanks. After all, there were few people around to use it.

They pulled up to a wire-mesh fence, the double gate closed but not latched. Both fence and gate were overgrown with the invading new plant that seemed to cover everything. Kenneth had seen some signs of it just outside Seattle, a bit more in rural areas. Carolyn had begun seeing it here and there before joining Kenneth, and from what she could tell at the time, it had been spreading rapidly. They had seen more since starting to Phoenix, more yet once they were beyond the Shylmahn province borders.

Carolyn managed to pull the gate open, but it wasn't easy. The vine had just about locked it into place. She hopped back into the Jeep as Kenneth drove in.

Despite having spent several years there, the Village was hardly recognizable. It appeared empty but for the vine, which had begun to blanket everything. Kenneth maneuvered the Jeep down the main thoroughfare for several hundred yards, steering around or over the thick vine, before finally forced to stop.

"This is crazy," he said.

Carolyn climbed out of the Jeep, took a few steps and studied the plant. "You know what I'm thinking?"

"Sure," said Kenneth. "The Shillies didn't do it, unless it was stuck to the bottom of their shoes when they got here."

"Phoenix. Joey and Jason and their team of mad scientists."

"That'd be my guess." Kenneth had to wonder now what this device Carolyn was hauling down to Phoenix was all about. Knowing Joseph, there were several irons in the fire.

Kenneth had stepped over a particularly thick vine and leafy mass of the plant. He was standing at the steps of a small structure.

"Susan's cabin."

"I remember." Susan and the two children had lived there at least up until the time Carolyn had escaped the Village, probably right up until the truce. She never did warm up to the family after Daryl had been killed. Carolyn could never figure out if she blamed the family for Daryl's death or just didn't want the reminder.

Kenneth climbed the steps and went into the cabin. He came out a few moments later.

"It'll do." It was as good a place as any to spend the night. The Jeep wasn't going any further into the Village, so they would have to scavenge for supplies on foot. There was no desperate need, they had most everything they needed, but one searched for supplies at every opportunity.

Carolyn opened the supply box and pulled out the sleeping bags. She tossed them to Kenneth, then brought out the two small duffels that held their personal gear. She walked to the foot of the steps and stopped.

The sound of movement to her right; Kenneth stood at the top of the steps, attention focused down the main thoroughfare.

There were moving shadows in the ever-thickening vines.

Someone or something was coming toward them.

First one, and then several shadows took the form of people approaching. They came into the open, continued towards them, stopping three or four steps from the front of the Jeep.

Carolyn recognized the woman standing in front of the small group. It was Brenda, one of the first faces she had seen when first opening her eyes on this place more than five years ago. Two of those standing with her were no more than teenagers, probably her kids, now nearly grown.

Brenda carried a rifle slung over one shoulder, as did one of the children and one of the other adults. The others held long staffs.

"Hello, Carolyn," she said. She looked up at Kenneth. "Long time no see, Kenny."

"Brenda," said Kenneth, moving down one step. "I didn't expect to see you here."

"It's home. Where else would I be?"

Kenneth took the rest of the steps down and passed Carolyn. Brenda reached out to him and they hugged.

"Love what you've done with the place," said Kenneth.

Joseph sat half dozing, the gentle, methodic movement of the train, the sound of the wheels on the tracks and the deep thrumming sound of the engine all working to put him to sleep. The world beyond the window was dark, the night sky overhead starless.

He was alone in the passenger car. He had transferred from the mainline train several hours earlier and was on his way to Weston, a small town well to the east of the primary north-south route. This smaller train running on this side track consisted only of the engine and tender car, the one passenger car, and a single box car to carry supplies and mail. It made weekly runs between Weston and an untended station on the mainline.

Miriam had remained on the mainline and would take it all the way to Phoenix Labs. They needed to know what had happened to Jason and Carolyn as soon as possible.

The train coming to a slow, screeching stop brought him fully awake, his fuzzy head quickly clearing.

They shouldn't be stopping; not for a long time yet.

Joseph slid the window open and looked cautiously out. The sun had recently set, dark clouds overhead made the early evening all the darker.

He stood and walked to the front of the car. Outside, the evening air felt warmer than he would have expected. It was actually comfortable. Stepping down onto the gravel bed, Joseph saw the engineer approaching from the front of the train. Looking in the other direction, he could make out the engineer's assistant just beyond the box car, walking the tracks.

"Is there a problem, Tom?" Joseph asked the engineer.

"Sorry 'bout this, Mr. Britton," said the engineer. "Tracks are blocked, but good."

"Blocked?"

"Yessir." Tom the engineer turned about and started forward again. He fully expected his lone passenger to follow him. He continued speaking over his shoulder as he walked. "We've got vegetation like you wouldn't believe. I forced our way through some thinner stuff up to now, but there's no gettin' through it, here on out."

They reached the front of the engine and took a few steps beyond. The engine light shone brightly, revealing thick vines criss-crossing the tracks for as far as the light-beam reached into the gray. Great walls of giant dark leaves and darker shadows pushed in toward the track line from either side.

"Never seen nothin' like it," said Tom. He kicked at the nearest vine lying across the track. It was at least a foot thick. "Never nothin' like it."

Joseph sighed. "I don't suppose you have."

"Like I said, with the guard here," he indicated the cattle guard at the engine's nose, "I was able to push us through the thinner stuff. But it's been gettin' worse by the minute."

"How much further to Weston?"

"Oh..." Tom thought about it. "I'd say three miles. A tad or two more."

"Not so bad, I guess."

"You thinkin' a walking it?" asked Tom.

"I don't expect we could take the train back the way we came?"

"We'd be pushing the vines we just come through." Tom pointed to the cattle guard. "Only without that."

The engineer's assistant appeared out of the shadows then, returning from his survey of the track line.

"Them vines is already comin' back across the tracks," he said. "Thick as my thigh and gettin' thicker. And the further I walked, the worse it got."

"That's it, then," said Tom. "Bessie's sittin' right here till I find a way to clear the way for her. We're hoofin' it to Weston."

The assistant glanced speculatively at Joseph.

"I'll be fine," he stated firmly. He looked up into the sky. Dusk would turn to night soon. They had better get started. "Get our gear, then?"

It may have only been three miles, but they had to scramble through the ever-thickening vine the entire way. They followed the railroad tracks well into the night, arriving outside Weston just as a half moon rose above the low mountain ridge to the east of the small town. A silvery shimmer was splashed across the rows of darkened buildings and dozen streets.

The town was nestled in a shallow basin with hills encircling it on three sides, the railroad tracks approaching it from a slight rise on the fourth. The group stood at the highest point of the approach and studied the scene below. The tracks led off to their right, taking the descent at a gentle angle and coming into the town from the south.

"Looks awful quiet," said the engineer.

"That it does, Tom," said Joseph. There were a few windows aglow with life, but there wasn't much at all going on outside.

"Ya' think this stuff has 'em spooked?" asked the engineer's young assistant.

"Maybe."

"It sure spooks me," said the engineer.

"Startin' to feel a bit fretful, myself," mumbled Joseph.

The engineer looked back the way they had come, turned and nodded sharply at the town before them. "Expect that's gonna be home for a spell, Mr. Britton."

"As pleasant a community as Weston no doubt is, Tom, I most sincerely hope not."

Chapter Nine

TohPeht and BehLahk walked a few yards along one side of the set of tracks, much of it now covered in the vine. The shuttle was in a wider stretch of the clearing a few dozen yards behind them. The pilot and the rest of the crew were milling about the craft.

"Another week and the Chehno railroad system will be useless to them," said BehLahk.

"If not sooner. A shame, really."

"Yes," said BehLahk. *Their brand new transportation system.*

He lifted his gaze and looked out at their surroundings. This had been an open plain, these tracks taking the human passengers from the Chehnon communities in the north all the way to their science facility fare to the south.

Now... now the Veltahk was everywhere, spreading and growing so very fast.

"Joseph held this one very close," he said.

"I believe only a very few knew what was to be unleashed on this world," said TohPeht.

"I must admit, I did not see this," said BehLahk. "I comprehended his other plans, saw them coming and have even calculated them into our own, but this... this I did not see."

"Nor I," said TohPeht.

BehLahk glanced behind them. They were well away from the shuttle. He stopped, and TohPeht stopped beside him.

"We may not have seen this coming," said BehLahk. "But now that it is here, we can use it to our advantage."

"My thought as well," said TohPeht. "This could bring EsJen and Michael Britton together as nothing else could; a common cause, the future of their shared world."

"It is clear that Joseph has kept Michael in the dark on much. Understandable, considering Michael's position, but that is also something we may be able to use."

They turned in unison and started walking again. The way grew more difficult, and they had to step over and around the vines.

They stopped again and TohPeht knelt down to study the large leaves. It really wasn't Veltahk, but the similarity was striking.

"You and I have taken very different paths to get where we are, BehLahk," he said, continuing to look at the vine. "But we both understand what must be done if the Shylmahn are to be one with this world."

BehLahk said nothing. TohPeht did look up then.

"I have observed you from afar, my friend. You have been very busy these past few years."

"As you say, we both understand what must be done."

"And now our paths converge," said TohPeht, rising again to his feet. "What remains is but a guiding hand; perhaps a nudge here and a wink there."

BehLahk grinned broadly. "I just love Chehnon turns of phrase, don't you?"

Phoenix Labs wasn't actually in Phoenix. Rather it was outside Phoenix, well outside Phoenix. A squat, square concrete structure eighty-eight feet on a side, it sat in the middle of a large empty parking lot, which sat in the middle of a very large, open field.

The building housed a number of offices, a large freight elevator and two stairwells. These led down to an underground laboratory complex of three wings each running several hundred feet from the hub of the facility.

At the end of one of these wings was a shorter side wing, this extension containing several large garages, a number of mechanic workshops and a vehicle elevator leading the surface at the far south end of the parking lot above.

The elevator slowly lowered now, settled into position level with the floor. Miriam drove the vehicle off the platform and maneuvered it into a nearby stall. She turned off the electric motor and climbed out, plugged the car into the wall outlet before getting onto the small, motorized cart she had waiting in the next stall. It was a long way to the central hub of the complex, and her leg was continuing to give her trouble.

She turned from the side wing and into the corridor of the primary wing. Most of the research in this section of the underground complex focused on transportation, both ground and air, and so the corridor here was much wider than those of the other wings. Most of the labs she passed were large and were either completely open to the passageway or had several oversize doors.

She parked the cart next to the freight elevator. The narrow stairwell just wasn't an option for her these days.

Carolyn and Kenneth were waiting for her in one of the upstairs conference rooms, as was Phillip Neville, the director of Phoenix Labs.

"Sorry to keep you waiting," said Miriam, settling into one of the chairs.

"I just got here, myself," said Kenneth. He glanced out the window at the scene outside. Asphalt stretched away several hundred yards, and beyond that a grassy field. There was no sign of the flyer, but there wouldn't have been; wrong side of the building. "How'd it go?"

"Fine, thanks."

"You'll be ready?" asked Neville.

"I'm ready now."

Carolyn was sitting directly across from Miriam. She said nothing. She seldom spoke to Miriam. Miriam was too close to Joseph, and Carolyn had a whole new set of reasons to be pissed at Joseph; and so Miriam by association.

Phoenix Labs was glad to receive the energy pod component she had worked so hard to get to them, but not for the reason she had been led to believe. Certainly, one of the downstairs labs was anxious to study the component, but it was not to become a part of some doomsday weapon. Rather, it was the intimation that was the weapon. Joseph had gone to great lengths to ensure the Shillies would draw the conclusion that such a weapon was imminent; dozens of carefully veiled clues that, when put together, would leave no doubt.

One prong of dear brother Joseph's grand plan. And from the way the Shillies had come after Jason and Carolyn, they believed what they had so carefully pieced together regarding the deadly Chehnon weapon.

And because of that, in the end, Carolyn had accepted the way she had been used, yet again.

And she had even gotten some pleasure in discovering that Joseph had spent a helluva lot of time placing all the bad that happened in the world directly at her feet.

No wonder the Shillies had it in for her.

Okay, being always in the Shillie headlights did have a downside; still, it was 'kinda' worth it.

But this? The Veltahk? My god...

Miriam had known about it, had gone along with it. But then, she would. Miriam looked on Joseph as some kind of holy man.

Phillip Neville leaned forward and placed his elbows on the table, clasped his hands.

"On schedule for the day after tomorrow, then." he stated. Neville was a large man with a deep voice. He was a hands-on director when it came to running Phoenix Labs. He was involved in everything that happened there to one degree or another.

"The earlier the better," said Miriam.

Neville gave her an affirming nod. He looked then to Carolyn. When she only stared back at him, he turned to Kenneth.

"With Miriam taking one flyer, we can spare you four."

Carolyn jumped in at that. "But we already agreed to six."

"I know what we agreed to," Neville said curtly. "But I have one flyer overdue, another not due back for at least a week. I won't have us without transportation."

"We'll make do," said Kenneth. "Thank you, director. We'll try to get them back to you in one piece."

"I would appreciate that," said Neville. "They would be difficult to replace."

Carolyn snarled. "Not to mention increasingly the only mode of travel."

"Exactly so." Neville looked from Carolyn to Kenneth. "I'm sending a team of research staff with you; they'll be investigating the vegetation en route."

"Of course," said Kenneth.

"Vegetation," growled Carolyn. "How innocuous. You mean the atrocity you unleashed on the world."

"Yes," Neville stated flatly. "We are monitoring its growth and studying the impact on various ecosystems."

"Why? You guys did a damn fine job. That stuff is taking over; like... everything, everywhere. You can say good-bye to all those ecosystems. Congratulations."

Director Neville said nothing. He unclasped his hands, studied them as he his fingertips together.

"Neville?"

"We did what needed doing, Miss Britton," Neville stated coolly. "It is done."

"Yeah, I get that," Carolyn said, wondering. "Say... you guys don't have like... some magic fairy dust or something?"

Neville had to smile at that. "No, Miss Britton. We do not have fairy dust."

"You sure?"

"I am sure."

Kenneth sat forward now, studied the director. "You guys got something. Don't you?"

"We have no fairy dust."

Joseph stepped out the front door of Weston's only hotel and out into the main street of the small town. The sky was a dull gray, the hills surrounding the village dark and heavy with shadows. He started up the narrow avenue toward the community center. There were very few people out, though it was already midmorning.

He had been in Weston a little over two weeks, and in that brief time this small island of humanity had changed. It was completely cut off from the rest of the world, and the evolving alien landscape around them was closing in on them, creeping ever closer minute by minute. The residents of the community were accustomed to living isolated and fending for themselves, but this threat was completely outside the norm; beyond that, it appeared all-encompassing, and the end inevitable.

Teams worked daily along the town perimeter, doing what they could to beat back the Veltahk. In these early weeks it was approaching from two directions; it followed the train tracks along one path and came in through a narrow valley along another. Reaching the outer edges of the community, the vines quickly spread into the side streets and in and around the structures.

A strategic decision had been made to abandon some streets and buildings in order to focus on others. Several neighborhoods had already been swallowed up, the streets now dark green tunnels. A few of the buildings were still being used, but it seemed to be only a matter of time.

The focus now was on defending the center of the community, pushing back the inevitable for as long as possible.

At some point, however, the decision would have to be made to either remain in a town fully engulfed in the Veltahk, or abandon Weston. Of course, then came the question of where to go and how to get there.

Joseph reached the community center and climbed the steps up to the front door. He could hear raised voices even before going inside.

The mayor of the town was standing on the raised platform at the far end of the hall. He was trying his best to calm a tall, middle-aged woman standing directly in front of him. She appeared unwilling to be mollified. The mayor maintained his soothing tone, she continued her sharp and impatient tone.

There were at least forty others in the large room, most sitting on benches or chairs, some gathered around tables. Several people had surrounded the agitated woman, though from the back of the room Joseph couldn't tell whether they were supporting her or trying to get her to sit down and shut up.

The woman was apparently of the mind that the mayor postponing their departure was putting them all in danger, and was letting him know in no uncertain terms that if he continued to waste time hacking away at vines that they would all soon be dead. They needed to leave now.

The mayor was calmly trying to explain that they hadn't yet determined where they were going to go, how they were going to get there, or even whether they should go at all.

As Joseph crossed the room, the woman replied to the mayor that that was the goddamn point. He needed to get off his fat ass and do something. Make a damn decision.

The mayor watched Joseph's approach with some sense of relief.

"Ah, Mister Britton," he said evenly. "Welcome."

Joseph found an empty chair, pulled it around and sat down. "Don't mind me, Mayor."

"Not at all, sir," said the mayor. "I would be interested in your opinion on this."

"I think I've already made that clear. Come or go as you wish."

The woman turned to look sharply at Joseph. "We should leave now."

Joseph nodded coolly at that. "Then do so, and the sooner, the better. Travel is only going grow more difficult."

"As I said," the woman said, turning back to the mayor. "We must leave now."

"Where would we go?" asked another in the crowd. "Won't it be the same everywhere?"

"The larger communities will have more support, more resources."

"It's a long way to Garden City. Further still to Freetown."

"Freetown," someone called out. "Underground. That's where we should go."

"What about a big city?" asked another. "Seattle."

"Seattle's empty," someone answered. "And it's deep in Shillie territory."

"All the more reason to go there," someone else said, somewhat light-heartedly.

The woman who had started it all turned sharply again to Joseph. "What about you, Mister Britton?"

"What about me?"

"Where do you think we should go?"

Joseph shrugged. "Freetown's good. They'll no doubt already be pulling their exterior population inside. With the limited access to the Inner Village, it should be easy enough to keep the vine out."

"Is that where you plan on going?"

"Me? Oh, I think I'll hang around here a while."

"But why? You said yourself, the sooner the better."

The town was already half empty, and Joseph had to assume a good portion of those still here would be leaving soon, probably within the next few days. Those staying behind would continue to move nearer the center of the town, until at some point every street and building would be covered in the vine. Rooms would become caverns.

"I expect it's going to get real interesting around here," he answered at last. "The few folks who decide to stay are going to need a hand. I thought I'd do what I can to help out."

"Very kind of you, Mister Britton," said the Mayor. He turned again to the group at large. "It sounds to me that the consensus among those choosing to leave is to head for Freetown. I suggest the members of the council meet this afternoon and we'll formulate a departure plan."

"Half the council's already gone," someone called out. There was scattered laughter among the crowd.

"Thank you so very much for volunteering," the Mayor said to the man. He turned to the woman then. "And you as well, Dorothy."

The laughter was more wide-spread this time.

Chapter Ten

Jenny knelt down to study the vegetation encroaching into the large clearing. She was only a few hundred yards outside Garden City, yet the small community was almost invisible from here. Looking back over her shoulder, she could only just make out the rooftop façade of one of the buildings.

Standing and looking about her, there was little visible beyond the clearing in any direction. The path leading back to town was almost gone. The wide trail continuing on toward the old highway would be gone in another couple of days, and she expected the highway itself would be nearly impassible in another two or three weeks.

What had they wrought?

She turned at the sound of someone approaching, relaxed when Monroe entered the clearing. He was leading his horse. The saddlebags were full, his rifle in the scabbard.

His face was stoic, his expression empty of emotion.

"Good morning, Jenny."

"Good morning, Monroe," she answered. "You're all ready, I see."

He was heading out to a farming enclave in the nearby foothills, would do what he could to help if needed.

"I don't feel good about leaving you here on your own."

"When in the last three decades have you ever felt good about leaving me alone?"

"I don't recall," he grumbled.

"Uh, huh. I'll be fine." She took a step toward him, reached out and gave him a hug. He managed an uncomfortable hug in return.

He indicated the vine world around them. "Never had this to deal with before."

She ignored the comment.

"I'll be at the station in five days." She then also glanced about them. "Okay, give me seven. Don't come looking for me for seven."

Monroe managed a very rare smile. "Same here."

They heard someone else approaching from the direction of town. Jenny gave Monroe a nod goodbye and he started away, leading his horse down-trail toward the highway.

Michael came into the clearing, his hands stuffed into the pockets of his light jacket.

"Jen," he said casually. He glanced at the retreating figures of horse and man. "Was that Monroe?"

"He's worried about some friends," said Jenny. "Farm in the foothills."

"Right," he said, distracted. "Hope they're okay."

"I expect they're fine. I've met them. Very resilient. Nice folks to boot."

"Wouldn't expect otherwise. Any friends of Monroe..." Michael let the statement fade. He looked about the clearing, beyond at the homegrown Veltahk that was swallowing up the native vegetation.

Jenny watched as her brother struggled with his thoughts. "What brings you out here, Michael?"

Michael hesitated, didn't look directly at her. "Saw you coming out this way. Thought it'd be a good time to talk."

Jenny didn't respond to that. She waited. Michael wandered over to the edge of the clearing, held a hand out and pulled at one of the large Veltahk leaves.

"You knew about this," he said at last.

Jenny continued her silence. She folded her arms across her chest and waited.

"You and Miriam," he said. "Monroe too, I expect."

"I knew some of it," she said softly. "Monroe less. Always best to assume Miriam knows a lot more."

"And yet you said nothing."

"Of course I said nothing. You know I could say nothing. We each have our—"

"This is different!" Michael turned to her, holding the leaf accusingly toward her. "This makes it different! My God, Jenny, look what the man did!"

Jenny answered precisely. "It was necessary."

"Necessary? Really?"

"Yes. Really."

Michael frowned, his expression dark. He stared down at the giant leaf without really looking at it. His focus was suddenly far from this clearing.

"What am I going to do, Jen?"

"Your part."

"And just what is that? What is my role in all of this?"

"You are the leader of the council. You are our representative, the face of humanity in our dealings with the Shillies."

"Great..." he said, almost to himself. "And the resistance?"

"We each have our role to—"

"Yeah, yeah." He cut her off with a wave of the hand, turned now and looked at her. "They're all insane, you know. All of 'em. Crazy. Our father? Head of the crazies. We held them up as these legendary warriors of humanity, standing against the monstrous invaders coming to take our world away from us, when in the end they would themselves destroy that world. Our world. Our home."

"It won't come to that, Michael."

"It already has. You may not have the full picture, what with your *role* in the grand plan," he was pointing to the Veltahk encircling the clearing. "But that's pretty damn clear to anyone who can see."

"I'm sorry," was all Jenny could manage. There really wasn't anything to say.

Michael sighed, then slowly turned away from his sister. He left the clearing without saying another word.

He had meetings. He always had meetings.

EsJen entered the room, the ever-present ShahnTahr probe hovering at head level beside and directly behind her. NehLoc stood waiting near the active holo-table. There was no other equipment or furniture, no windows and no other doors.

The door closed as EsJen continued across the room. NehLoc said nothing as she approached. She walked slowly around the holo-table, studying the image that was floating above it.

"The Chehnon Phoenix Labs," observed EsJen. She stopped directly opposite NehLoc, who took a step nearer the holo-image.

"That is correct," he said. It was the facility as seen from high altitude; a single, ugly building surrounded by asphalt surrounded by dry, weedy fields. "The facility itself is underground, an extensive complex with thick walls of concrete and steel."

"I already know this."

"Pardon." NehLoc stepped a bit to one side, glanced once at the Shahn-Tahr device hovering nearby, always observing. "Our improved surveillance probe is providing us with greater detail of the underground labyrinth, which should help us in eliminating this threat once and for all."

"Understood," said EsJen absently. She reached out to a panel and swiped a finger across a pad. A display of text and numbers swam in the midst of the image. "I see."

NehLoc waited a polite interval of seconds. "There has been an increase in activity over the past few weeks; their new hybrid flyers as well as ground traffic."

EsJen removed the data display from the image, zoomed in the visual until she was near enough that the tracks worn into the pavement were visible. She could see the steel plating sheets set into the asphalt that were undoubtedly elevator platforms.

"And you are ready?" she asked, running her finger across the pad. The image zoomed back out.

"Yes, EsJen."

EsJen stared intently at the image. She didn't want to look at NehLoc just now.

This action will change much...

When it was clear that EsJen was not going to speak, NehLoc continued. "We should have taken out the facility three years ago, the very day we identified its location."

"Allowing them their technologies was part of the truce," said EsJen. "The Chehnon better serve if they can stand on their own and are not totally dependent upon us. It was believed that without Phoenix Labs they would have been thrown back a hundred years."

NehLoc had never liked that argument. "The primary purpose of the facility has been to develop technology to be used against us rather than for their own benefit. And look where we are now... we are taking out the facility as we should have done years ago, and we now have the additional threats to deal with."

EsJen would not be baited. She knew the circumstances surrounding the previous decisions, the reasons behind the choices made. They had made sense at the time. It had been logical.

Now, however, they had to deal with the results of those decisions.

"Given the improved data derived from the new surveillance probe, how certain are you that the... *contents*... of the facility will be eliminated?"

"I am certain that whatever remains will no longer prove a threat."

EsJen stepped the rest of the way around the holo-table, side-glanced to the probe coming around to stay beside her. ShahnTahr picked up her subtle facial expression. She wanted his opinion of NehLoc's assessment.

"I agree," said ShahnTahr.

EsJen accepted this. She started toward the door. "Very well, NehLoc. I will send word. I have to visit Michael, and I have several stops to make along the way."

NehLoc was unable to hide a sense of alarm. "You are not going to warn them, are you?"

"I am not. I want to measure the current situation with the Chehnon, try to determine which way things are likely go when we eliminate Phoenix Labs." She looked back over her shoulder as she reached the door. "No matter what I find, NehLoc, this will happen. Stand ready."

"Thank you, EsJen."

EsJen settled into her seat in the shuttle's main compartment, stared quietly out the window as the craft lifted off. She said nothing for some time, and ShahnTahr did not disturb her. He hovered nearby, hundreds of internal processes going about their individual duties, actions rising to a higher function level for specific, direct action only when deemed necessary.

EsJen's facial expression changed very faintly, but it was enough to alert ShahnTahr that EsJen would soon speak.

She spoke without shifting her gaze. She continued to look out the window.

"Their doomsday device, the Veltahk, the unrest... all due to the Brittons, all of which could have been avoided had the Brittons not been allowed to survive the island all those years ago."

She looked briefly from the window, to ShahnTahr. He was hovering at the precise comfortable distance before her. She turned back to the window, to the world beyond the window.

ShahnTahr held silent. He knew when to speak and when to wait.

"They should have been eliminated," she stated flatly. "My particular attachment to the Brittons, to Joseph Britton, is why we are here now, why we are having to deal with this now."

"Perhaps that is true," said ShahnTahr. "However, while it was at your suggestion, the decision not to eliminate the members of the Britton family while they were together on the island was not yours. It was mine. Chehnon are a resource that should not be destroyed indiscriminately. You understand this."

"And yet—"

"It was deemed their potential value to service outweighed the potential risk."

"As I recall, that hadn't always been so. It was at my insistence that their elimination order was reversed."

"Insistence?"

"Suggestion, then."

"We serve the purpose, EsJen," said ShahnTahr.

"Yes... the purpose," EsJen sighed.

"The survival and wellbeing of the Shylmahn. All that is, exists to serve the purpose. These Chehnon, they exist to serve the purpose. We are accountable for assuring this resource is in the best position to serve that purpose."

EsJen couldn't help but smile, as thin and contemplative as that smile might be.

"You're beginning to sound a bit too much like BehLahk, my friend."

BehLahk was enjoying his walk, his sample case in one hand, a toolkit hanging from one shoulder. The weather was pleasant, and the world quiet. The center of the wide thoroughfare of this long-abandoned Chehnon community was still easily traversable. The Veltahk, or rather the Chehnon's idea of the Veltahk, had begun enveloping itself around the buildings that lined both sides of the street, but had only just started to work its way across the weathered and broken asphalt. The only obstacles in his path were the dry native weeds growing up through the cracks.

Up ahead, he saw TohPeht turn into an alley and disappear. At that, BehLahk worked his way over to a metal bench that looked to be only days from being swallowed up by the vine. He set his case and toolkit down and settled in to rest for a bit.

He and TohPeht had been just about inseparable for weeks. TohPeht referred to the two of them as 'traveling companions'. Each had come into the relationship for different reasons, with their own ulterior motives, but BehLahk genuinely liked TohPeht and believed the feeling was reciprocated.

TohPeht was curious about everything, was fascinated by everything and enjoyed each and every discovery.

All the while, all along this amazing journey that TohPeht had undertaken and from which he drew so much pleasure, TohPeht observed the evolution of the migration of the Shylmahn, the integration of the Shylmahn into this world that he had grown to love.

And it was through these observations that he was drawn to BehLahk.

A shuttle appeared overhead, slowing and descending as it passed, landing finally some distance up the street, probably very near BehLahk's own shuttle. He could see neither from his place on the bench.

He waited. Some while later he saw EsJen coming up the street, walking toward him. She appeared to be by herself, except for the ShahnTahr probe, but of course BehLahk knew there would be a small escort not far behind her.

He stood as EsJen came nearer. He gave a warm and genuine smile.

"My dear friend, EsJen. How are you this pleasant day?"

EsJen's response wasn't quite as cheerful. Her tone betrayed no emotion. "I am well, BehLahk."

"That is good." BehLahk looked at the hovering probe. "And you, ShahnTahr? How are you doing?"

"I have no issues of concern, BehLahk. I thank you for asking."

"But of course, but of course." BehLahk indicated the bench and he sat. EsJen sat beside him. She looked up the street, then all about them.

"TohPeht is well?" she asked.

"Quite well; in both mind and body."

"I am glad to hear that," said EsJen. She glanced at the sample case and the toolkit. "Do you have news regarding the Veltahk?"

BehLahk pursed his lips and grew thoughtful. He had mastered the human gesture. "As we already knew, beyond some slight resemblance the plant has nothing in common with the Veltahk we left behind... other than the obvious similar invasive impact on whatever ecosystem it moves into."

"I find the resemblance most startling."

"I have identified several small visual similarities that do trigger such a response in many of us. However, I can assure you they are slight and quite superficial. This is not the Veltahk."

"As you say, we knew that. Veltahk or not, have you made any progress in ascertaining a way to destroy it?"

As with its namesake, BehLahk found that they could cut it, hack it, pull it, spray it, poison it, burn it, even irradiate it... but short of salting the top eight feet of the earth worldwide, the Veltahk was here to stay; all the more so due to the many variations that existed, seemingly as many varieties as there were ecosystems on the planet.

"Only insofar as we have identified a number of methodologies that do not work," he said. "I am sorry, EsJen. We have only just begun our research. There may yet be a breakthrough, but to be quite candid, I believe this will be with us for some time."

EsJen didn't respond for a very long time. When she did, she spoke barely above a whisper.

"It is going to get so much worse, BehLahk."

"Yes it is. We are only seeing the very beginning of it."

"We will be able to keep it from the dahlsehts, but the world beyond our city walls will be lost."

"I am afraid so. Travel by ground is almost impossible. Air travel will soon only be possible between maintained landing fields."

"So I have already experienced."

"And as for agriculture... we must establish perimeters as we did on Shylmah."

"I have already issued directives," she stately flatly. She went silent again, and BehLahk waited. At last, after several minutes at least, EsJen leaned forward and slowly stood up. She took a step away from the bench.

BehLahk watched and continued to wait.

"ShahnTahr," said EsJen.

"Yes, EsJen?"

"I see no benefit to visiting Michael. Send word to NehLoc. He is to remove Phoenix Labs from this world."

"Yes, EsJen."

BehLahk stood now and stepped up beside EsJen, his mind racing.

"EsJen," he began. "I understand the assault on the Chehnon research facility. If you consider it necessary, very well. Remove it. But you really must reach out to Michael. Joseph Britton has put Michael, and all Chehnon, in circumstances at least as difficult as our own. You and Michael should work together, should work for the benefit of both our people."

EsJen refused to look at BehLahk.

"They are not people. They are a resource." She started away. "A resource of diminishing value."

Victoria waited beside the door as the members of the council filed out of the meeting chamber. She nodded politely to each as they passed. None looked directly at her. None spoke.

Not a good sign.

When the last of them left the room, Victoria looked across at Michael. He was sitting at the far end of the table, frowning and staring at the pencil that he was slowly, methodically tapping on the tabletop.

"They blame me," he said, without looking up.

"I'm sure they don't."

"Yes. They do. They believe I knew of it, that I was a part of it." Michael continued to stare at the pencil. "How could I not? My father, after all…"

"All right; if that is so, then prove to them otherwise." Victoria pushed away from the wall, started toward Michael. "You cannot continue to serve two masters, both the resistance and your role as the head of the council."

"We've seen how that went," grumbled Michael.

"It was inevitable. Whatever the intent, the two roles serve at cross-purposes."

"And?"

"With every decision you've made these past five years, you've always had an eye to the resistance. How might this effect the resistance? Oh, you've tried to do what's right by both, you took your position as head of the council to heart, but the goals of the resistance were always there. They shadowed every move you made."

"Let's say that's so. What are you suggesting?"

"You have to take a side."

Victoria settled into a chair near Michael. He looked up at his wife, tossed the pencil aside and took Victoria's offered hand.

The flyer was resting on the platform, the platform itself rising smoothly up into the open. Reaching ground level, it locked into position.

Miriam reached out and flipped a switch, powering on all systems. She could hear a low hum coming from the back of the little shuttle. She set her fingertips on a small panel directly in front of her and it illuminated. She gave it three taps and the shuttle lifted.

It hovered several feet above the platform.

She pushed a button and a square section of panel lifted from the board. She slid a fingertip in a smooth arc across the face of the panel. The flyer turned about, mirroring the movement of the fingertip, without leaving its position above the platform.

She reached above her and tapped a small overhead panel.

"Phoenix, this is flyer four. I'm outta here, over."

"Flyer four, this is Phoenix. Roger that." It sounded like Phillip. "Good luck to you, Miriam."

"Thank you, sir. It's been a pleasure."

Miriam swiped at the overhead panel and cut their communication. She moved her hand then above a thin strip of panel set into the console beside her. She rested the pad of a fingertip on the surface. As she moved it slowly forward, the ship moved slowly and silently forward. She made a few adjustments and the flyer began to rise up into the sky at a steep angle.

Chapter Eleven

Carolyn came into the conference room, saw Phillip standing over by the window. A few moments earlier, he had watched three flyers come up from below ground and take off. Earlier that morning, he had seen Miriam off.

He spoke to Carolyn without turning. "I see that Kenneth made it away on time. I look forward to the reports." The people Phillip had imbedded in Kenneth's team would be studying conditions en route and reporting back their findings.

"I'll be leaving myself soon." She would be meeting up with Kenneth in a few weeks. First though, she would return to her keep. She had been away far too long. She feared what the conditions would be like there. She had been following the reports coming in from other parts of the world, from other teams. Things were getting bad everywhere, and not just for the Shillies. This stuff was impacting everyone.

Phillip turned from the window. Carolyn was looking at him. She had a detached way about her, while at the same time managing to be right in your face. She stood cool now, chilly in fact. There was a catlike intensity in the way she was watching him.

He felt sorry for her. She had been such a critical part of all that had been happening and yet had been left almost completely out of the loop. As much as he understood the reasoning behind that decision, he had also disagreed with the reasoning, and with the decision.

"There is something you should know," he stated calmly. He stayed near the window, waited for some acknowledgment from Carolyn. He believed that conversations should have a back and forth to their structure. This wasn't always the case when it came to Carolyn.

Phillip patiently waited. Carolyn finally nodded once and started over toward the table.

"Is that what this meeting is about?" she asked, pulling out a chair and sitting down. "I mean, there's a lot I should know."

God, she's a pain in the ass, he thought. He liked her. Things being what they were, that liking would never be reciprocated.

"I wanted to be sure you were brought up-to-date before you left," he said. "I believe it is important that you know, and the world being what it is, I may never get another opportunity."

"Okay," she said, truly curious now. She placed her arms on the table and intertwined her fingers. "I'm listening."

Phillip nodded, hesitated.

Here goes...

"Only five people on the planet know what I'm going to tell you. You will make six."

Carolyn didn't change expression, said nothing. She looked calmly over at Phillip, still standing beside the window.

"You should have been in on this from the start, but it wasn't my call to make."

"Get on with it."

"Right." Phillip held his palms together, almost in prayer. "You can tell no one. I mean absolutely no one."

"I kinda got that."

"Good, good..." Phillip stepped forward now, sat at the table opposite Carolyn. He leaned forward. "We developed the Veltahk, or what we call the Veltahk, here in the labs; dozens of variations to match the wide variety of ecosystems here on Earth. We produced and distributed thousands of seeds. Tens of thousands."

"Uh, huh. And?"

"They all have a defect coded into their genetic makeup. You might think of it as an extinction gene."

Carolyn stiffened, straightened. "What?"

"There are two components to the design. First, the plants cannot re-seed. Zero propagation. All the vegetation out there are the original plants from those original seeds. Oh, the first generation plants will grow and spread like a sonofabitch, but there will be no second generation."

Carolyn's expression was hard to read. It was dark and intense.

Phillip went on.

"Second component... the existing plants have a greatly shortened lifespan."

"Holy shit."

"They will die out. Combine the shortened life span with the lack of reseeding, and—"

"I get it. You goddamned bastards."

"Yes."

"I think I hate you even more. If that's possible."

"I don't blame you. Not one bit. You should have been in on this from the beginning." Phillip stared down at his hands. "The ecosystems are taking a helluva hit. But I have been assured that they will recover. It will take time, but I am confident..."

He let that last fade out. Confident? How confident could he be? How much had he accepted on blind hope? How much did they really know about what they had done?

He waited for Carolyn to ask the big question. *How long before the plants start to die?*

The Veltahk had to survive long enough to freak out the Shillies, not so long that the ecosystems wouldn't be able to recover. There had been a lot of back and forth, and none of the inside group really knew enough about ecosystems to be sure, but in the end they decided to let the Veltahk start to die out in six months, which would put it mid-winter in the northern hemisphere.

That assumed the plant would actually die.

Carolyn didn't ask the question. She didn't ask any question.

She slid her chair back and stood up.

"If I'm going to get to the keep before dark, I better leave."

"Oh, yes, of course." Phillip quickly got to his feet and started around the table toward the door. "Let me see you to your flyer."

"I know my way."

"Of course, of course." Phillip opened the door. "Nonetheless... please."

Carolyn said nothing, followed Phillip out into the hall and to the door to the stairwell.

They made it to the first landing, midway to the downstairs complex, when the first CEB struck Phoenix Labs.

The concussive blast resounded heavy and intense in the narrow stairwell, pounding deep into Carolyn's body. She was thrown forward and down the next set of stairs, Phillip plunging headlong ahead of her. Cracks spidered and widened across the walls and the slanted ceiling.

Carolyn found herself lying forward and face-down on the stairs. She took a moment to orient herself, then twisted around and pushed herself into a sitting position. Her ears were hissing and ringing at the same time. Her skin and flesh was numb and she felt her heart pounding against her ribs.

Phillip was lying at the foot of the stairs, just starting to move. He looked worse than Carolyn felt, and Carolyn didn't' feel well at all. When he looked up at her, he had to wipe blood out of his eyes to see. There was a deep gash across his forehead that was starting to swell and discolor. Shifting position, he winced and took hold of one arm.

"How bad?" asked Carolyn.

Phillip's arm and shoulder hurt like a sonofabitch. That was obvious to Carolyn. He tried to wave that off with his good arm and said only, "I could probably use a new skull."

"You know head wounds, bleed like a garden hose." She looked about them, at the stairwell above them. At least the lights were still on. "What the hell, huh?"

"CEB."

"Yeah, I got that. Helluva time for the Shillies to get pissy." Carolyn had experienced CEBs first hand on a number of occasions, but this one took her back to the very first... to Joseph's house, to the first day of the invasion; the first moments of the invasion.

That seemed like a couple of lifetimes ago.

There was another blast. This one sounded more distant, more hollow, but the stairwell shook and heaved and one wall burst in, exploding bits and chunks of concrete.

"Time to go," said Carolyn. She got to her feet and stepped down to the bottom of the stairs as Phillip slid aside, away from the door.

The door frame looked distorted and off square. When she tried to open it, it wouldn't budge.

"Crap." She spread her feet, took a solid stance and tried again. There was a screeching sound, and the door moved just enough that Carolyn could get her fingers in the gap. She got a firm grip and pulled.

More creaking and screeching. Another inch of movement.

Behind her, Phillip was slowly getting to his feet, his back pressed against the wall for support.

With that shoulder injury, he wasn't going to be any help to Carolyn.

Carolyn lifted a leg and held her foot against the wall beside the door. She took another firm grip on the door and using arms and legs and shifting balance pulled with everything she had. The gap widened to the accompanying horrific sound of the metal door scraping across the floor and the twisted frame and the bowed ceiling.

It didn't look like much of an opening.

"You might just make it through," said Phillip. "You go on ahead."

"Nope," she stated flatly; another long, steady pull. Another two inches.

She tried again. This time... nothing.

She stepped back, studied the jamb, the door.

That was it. The door was as open as it was ever going to get.

Carolyn turned to Phillip and indicated the opening. "Let's go."

"You first."

Carolyn had to grin at that. Yeah, right... she works her way through only to have Phillip decide to hang out in the stairwell for a spell.

There was another CEB blast and then quickly another, both striking at the far end of the complex. Dust and particles rolled down the stairwell toward them.

"I don't think so," said Carolyn. "Come on. You wanted to see me to the flyer, so see me to the flyer. Get moving."

To be honest, Carolyn didn't think Phillip had enough left in him to make it all the way to the hangars, but she wasn't about to leave him lying here in the stairwell. She reached out to him and supported him as he moved to the narrow opening.

He was midway through, sliding through as delicately as he was able, when a voice came from to the other side.

"Director Neville?"

Phillip had his face turned back into the stairwell, but he recognized the voice. It was Doctor Lansing, a researcher from one of the labs.

"Jack?"

"Yes sir," said Lansing. "Let me help you."

"Thanks. Watch the shoulder."

It took another half minute to get him through, after which Carolyn slid through without much trouble.

While Lansing, a thin, elderly man, looked after Phillip, Carolyn stepped through the rubble and debris and moved into the heart of the central hub, from which spread the three wings of the underground complex.

The south wing corridor was completely blocked, the walls and ceiling having collapsed, filling the long hallway. The northeast wing had gone dark, but from what she could see, that corridor was only partially blocked. The ceiling had collapsed in places, and here and there the lab walls had fallen into the hall.

Carolyn looked to the northwest wing. The flyer hangar lay at the end of the northwest wing. For the moment, the corridor looked passable. Lights flickered and threatened to go out. Dust hung in the air like a misty fog.

So... not very inviting, but passable.

Carolyn returned to Phillip and Dr. Lansing. Phillip was sitting in a metal folding chair and the scientist was binding his arm tight to his side in an attempt to immobilize the shoulder.

"How's it looking, Doc?"

"I'm not much in the ways of the medical sciences Miss Britton, but we'll make do until we come across someone who is."

"I'll be fine, Carolyn," said Phillip. "You need to go."

Carolyn gave a questioning look to Lansing. He gave a nod over his shoulder in the direction of the first lab in the northeast wing.

"We'll ride this out in my shop," he said. "You don't worry about us."

There were several more deep, rumbling concussive blasts. Powdery dust billowed out from the two wings that had not as yet fully collapsed. Bits of concrete and glass and other debris slowly settled to the rubble-strewn floor.

Twenty seconds passed and the world grew eerily silent.

"I'm not so sure that's a good idea, Doc," said Carolyn. "Maybe you two should come with me."

"I'm not going down there," said Lansing, indicating the ominous mouth of the tunnel that led to the hangar. "And in any case, Director Neville couldn't. Not in his condition."

Carolyn looked down at Phillip. True enough, he didn't look in any condition to make the journey all the way to the hangar. And she doubted that she could get him to leave Phoenix Labs and abandon whoever might survive this attack.

"Maybe I'll hang around a while longer," said Carolyn.

"Absolutely not," stated Phillip. It was very much an order. "You've important tasks to complete. And you are in possession of certain facts that must survive, should the facility succumb to this assault."

Crap and double crap, she thought. *How in the hell do I always end up in these situations?*

This was Jason all over again.

"Damn you," she said, but there wasn't much behind it. "Damn all of you."

Carolyn stumbled over the last of the rubble and into the hangar. Dust continued to waft out of the wide corridor from the most recent rumblings, and she knew the entire length of the passageway was doomed to collapse at any moment.

She was a bit surprised to have made it through alive.

I'm not outta here yet...

The ceiling in the hangar was quite a bit higher than that of the corridor behind her, with metal plates set into position directly above each of the landing pads that were set all about the hangar floor.

The hangar hadn't survived the assault completely unscathed. A steel scaffold had collapsed onto one of the two remaining flyers that were sitting on their pads. And one of the swing arm lifts had also been damaged, had fallen forward and into the wall of electrical panels. Many of the panel covers were blackened from recent electrical fires.

Carolyn hurried over to the last surviving flyer and up the ramp, went inside. Sitting in the cockpit, she powered on the systems. Everything appeared okay. She raised the ramp and closed the exterior door.

With no one manning the landing pads, she would be doing that from inside the flyer. A panel on the bulkhead immediately to her left interfaced with the hangar systems. She swept a finger across the panel and activated it. She touched an indicator to initiate the pad that the flyer was sitting on.

Nothing.

She tapped the panel again.

Sonofabitch.

She leaned forward and looked out at the wall of electrical panels. No power to the landing pad? It was either that or the computer interface between the flyer and the hangar systems was out.

She hoped it wasn't that. The overhead panel in the ceiling above was set to trigger and slide open when the corresponding landing pad beneath began its ascent. However, it could be done independently, directly from within the flyer cockpit, if the interface was working.

Carolyn swept her fingertips across the interface display to brush the current indicators aside and tapped at another that had moved onto the display. She made a couple of adjustments and initiated the trigger sequence.

She heard the welcoming sound of gears and slides maneuvering into place and starting to shift the overhead panel open.

She didn't wait, quickly powered on all flight systems. She turned to the panel set in the dashboard directly in front of her, activated it and tapped at several indicators. The flyer lifted slowly from the unmoving pad and then hovered. She rested a fingertip on the surface of the panel in the console that was set between the pilot and copilot seats and the flyer began rise. It drifted slightly from side to side as it rose, but with slight movements of her fingers on the panel she continued to guide it toward the still widening opening above.

Carolyn carefully maneuvered the flyer through the opening and rose up above ground level, continued another forty feet before easing the flyer into a hovering status. She quickly took in the scene, and not seeing any immediate threat guided the flyer up another forty feet, hovered again.

The building was gone. The acres of asphalt looked to have collapsed into the underground complex. The only movement was dust and smoke rolling up from several dozen craters and drifting across the landscape.

She spun the flyer about and started north, keeping to eighty feet of altitude until she reached the trees and was forced to take it higher.

EsJen climbed the steps up to the top of the high wall that enclosed the dahlseht, this the central Shylmahn city in the province. She spent very little time here, traveling as she did from province to province and from command center to command center. This was, however, the recognized governmental capitol of the Shylmahn and there were expectations.

The land beyond the wall had been cleared years ago, at the time of the dahlseht's initial construction, as part of the defensive measures that had been taken during those first turbulent years. The cleared land had later been put into cultivation.

The agricultural landscape was now besieged by the Veltahk. The perimeter enclosing the open land was thick with it, the vine choking out and rising above the surrounding forest and beginning now to spread out across the fields. Crews worked day and night to beat it back even as they brought in heavy equipment to dig wide, deep channels. Back on Shylmah such saltwater-filled channels had been used with some success as barriers against the Veltahk.

EsJen stood unmoving atop the wall, silently watching a number of crews working along the distant perimeter.

ShahnTahr hovered beside her.

"NehLoc has provided a preliminary report regarding the assault on the *Phoenix Labs* facility," he stated. "Once his team is able to safely enter the ruins, a more detailed report will follow."

"Then I can assume the action went well?"

"So the early indications suggest. The advanced imagery from the low-orbit probe was very beneficial in providing effective targeting. The first post-assault images indicate near-complete destruction of the facility and the elimination of the resources within."

"Let me know when the team goes in. I want visual confirmation."

"They will soon arrive on site," said ShahnTahr. "The precarious circumstances produced by the destruction will necessitate caution in their investigation."

"I understand that." EsJen continued to observe the work going on beyond the fields. "We need to know with certainty the status of Joseph's doomsday device."

"Joseph Britton has certainly made things difficult of late," ShahnTahr stated flatly. "The removal of such a device from the state of affairs would indeed lessen much of that difficulty."

"Everything else can be dealt with. That cannot. It must be eliminated."

"I have been evaluating possible options should the status of the device not be determined with certainly. Options are few."

"We won't leave," EsJen stated. The remark was cold and matter-of-fact and it came rather unexpected.

"And the transport ships in orbit?" he asked. "I have completed what observations I am able from here. Some are serviceable. MehnTec is preparing a team to investigate further."

"Yes, yes... a worthwhile endeavor," she droned distractedly. The comment acceded nothing.

ShahnTahr hovered in silence for several moments, updating his database to include this new information, processing and then reevaluating the topic.

"And yet we will not leave?" he asked at last.

"No."

§

Victoria passed a number of council members in the hall on her way to the conference room. The room was empty, but she found Michael just outside in the enclosed plaza.

Hearing her come through the door, Michael stopped his slow, aimless pacing and turned to face her.

"You heard?"

"I heard," she said. "I've been expecting it. Everyone has."

Michael nodded sadly.

"Are you all right?" asked Victoria.

"Fine," he mumbled. He frowned. "I'm going to miss this town."

"You hate this town."

"Well... I guess I can't argue with going home." He looked side-glance at Victoria. "I grew up there, spent most of my life there."

"I know," grinned Victoria. "I was there."

Michael grinned right back. "Right... that's where I remember you from."

"Does your memory need some jogging? I can do that."

"I'll bet you can."

Michael grew silent. Victoria waited.

"The Inner Village should be defensible against the Veltahk," he said then.

"I would think so. Freetown is a long way from here on foot, Michael."

"Not much choice, really. And it's only going to get worse."

"I know. But the whole town... it's not going to be easy."

"I'm sending a team out ahead of us; I'm hoping we'll have a route that will allow supply carts." Michael had given orders to construct as many two-wheeled carts as they could. Small two-wheelers would be easier to take through the vines than large wagons.

"We do have a few pack animals," said Victoria. The stable at the south end of town was home to a handful of mules and horses; there was even a pair of alpacas.

"The stable master is already making preparations." Unable to stand still, Michael started walking again along the plaza's outer walkway. "Did you find Jenny?"

"Sorry, no. No one has seen her since breakfast, in the cafeteria."

Michael stopped near one of the benches lining the walk. He started to sit down, changed his mind and turned about. He stuffed his hands into his jacket pockets.

"She's leaving, then," he said. "If she's not gone already."

"Without saying a word? I can't imagine that."

"I can. Our last few conversations were less than cordial. Who knows what's going through her mind?"

"Is she going to your father, do you think?"

"Or where she's always felt most comfortable." If Michael had to guess, he would guess that his sister was heading for her cabin, the way station that she had run as part of the underground railroad, the operation he had overseen all those years ago. A lifetime ago.

He grew very quiet. Victoria slipped her arm through his, started him forward again. They circled the plaza in silence.

The sun was just beginning to set when Jenny left Garden City, slipping quietly out through the north gate. Dressed in hiking pants and her most comfortable boots, a full pack on her back and a hiking staff in hand, she wasn't exactly hiding the fact that she was leaving. It wouldn't take long for word to get back to Michael that she was gone.

That would have to serve as her goodbye. She had considered attempting a last conversation with her brother, but in the end had dismissed the idea. It wouldn't have ended well. Better to let the dust settle and then mend the relationship later under better circumstances. They had been through a lot together; there had been so many positive shared experiences. The healing would come.

The fields north of town were already being encroached upon by the vine, but hadn't yet been fully overwhelmed. Jenny crossed the open expanse with no trouble and reaching the other side, she worked her way along the perimeter until she found the trail. It had once been a paved road, but with the vine, and the more familiar earthborn vegetation that had come before it, the path was now barely arms-width wide and was criss-crossed with thick tendrils.

She took one last look behind her before going into the shadows of the forest and vine, looking back across the field at the silhouette of buildings that had served as the administrative headquarters of all the humans on Earth over these past five years.

The town didn't look like much. Still, it tugged at Jenny's heart; perhaps more so because it really did not look like much.

She turned and disappeared into the dark.

Carolyn Britton set up camp for the night beneath a thick canopy of trees, maneuvering the flyer into the vine-choked forest and out of sight as far as she was able. It may all have been for naught, of course, if eyes had been watching her from above, but she had done what she could and at this point was going to try her damnedest not to stress about it.

She settled before her small campfire and prepared a meal from her rations; a watery stew of potatoes, carrots, celery and some unrecognizable meat.

Once she had made it away from Phoenix Labs, she had sought out the railroad tracks that ran north all the way to Garden City and then on to Freetown beyond. She had found the line readily enough, despite the fact that it was quickly being covered in the Veltahk. Positioning the flyer above the tracks, she lowered her speed and then lowered her altitude to just thirty feet, well below the tops of the nearby trees, occasionally rising to forty or even fifty feet when the vine reached up into the sky and became an aviation hazard.

She traveled until dusk and then sought out a place to spend the night. A shadowy opening in the treeline to the right appeared as a safe harbor in a dangerous landscape.

At the speed she was traveling, Carolyn figured she would get to within walking distance of the keep by midday the next day. The tracks she was following didn't go directly to the keep, but that suited her fine, as she didn't plan to take the flyer all the way home. She would set down several miles out and make the rest of the way in on foot.

She didn't know whether the Shillies had seen her leave the facility, but if they had they couldn't know for sure that it had been Carolyn Britton in the flyer. No sense drawing attention to herself by parking outside her keep.

She set her empty dinner bowl down on the ground beside her and picked up the water bottle. She took several swallows, then held the bottle out over the small fire and poured the contents into the flames. This brought up a cloud of smoke. She casually stretched out a foot and pushed dirt over the embers.

Black shadows reached into the camp from the surrounding trees and brush and vine. She sat in the dark, listened as the sounds of the night began to creep in.

Some of it didn't sound all that hospitable.

Carolyn glanced over at the flyer, at the extended ramp and the side door open and inviting.

Yep, she thought, standing and starting toward the flyer. *That looks like a plan.*

Chapter Twelve

Miriam guided the flyer over the ridge and then down into the valley, keeping her altitude as low as she felt was practical; still well above the tree-tops, high enough to give her a good view of the community that she was approaching and no higher.

The little town of Weston was being consumed by the vine. The outer perimeter and all the side streets appeared buried in it. Several of the higher rooftops poked above the vegetation, many of the single story structures were lost beneath it.

She brought the flyer in along the town's main street, looking for a place to land. Asphalt was still visible, but nothing open enough to set a flyer down. Many of the building fronts were still mostly clear of the vine, though the alleys and the sides of every building along the main avenue were covered in it.

She approached the far end of town and was considering a rooftop landing when she saw the train station's parking lot was clear enough that she calculated she could land the flyer with plenty of room to spare.

Coming down the ramp out of the flyer, leaning heavily on her cane, Miriam saw Joseph sitting on a bench set against the station's back wall. A middle-aged man was standing beside him, his arms folded across his chest.

Joseph rose up from the bench as Miriam reached the foot of the ramp. They were only a few yards apart.

"Miriam, glad to see you."

"Hello, Joseph," she said, smiling. She looked to the other man, nodded a silent hello.

Joseph introduced him. "Miriam, this is Mayor Tomlinson. The man is hospitable to a fault."

Miriam held out a hand and they shook. She gave him a second nod and then a smile. "Quite a little hideaway you have here, Mayor."

Mayor Tomlinson held a welcoming hand in the direction of town. "Let me give you the five cent tour, Ma'am."

The three crossed the parking lot and started up the street. As they skirted around and clambered over vines, the mayor pointed out the different buildings, described the functions they once served.

Joseph waited for an opening in the conversation to ask about conditions outside.

"Pretty much just like this," she said, almost indifferently. "Just like this everywhere."

"And how's business at the Labs?"

"Everything exactly as you would expect," she said noncommittally, smiling to the mayor. She gave a knowing smirk then to Joseph. "Carolyn sends her best."

Joseph barely managed to hold back a chuckle. "How thoughtful. I should send her a card."

As they continued to work their way up main street, Joseph and the mayor described the situation in Weston; the mayor giving Miriam the lay of the town, Joseph the current situation.

The population was continuing to abandon the town, originally leaving in larger groups, over the past few days in small bands of half a dozen or fewer. Most were heading for Freetown.

As of this morning, thirty people remained.

The three of them stopped in front of what had once been the town's only hotel.

"Too few of us left to keep back the vine," said the mayor. "Instead, we adapt."

"How so?" asked Miriam.

He pointed toward the open door of the hotel, a black, yawning opening in the vine. He pointed then across the street to the alley, a tunnel in the vine seven feet high, five feet wide.

"We train the vine," said the mayor. "Rooms, passages, even windows of a sort. It's not easy, but it's easier than hacking at it with machetes."

"Does it work?" asked Miriam, as much to Joseph as to the mayor.

The mayor cocked his head to one side and half-smiled, half smirked. "If you're willing to let the vine have its way when it gets stubborn." He excused himself then, mayoral duties to tend to, and continued on up the street, leaving Joseph and Miriam.

She watched the mayor struggle around, over and through the vine, disappearing finally through another dark opening that had once been the door of the building several doors down.

Miriam shook her head and looked side-glance at Joseph. "Adapt?"

"Yeah, well, it's not as bad as you think."

"We're climbing back into the trees from whence we came."

"Remember the cavern that we turned into Freetown?"

Miriam had to give him that. Freetown had turned out okay. But then, she had chosen to live in the Outer Village, not inside.

She and Joseph had been close for decades, since Joseph and his wife had taken her in as a little girl. She trusted him implicitly.

Miriam hesitated. She turned and faced him.

"What if they don't leave, Joseph? What if this isn't enough? What if none of this is enough?"

"I don't know what more I can do, what more any of us can do, but I do not see the struggle ending. I don't think it can." Joseph had been contemplating these very same dark thoughts for some time. "While the Shillies are here, this world will not be at peace until every human being that was alive at the time of the invasion has passed on. Our memories of what was before, and of what happened during those first months following the Shillies arrival, will not allow it to be otherwise."

This shook Miriam. She sensed the truth of it. "For there to be peace, we'll have to die."

"I think so." Joseph hesitated, forced a sad smile. "At least, that's pretty much what BehLahk told me, a very long time ago."

Back before the invasion, the area some distance southwest of Carolyn's Keep had been apple orchards, sloping hillsides and vast level expanses, row upon row of trees carefully maintained to produce the perfect fruit for a very finicky consumer.

In the years following the invasion the trees had gone wild. Most still produced fruit, even decades later, but the fruit was less than pristine; small, misshapen and blemished, still perfectly edible, but would never have made it anywhere near the fresh fruit department of any truly civilized pre-invasion grocery store.

Under normal circumstances, given the right environment, apple trees could live eighty years or more. These orchards had done fairly well on their own up to now, all things considered. Quite a number of young tree volunteers had even taken root between the old, carefully laid out rows.

But circumstances had now suddenly and quite drastically veered far from normal. The orchard rows Carolyn traveled through were thick with the vine. The ground was covered with it, the tree branches overhead choked with it. She didn't see how the trees would survive even a single season of this invasive takeover of such a quiet ecosystem.

This was the worst that Carolyn had seen. Travel was difficult. She had landed the flyer some four miles from the keep, and two hours later she estimated she still had two miles to go.

She scrambled over another particularly thick vine and then dropped back and sat down. She needed another break. Middle-age was showing, though she was certain this little excursion would wear out even the youngest whippersnapper. At least she hoped so. She couldn't bear to think it was just her.

Glancing up, she saw several wild apples in amongst the bizarre, twisted mix of apple branches and the vine. A moment later movement deeper into the vegetation caught her eye. Birds, hopping and fluttering in the branches.

What a strange new world...

She wondered then what would happen when the vine started to die out. Millions of tons of vegetation all around the world dying and decaying, this after months of choking out all the ecosystems that it had invaded.

What might survive?

Enough of this... Carolyn pushed herself from the vine she had been sitting on and started out again.

Jackson led the way through the vine, hacking at the vegetation with a machete, the others of his team following at a safe distance. Machetes didn't do much when it came to the thicker vines, but taking out the leaves and the thinner creepers did help clear paths through this nightmare of an alien jungle.

They were on their way back to the keep, returning from a morning hunting and gathering excursion. The hunting had been less than successful, but the gathering had gone well enough; blackberries, huckleberries, mushrooms, several varieties of the ever-popular apple.

They were within a few hundred yards of the main gate when Jackson came to a sudden stop, bringing those behind him up short.

Carolyn stood in the small clearing, looking a bit ragged but very much alive. There had been some question of that. She had been gone for several months, and the mission had been a dangerous one.

Jackson tried and failed to minimize his surprise. "Carolyn," was all he could manage.

"Mr. Jackson," she said calmly. "Good to see you."

"Yes," said Jackson. "You too."

"So I'm not lost, then." Carolyn indicated the way ahead. "We're that way?"

"As the crow flies. The actual course deviates somewhat. And is never the same path twice."

"I'll let you lead the way, then."

They traveled the rest of the way with only brief exchanges; how have you been, is the keep holding up well... Responses were pretty non-committal, but apparently Steven was keeping the home hearth warm for Carolyn's return.

As Jackson had warned, the path to the main gate was roundabout. Even with the machete, the team had to veer off-course a number of times over those few hundred yards. And Jackson pointed out that whatever they cleared one day was inevitably and quickly overgrown the next.

Joseph and his mad-scientists had done their job all too well.

She wondered for the hundredth time about Phillip.

They were nearly upon the main gate before they saw it, stumbling into the small clearing directly before it.

The double-gate and the area in front of it was kept clear. The timber walls of the keep to either side of the gate were covered in the vine, reaching to the top and threatening to climb over and down into the keep itself.

The gates slowly opened at their approach. Jackson stepped aside and indicated that Carolyn should lead them inside.

The grounds of the central square were clear, but Carolyn could see the vine reaching over the outer walls on all sides. There were men and women on the upper gangway all around the square working machetes. Carolyn guessed that keeping the vine from getting inside was becoming a fulltime job.

Steven stepped down from the porch of the keep's small headquarters building and walked as calmly to Carolyn as he was able. He stopped in front of her, gave her a welcoming nod and fought back a big smile.

"Welcome home, ma'am," he said.

"Thank you, Steven."

Jackson backed away. "We'll get these provisions stowed," he said, and silently ordered the others of the team to follow.

"You never write," said Steven, now wearing a full grin.

"Yeah, well, you never call," answered Carolyn. She started forward and the two of them headed back to the headquarters building. "It looks like you're taking care of the place well enough."

"I did my best. Not easy."

"I hear ya'."

"How are you?" he asked.

"Well enough."

"You look like shit, you don't mind my saying so."

They reached the steps and Carolyn climbed up onto the porch. "You're a good lad, Steven."

Cleaned up, a hot meal and a few hours rest, Carolyn called an evening meeting of her team leaders. After being briefed on the status of the keep, it was her turn to give them the highlights of her own recent experiences. She kept it succinct and to the point. They needed the facts, not the color.

They were very curious about Kenneth's community in Seattle, and were desperate for any and all news about the vine. She told them of the design of the Veltahk and of the global distribution of the seeds.

For the moment she said nothing of the planned death of the plant, nor of the virtual nature of the doomsday device.

While they were as horrified as she on hearing the origin of the vine, they were more devastated by the news of Jason's death and the destruction of Phoenix Labs, questioning aloud on how they might retaliate.

That may come, she thought. *For now, considering the price we're paying, I'll give Joseph's insane plan a chance. It doesn't have a snowball's chance in hell, but I'll let it play out.*

Once all other subjects had been thoroughly gone over, Carolyn casually brought up the matter of her observation that some of the smaller communities had begun migrating to the larger communities. Still others were moving back into the pre-invasion cities; specifically into the inner cities. Doing so was affording them a larger support base, greater resources, and the ability to work with the vine much more effectively than hacking at it when it crawls over the wall.

"You want us to leave the keep?" asked Jackson.

"I don't want to, but circumstances advise it."

"Are you thinking on having us join up with your brother?" asked Steven.

"Let's just say I'm thinking we play house in the same neighborhood."

"Seattle," Jackson said with a sigh. "We can't move everyone and all our equipment and supplies with that one little flyer of yours. We'll have to go overland."

"I'm hoping to get a little help with that, but you're right. This won't be an easy operation."

Brown, another of Carolyn's leaders, let out a noisy breath. "You're talking about taking an entire population across the mountains. And into the Shillie province."

Jackson chuckled. "When has going into the province ever been an issue?"

That got a brief round of nervous laughter.

"We weren't moving in before," said Brown. "I'm not opposed to the idea, just pointing out a few of the more obvious obstacles. Like for instance the vine between here and there."

"I know first-hand the difficulties in traveling the vine," said Carolyn. "But it's the vine that makes this an option at all. The Shillies have a helluva lot to deal with right now. They're not gonna be overly concerned with a few humans trekking over the mountains."

"If they see us at all, under all that vegetation," said Steven.

"And like I said, they have their hands full at the moment."

The room fell silent. Carolyn leaned back in her chair and studied the faces of those sitting around the table. They were all solid people. They would speak their minds, voice their objections, but once the issues were sorted out, they would reach a consensus.

"When?" asked Steven.

"Right away."

"What's the rush, Carolyn?" asked Brown.

"We can't stay here," said Carolyn.

"She's right," said Steven. "Keeping the vine out is growing more difficult every day. And it's starting to work its way in between the wall timbers."

"The keep is too small and we are too few."

"And traveling through the vine will grow more difficult the longer we wait," said Jackson.

Brown nodded thoughtfully. "So if we do this, we do it now."

"I'm afraid so," said Carolyn.

The discussion continued for another few minutes, but the meeting was basically over. Next steps were gone over and then chairs began sliding back.

Carolyn leaned back in her chair at the head of the table and watched her council members drift toward the door.

"Steven, would you hang back a minute?"

Steven stepped out of the way and let the others pass. Once they had left, he closed to door and returned to the table. Carolyn indicated the chair nearest him. He settled into it and scooted it forward.

"Something dark and gloomy?"

"Maybe. Maybe not."

"Okay, that doesn't make it ominous and scary at all."

"It gets worse," Carolyn grumbled. "It's about the vine."

"Your brother is probably in need of psychiatric care, but his plan might work."

"That's very generous of you, Steven, but we both know the Shillies aren't going anywhere."

"But if Joseph convinces that AI of theirs that—"

"It won't matter. EsJen is running things." She waved away the thought. "But that's not what I want to talk to you about."

"Right. The vine."

"Yes. The vine." She hesitated, then leaned forward, placed her forearms on the table and clasped her hands together. "There's something you need to know. And I hate to say this, but for the moment it's gotta stay between you and me."

"All right."

"I mean, considering what we're going to do, if we were to be taken by the Shillies, the fewer who know, the better. To be fair to the plan."

Steven frowned. "Then should you tell me?"

"Most of those who were in on this are probably dead. If anything happens to me... tag, you're it."

"Okay... got it."

An access had been created leading from the surface down to the complex that the Chehnon had called the Phoenix Labs. From what NehLoc's linguistic expert had been able to interpret, a *phoenix* was a mythical bird and *labs* referred to a Chehnon facility for research and experimentation.

The opening from the surface was directly above the central hub. From there three long underground corridors stretched away like spokes in a wheel. All these corridors had collapsed under the bombardment and NehLoc's teams had spent several days clearing paths through the passageways wide enough to allow his people to get into the laboratories and search for evidence of what the Chehnon had been working on.

NehLoc followed one of these corridors, maneuvering his way through and around the rubble, until he reached the laboratory outside which waited one of his team.

"Well?" asked NehLoc.

"Right this way, sir." The young Shylmahn led NehLoc into the lab. Chairs and counters and equipment lay strewn about and broken. Much of the ceiling had collapsed and overhead lighting hung precariously from thin metal framework.

They reached another Shylmahn who was kneeling before a broken cabinet and pulling out laboratory equipment and grousing to himself.

"PahLen," said NehLoc.

PahLen pulled himself away from the cabinet and stood up. "Ah. NehLoc. I appreciate your coming. This way, please." He stepped over to a counter that was set against the back wall and picked up a small metal box. He handed it to NehLoc.

NehLoc opened the box. It was empty.

"You hand me an empty box."

"Yes," said PahLen. "Empty."

"I trust you will explain."

PahLen pointed at the box in NehLoc's hands. "That container once held the energy pod component the Chehnon intended to use in the development of their doomsday device."

"You are sure?"

"I have examined the recording that you provided of Carolyn Britton bringing it out of hiding. I am confident it is the same container."

NehLoc handed the box back to PahLen as he looked about the room. He could see the bodies of several Chehnon still half-buried in debris, but there was little of interest here.

"And no sign of the component itself..."

"It is not in this laboratory. We may yet find it in another. The level of destruction has complicated the search, but if it is here, we will find it."

The Shylmahn who had escorted NehLoc into the room spoke up now.

"Several of the Chehnon creatures managed to survive, NehLoc. They are being delivered to the regional security facility for interrogation."

"Yes, of course," NehLoc stated absently. "I will be taking charge of that myself." He looked to PahLen. "Documents."

"All are being collected. The linguistics team is translating the scribblings even now."

"I refer to what might be recovered from their digital storage. If there is anything, it will most likely be found there."

"Of course."

NehLoc had already turned about and was starting across the room. He spoke without looking back. "And find that component."

"Yes, NehLoc."

MehnTec and young JoVahn floated into the primary control room of the transport ship, the small lamps on the sides of their helmets piercing the darkness. MehnTec glided over to a handhold mounted on one wall as JoVahn slowly settled into the seat in front of the environmental control panel. She slipped her booted feet beneath a floor railing, brought a gloved hand up and activated the board. Several subpanels lit up. She brought the ship's lights up, then looked over at MehnTec and gave a curt nod.

MehnTec tapped a small plate on his left sleeve near his wrist.

"This is MehnTec," he said, speaking through his helmet's comm link to the other members of the team. They were working their way to various locations throughout the great ship. "Stand ready, everyone. Gravity is being initiated in... 3, 2, 1..."

JoVahn flipped a switch and brushed a gloved finger across a touch pad. A faint hum and slight vibration drifted through the ship as the gravity plating came alive.

Both sound and sensation faded after several seconds. MehnTec's feet drifted to the floor as standard gravity was restored throughout the ship. JoVahn next began activating the atmospheric systems. MehnTec walked over to stand beside her, watching the indicators on the panel. They came alive one by one, each initially barely registering but slowly rising to safe levels. He gave it a few moments more, then unfastened his helmet and lifted it off.

The air was stale and bitterly cold, but breathable.

He unfastened and pulled off his gloves as he stepped over to the communications panel, brought up the ship's intercom.

"This is MehnTec. All environmental systems are online. It's safe to climb out of your suits, should you choose to do so. Air is now breathable and improving; it is cold but warming."

MehnTec turned off the intercom and looked over at JoVahn, who by now had removed her own helmet and was slipping out of her gloves. She appeared to be shivering.

"Are you all right?" asked MehnTec. He wore the hint of a smile.

"You weren't exaggerating about the cold. Really, really cold." She glanced over at the environmental indicators. Yes, cold but well into the survivable range, and the temperature was continuing to rise.

"No colder than any of the other ships we've visited, JoVahn."

"Well, it sure feels colder."

MehnTec moved over to the primary systems panel. "Let's get to work. It'll take your mind off it."

The team's assignment was to board each transport ship and ascertain its viability should the Shylmahn need to leave their home of the past thirty years. This included all internal systems, power core, structural integrity, and cryo support.

A number of ships had been virtually stripped to the bulkheads during the first years of the migration, while others had been carefully mothballed, having had equipment, components and supplies removed while maintaining a base level of restoration should the Shylmahn one day have the need of a massively large transport ship.

ShahnTahr had identified the ships to be inspected. Since the ships had been completely shut down, even having the individual the ShahnTahr entities belonging to each ship removed, he wasn't able to investigate these potential transports beyond the most basic cursory examination. A true determination required in-person visits.

This was the sixth ship that MehnTec and his team had visited. Of the previous five, three showed promise, with some restoration required. The other two were considered derelicts, to join the fleet of derelicts ShahnTahr had previously identified.

Small programmable thrusters were being attached to the hulls of the derelicts, which were destined to be sent into the sun.

The numbers didn't add up. They had never added up. ShahnTahr had originally tagged forty percent of the transport ships in orbit as derelict; unusable, scrap destined for the sun.

Right from the start, the ships remaining couldn't possibly transport the entire population of Shylmahn.

And of the five ships that MehnTec had inspected, only three had been identified as possibly viable. That was sixty percent. Assuming that held up for the remainder of the inspections, that meant sixty percent of the sixty percent.

That meant only fifteen of the great transport ships. And that calculated out to less than forty percent of the population of Shylmahn currently living on Chehno.

No one talked of it. MehnTec was certain everyone was thinking about it.

Should it come down to it, should they have to leave Chehno, just how would they decide who was to leave and who was to stay behind?

MehnTec and JoVahn completed the initial systems checks. On first inspection, everything looked good, so they initiated ship-wide diagnostics. The processes would take some minutes.

MehnTec leaned back in his chair, looked casually over at JoVahn. She was watching him. She smiled.

"It's finally warming up," she said.

"Almost comfortable." MehnTec liked JoVahn. He was more compatible with her than he had been with EsJen. As he and EsJen had drifted apart, were no longer together, there was no reason he couldn't pursue a relationship with JoVahn.

And yet he had never seriously considered it. He did like her, and they got along very well, but there was nothing beyond that. He had never felt the extra *something* that he had with EsJen.

He looked away, focused his attention on the indicators and monitors. Data had begun coming in, and for the most part it all looked positive.

Communications began coming in from the teams throughout the ship. There was still much to be done, but the initial physical inspections had revealed no issues and the first engineering and cryo system tests were running.

Even if every inspection and test came back positive, making one of these transports ready would be a significant undertaking. Making all of them ready would be a huge undertaking.

Just one more thing that MehnTec wasn't ready to wrap his head around.

He looked again at the indicators as he listened to the teams checking in.

Michael stood alone and silent at the north gate, watching as the residents of Garden City streamed out. Most wore backpacks and were dressed for a hard journey. Hand carts were mixed in amongst the procession, and the occasional horse, mule and alpaca.

Some of the folks acknowledged him as they passed, sometimes with a simple nod, sometimes with a noncommittal greeting. Many pointedly ignored him.

Guilt by association.

It was going to be a long, difficult journey, and at its end they would be refugees begging at the gates of Freetown for permission to enter and live in a hole in the ground.

And it was his fault.

Guilt by association.

It took almost three quarters of an hour for everyone to pass through the gate. The stablemaster and his wife brought up the end of the procession, leading several mules packed with supplies.

The stablemaster brought his mule to a stop, let his wife continue on.

"That's it then, Michael," he said poignantly. He loved this town. He also knew this wasn't Michael's fault. "S'pose we're done here."

"For now, George."

"You don't figure we'll be coming back, do you?"

"I want to think so. I have to hope things will get better."

George studied Michael's face, the sadness behind the eyes, for a long moment. He gave a very faint nod.

"Yes... yes, I suppose you do." He looked ahead then, at the slowly receding procession. His wife was midway across the field, the line ahead of her disappearing into the thick foliage beyond. He gave another nod to Michael, moved ahead of his mule and gave a tug at the reins.

Alone now, Michael stepped fully into the gateway and looked back into town. Empty, abandoned, much of it already besieged by the vine.

The backdrop of the night sky was jet black, the intensity of the thousand visible stars obscured by the bright glow of an almost full moon. The wide-open field below shimmered in moonlight, the color of the yellow grass washed out to a light gray.

EsJen stood in the very center of the field. She was alone. Her escort, and even ShahnTahr, waited in camp a hundred yards behind her, near the shuttle.

She brought her gaze down from the moon and looked west. They were a long way from the province. This was considered *the wild* by most, where the Chehnon creatures dwelled; out there, hidden in the dark.

EsJen turned about in a slow circle. There was no Veltahk here. The open expanse reached hundreds of yards in every direction, the grass gently shifting and drifting in a slight breeze, her black shadow created by the moonglow alive and moving as the grass moved.

This was nice. She could get lost here. If only she could keep the world away.

But she could not. Even now the Chehnon-born Veltahk was creeping ever closer, with every passing second. And the Britton clan was out there, an ever-increasing threat, creeping ever closer. The truce had meant nothing to them beyond a fertile landscape upon which to grow and spread their brackish subversion. And now they would destroy this magnificent world rather than live in peace and harmony as part of it.

EsJen turned about again at the sound of rustling in the grass, saw one of the escort approaching, with the ShahnTahr probe beside him, gliding above the whispering grass.

"EsJen," said the escort. "The evening meal is ready."

EsJen nodded in answer, said nothing. The escort looked warily about for any signs of threat, turned around and returned to camp.

ShahnTahr remained with EsJen. The probe hovered near enough for comfortable conversation.

EsJen turned away. "What is it, ShahnTahr?"

"We have not spoken since receiving the latest reports from MehnTec."

EsJen brushed a hand across the tall grass, looked out across the rippling waves. "We seldom take the time to appreciate what this world has to offer. Not like we used to. Not like before."

ShahnTahr hesitated only very briefly, as if but a second's pause was what was called for at that moment.

"I have outlined the schedule necessary to make the transports ready, should it be decided that we must leave. There is much to be done. The workable ships are far from travel-worthy."

"I see." EsJen had yet to look in ShahnTahr's direction. "And have you a schedule to determine those whom we are to leave behind? Should we find it necessary to leave?"

"I have completed designs on adapting the remaining ships, EsJen. As I said that I would. Using the cryo equipment from the derelict ships, and with additional materials from here. Extrapolating a final number of viable ships from the current projections, the percentage of Shylmahn remaining behind would be five percent."

"Five percent."

"The time, resources and infrastructure necessary to design and develop the additional ships required to include—"

"Yes, yes. Will never happen," EsJen cut him off. "Send the ships into the sun."

"The derelicts are being fitted with maneuvering jets," said ShahnTahr. "Once we remove the equipment—"

"All of them."

"EsJen?"

"All of them."

"I don't understand."

EsJen breathed in deeply through her nose. The smell of warm grass soothed her, calmed her. She stepped away from ShahnTahr, away from the shuttle in the distance, and away from the noise that threatened her world.

Her world...

"We will not leave. Send them all into the sun."

Chapter Thirteen

BehLahk and TohPeht allowed one of the escort to lead the way, following several paces down the ramp of their shuttle. While their wary guard took up watch, they walked several yards ahead and stopped at the edge of what had at one time been a parking lot, the building that it served hidden from them now behind the shuttle.

The lot was surrounded by the vine, which was continuing to creep in and was slowly engulfing it. Directly ahead, the main street of the small Chehnon community was all but lost to it. The buildings were covered in it; it ran along the overhead wires, forming an enclosing shell above.

A lone Chehnon approached them, walking calmly up the street toward them.

"Hello, my dear friend Joseph," said BehLahk. He smiled broadly.

"Doctor BehLahk," said Joseph, with much less emotion. He looked coolly over at the other Shylmahn. "Hello, TohPeht. It's been a long time."

TohPeht nodded in greeting. "Joseph Britton."

Joseph looked at them both. "What brings you to Weston?"

"You, my friend," said BehLahk.

"Is that so?"

"Yes. Dropping in for a visit; *dropping in to say hello*, as they say. Although, you were rather difficult to find, which I imagine casts a shadow on the credibility of that statement."

"I'm willing to overlook it."

"That is very kind of you." BehLahk looked beyond Joseph toward the small town. "A pleasant little community, is it? Rather out of the way, though, I would think."

"Home away from home." Joseph turned to one side and held out a beckoning arm. BehLahk and TohPeht accepted and they started walking along the main street. The escort stepped in quickly behind them.

BehLahk and Joseph continued to exchange meaningless pleasantries, brought up reminisces from their occasional meetings over the years. Toh-Peht mostly remained silent, though he listened very carefully to what was said and how it was spoken. Tone and inflection were important.

They passed several buildings, the doorways now dark openings all but lost deep within vine and leaf. The Shylmahn visitors noted pale Chehnon faces peering through the leaves from half-hidden second story windows.

BehLahk stopped. The others came to a stop and they faced each other in the center of the street. BehLahk grew thoughtful.

"I must say, my friend Joseph... this home away from home... it no doubt places you, as they say... *well out of the loop.*"

"I admit that news is sometimes late in coming," said Joseph.

"I should think you would want to be more on top of current events; as involved as you were in their... initiation."

Joseph gave a calm, easy smile. "I enjoy the quiet."

"Most interesting." BehLahk turned about and started back in the direction of the shuttle. The others followed.

"You know..." BehLahk continued. "Your stratagem and mine, as complex and as covert as they were, had a number of similarities."

"Stratagem?"

"And yet, our ultimate goals are quite different. I find that most curious."

"Really..." Joseph said dryly.

"Yes. I must say, Joseph, I was rather impressed. You surprised me."

"Really," he stated again. "How so?"

The hint of wry humor that BehLahk had been showing faded. There was nothing threatening, rather it was introspective. "I reasoned the other components of your stratagem, your plan... but I missed this. I did not see this at all."

Joseph didn't respond. They walked in silence for a few moments. BehLahk gave out a rather sad sigh.

"In the end, my friend, your goal will not be realized. And the cost... the cost is so very high."

"A price we are willing to accept."

"Time will tell." BehLahk glanced up into the sky, his pace slowing. He stopped then, turned and faced Joseph. "If you have no objection, we will spend the night and get an early start in the morning."

"Fine by me. You might want to hang close to your shuttle."

"We will do that." He started away. "We may speak again before we leave."

"If not, good luck to you."

Joseph started back to town. BehLahk and TohPeht continued on toward the shuttle, their escort continuing to follow a few paces behind.

"You sounded quite confident that Joseph's plan will fail, BehLahk," said TohPeht. "Was that wholly for his benefit?"

"Not at all," said BehLahk. "It will fail."

"But if ShahnTahr crunches all the data and the data says to leave—"

"That would have worked in the past, but it is no longer just about cold logic. This is between Joseph and EsJen."

"Certainly not at the expense of the Shylmahn. We serve."

"We serve. Yes." BehLahk spoke softly, introspectively. "Our very soul. It is what makes us Shylmahn."

"Precisely," said TohPeht. *So it is not possible for EsJen to act in any way detrimental to Shylmahn.*

"I know what you are thinking, TohPeht. But it is your very logic that leads you astray. Look beneath the facts being presented. Study the landscape. EsJen does not realize that this is what she is doing, but in truth the actions that she will take will be based on the landscape that lay between she and the Chehnon Joseph Britton. She does not realize it, but she has come to understand him."

"So... our own efforts have been successful."

"Such an observation is probably premature," said BehLahk. "But I am optimistic."

§

The flyer glided just above the canopy of trees. Reaching the edge of the forest, Carolyn turned the tiny hybrid shuttle due east and took it out across the open expanse, descending to forty feet. Double-checking altitude and course, she settled back and relaxed.

Seated to her right, Steven finished his notes and slipped the notebook into the copilot's seat side pocket. He leaned back then as well and took in the view.

It was mid-afternoon. They had spent the day reconnoitering a route from the keep to deep into the Shillie province and within spitting distance of Seattle. Surprisingly, once they got well away from the basin in which the keep was located, they had been able to map a clear route for most of the way, with only a few difficult stretches. They were well aware that any survey would have a very limited life expectancy, and they could expect the way to grow increasingly difficult with each passing day as the vine continued to spread, but there didn't look to be any insurmountable obstacles.

"It's hard to imagine all this vine dying out," said Steven. There were signs of the Veltahk on the plain below.

"I'll go with the scientists on this one, until I see different," said Carolyn.

"So... I've been wondering... if it's going to die out this winter, why don't we ride things out in the keep? I mean, why move to Seattle?"

"I don't think the keep is going to survive the vine through the winter."

Steven thought about that for a moment, finally shook his head. He didn't look at Carolyn, kept his gaze out the window. "No... no, there's more to it than that. If you wanted to make it happen, we could fight off the Veltahk for one season."

At first, Carolyn said nothing. Steven didn't think she was going to respond. Her head leaning back against the seat, her focus straight ahead, she made no sign that she had even heard him. She wasn't really looking at anything, at least not at anything out there.

"The timing is right," she said at last, her words soft and distant. She fell silent again. She turned briefly, looked over at Steven, then let her head roll back.

She didn't know what else to say, how she could put it into words that he would understand.

Whatever happened, however this all played out, there were big changes coming. The world was changing. Everything was changing. In a year's time, whether the Shillies were still here or not, whether the vine was still here or not, the world was going to be a very different place.

Till now, the world being what it was, Carolyn's choice had been to isolate her people from the rest of humanity. She had walked away, years ago, walled herself and her people up behind the timbers of the keep, and was only occasionally dragged out by her brothers to help with one fool adventure or another.

But now... the world was being reborn. She didn't yet know what form this new world would take, but she could foresee that her keep would have no place there.

It was time to rejoin the human race. For her, at least for now, that meant moving into one of the cities of the past.

"The time is right," she said.

They were able to set the flyer down in the same clearing from which they had departed that morning, which gave them a four mile hike back to the keep. Carolyn had considered finding a landing site closer to home, but decided best not to tempt fate this close to the move.

The gate opened as they approached and Jackson stepped outside.

"I hope all went well," he said.

"There were no problems," said Carolyn. "We have mapped a passable route."

"Very good. And did you meet with your brother?"

"Kenneth is sending flyers over to transport what they can to Seattle," said Carolyn. They had met Kenneth near the city and had made arrangements for his people to assist with the move. He was looking forward to having Carolyn as a neighbor. "They'll be here in the morning."

"More good news," said Jackson. "That much less that we'll have to leave behind."

"I don't know what kind of reaction this'll get from the Shillies. Maybe none, but I want us miles away before those flyers land."

"Yes ma'am."

They stepped through the gate and it slowly closed behind them. Carolyn continued toward her office.

"I want you and three volunteers to meet the flyers. Load 'em up and get outta here."

"You got it."

Jenny's way station consisted of a small cabin, a barn and a utility shed. Jenny came into the yard just after sunrise, found Monroe sitting on the porch. He had a cup of coffee in hand, was quietly taking in the morning. He slowly sat forward when he saw her, filled a second cup from the carafe on the small side table and had it ready when Jenny climbed the steps.

"Good morning, Monroe," she said. She took the cup.

"You didn't travel through that in the dark, did you?" He was nodding in the direction she had come in from. Though the way station itself was still clear, the surrounding forest was starting to see a lot of the vine.

"Not so much. I was camped two hours from here, got an early start." Jenny took a sip from the cup. She looked once behind her. "It's still not too bad out there; still passable."

"How's Michael?" he asked.

"Irritable." Best to get off that subject. She asked about the family that he had gone to check on.

They were doing well enough for the moment, had supplies and stores to last them a while, but the farm was all but lost. This was to be the last season.

Their plan was to stay on for now, harvest what they could, and then hunker down for the winter. Come spring they would be moving on.

Jenny wasn't sure what her next step was and was considering doing the same thing herself. There had been no word from Carolyn for quite some time, and her father and Miriam had apparently fallen off the edge of the planet. With Michael soon to be heading north to Freetown, Jenny's immediate assignment was complete.

When deciding to leave Michael and Garden City, the way station had been the first and only place she had sought to go to. Now that she was here, she could convince herself that it was as good a place as any to lay low for a while, at least until there was some sign, some indication as to what to do next.

And anyone looking for her and not finding her with Michael, this would be the first place they would look.

She had supplies to last two to three weeks, and could stretch that out indefinitely with hunting and foraging.

"How are you supply-wise, Monroe?" she asked.

"I got no immediate concerns."

"Plans?"

"About run out."

"Me, too." She turned about and took the first step down off the porch. She looked about her. Yes, she could see the vine in the shadows of the surrounding forest, but for the moment the way station looked much as it had years earlier. "It's good to be home, Monroe."

"I imagine so." Monroe took another swallow of his coffee, watched Jenny take the last step down and move out away from the cabin.

Jenny stopped then, turned her head and listened. There was a sound... a strange humming noise, distant but getting nearer.

Monroe heard it too. He stood and started down from the porch.

They came then, from the west. Several small flyers, traveling fast, only a few dozen feet above the trees. They passed directly overhead and continued east.

Overhead and then quickly gone; the sound of their engines quickly faded.

"Ours," she said absently. She knew about the hybrid flyers of course, though she hadn't actually seen one until now.

"Yep."

Jenny looked back west, from the direction they had come, then east. Where had they come from, and where were they going?

"Our little timeout here may be short-lived."

NehLoc and EsJen stood before a stone half-wall near the edge of the precipice. Behind them their two shuttles sat side by side in the center of a paved parking area, this a vista point midway along a mountain ridge. Further back were the remnants of an old Chehnon highway, now broken asphalt and faded metal signs.

The vista that was spread out before them was of a lush green valley below and beyond that a high, snowcapped ridge of exposed rock that rose up several thousand feet and spanned the length of the valley.

And spread out across the floor of the valley was a Chehnon community. It appeared to be in the final throes of a violent assault. Many of the buildings were on fire, bright flame and pillars of smoke billowing up in ugly dark whorls.

Even at this great distance, EsJen could hear the hollow echoes of gunshots, and when the wind was just right she thought she heard human screams.

The Chehnon were killing each other.

NehLoc appeared pleased by what he saw.

"They've been working their way west for several months; their method is always the same. A hunting party locates the next town, the army descends, murders, pillages, plunders the community of anything of value, then moves on to the next town."

"To what end?"

NehLoc shrugged. "The leader states that he is bringing order, that he is creating an empire spanning coast to coast. I see no evidence of that. I see only the Chehnon penchant for violence and self-destruction."

EsJen looked down upon the scene, wore a look of revulsion at what these creatures were capable of.

She spoke very matter-of-fact. "Is there any indication that this poses a threat to us?"

"None as yet; we continue to monitor, and we are prepared should the situation change."

"Very good."

NehLoc smiled now. "Do you see, EsJen? Do you see? Every aspect of Joseph Britton's scheme will fail at the hands of the Chehnon themselves. They are their own downfall. They will bring about their own demise."

"I find it very sad." EsJen turned away from the scene and started back to her shuttle. NehLoc watched the spectacle a moment more before following.

"It was inevitable," he stated coldly.

"I suppose it was." She reached the foot of her shuttle's ramp, hesitated before going inside. "I have heard nothing further regarding their doomsday device. Why?"

"There is nothing more to report, as yet. The few captives we collected from their *Phoenix Labs* have been delivered to a nearby facility, and are awaiting my arrival. I will be seeing to the interrogations myself."

"As soon as you have word then, NehLoc."

"Of course, EsJen. I serve."

Joseph and TohPeht stood at the edge of the train station's loading platform, which ran the length of the building. The tracks before them were covered in long, twisted vine than grew unimpeded along the track line. They could see the receding figure of BehLahk a hundred feet or so to their left, absentmindedly exploring his way along the tracks, stopping to look at this and then at that.

The station behind them was beginning to look much like the other buildings in town, covered in vine and leaf, but the platform they were on was still mostly clear. The faded brown wooden deck was a small island in a sea of varied greens and yellows.

TohPeht had asked to meet with Joseph, wanting to talk with him before he and BehLahk left. The three of them had wandered away from the Shylmahn shuttle, working their way around the train station, TohPeht being ever curious of the world around him. BehLahk had excused himself and left the two of them alone on the platform.

TohPeht had fallen silent. The silence didn't seem to bother him at all. The quiet contemplation was good for the soul.

After some time had passed, a minute or more that felt much longer to Joseph, TohPeht lifted a hand and rested it on Joseph's arm.

"So many shadows, Joseph Britton," he said, the words sounding as if they had come from very far away.

"I'm not sure I understand."

TohPeht looked away, looked forward and beyond, to someplace else.

"That is quite all right," he said.

A moment then, and then Joseph started to feel lightheaded. The scene around him grew fuzzy, veiled. There was a glassy shimmering and then the tracks faded, the platform faded, the world around him was gone.

He stood on a hilltop. TohPeht stood beside him. They were looking out across a neighborhood, and beyond that the skyline of a city far in the distance.

Joseph recognized this place. He quickly turned and looked behind him, then forward again at the neighborhood below.

This was the hilltop park. He had spent a lot time here, so many years ago. Down there somewhere was Elizabeth's house, and his own.

This was where he had had the vision. He had seen the destruction resulting from the invasion long before it had happened.

The world he looked out on now was sometime before the Shylmahn. The sky overhead was crisscrossed with the contrails of half a dozen jets. The skyline of the city in the distance was intact. The homes and yards of the neighborhood below were well-kept.

The world still belonged to us.

He looked back behind them again at the park. It was small, enclosed on three sides by trees and shrubs. There was a small parking lot off the left.

There was no one else in the park, but there seldom was.

The lawn had been recently mown Joseph could smell freshly cut grass.

He felt a slight breeze on his face.

He looked at TohPeht. TohPeht was looking out across the panoramic view.

"TohPeht," said Joseph. "How did—"

There was a sudden rush of air, the world shimmered and swam, everything turned misty and gray...

Joseph was again standing on the train platform. The smell of freshly cut grass was replaced with the earthy smell of the Veltahk.

Joseph was still looking at TohPeht.

"What did you do?" he asked. "I was there. We were there."

"Yes."

"That's it? Yes? What does it mean?"

TohPeht shrugged. "I don't know."

Joseph studied TohPeht's face, the expression he wore. TohPeht believed what he was saying. But there was something else there. What was it? Joseph knew the history of this being, this hybrid of TohPeht and Shahn-Tahr.

"No Shylmahn can do that. An AI can't do that. What are you?"

"I simply am."

"That's no answer. You're TohPeht, but not TohPeht. You're the AI, but much more."

TohPeht studied the Chehnon a few seconds, analyzing the comment.

"That which was ShahnTahr is within me, but I am not ShahnTahr."

"But how are you doing this? That place, that vision, that's been with me since before the invasion. It was you, even back then. I saw what was going to happen. You gave that to me; like you did just now."

"I am in many places."

"You mean times? You're in different times?"

"I am a part of this world. I am one with this world."

"No," said Joseph resolutely; with finality. "That is not true. This is not your world. It will never be your world."

The transition came quickly this time. A blast of air, a sudden shimmering, shifting of scene and vision...

Joseph and TohPeht stood again at the very edge of the park, a few feet in front of the small bench. It was evening, sometime before the invasion. The neighborhood below was transitioning to evening activities. One window and then another began to glow yellow or white as lights were turned on. An occasional car pulled into a driveway; a mom or a dad climbed out and went inside to join the family.

The scene shifted suddenly, starkly. The sky was a dark, pasty gray. Smoke drifted across the neighborhood. Fires burned untended. The skyline of the city in the distance was a silhouette of twisted shards, all that remained of the tall buildings.

The invasion had come.

"Look at what you did to us," said Joseph sadly.

The scene shifted yet again, a dizzying transition.

It was daylight in the neighborhood below. Decades had come and gone. The long-abandoned middle-class homes were being swallowed up by the vine.

The earthborn Veltahk had come.

"What you did, Joseph," said TohPeht.

"You can't compare the two. You left us no choice."

"*There is always choice.* I believe those were your very words. Choice is what makes you human."

The scene slowly faded in a shining, drifting fog. Joseph and TohPeht stood again on the loading platform outside the train station.

Joseph let the argument go. What was to be gained?

"I still don't understand," he said tentatively. "How..."

"One with the world, one with you."

"You? Me?"

TohPeht looked to Joseph, then looked away, looked down at his feet, at the earth beneath his feet.

The Shylmahn... and me... and this Chehnon. It had always been so. EsJen had felt it too, had a sense of it, unknowing but there.

TohPeht had only recently come to fully realize it. It had taken the amalgamation of TohPeht and ShahnTahr for such realization.

"Yes," TohPeht stated simply. "We."

"Is this why you are here? Why you come to me now? You and BehLahk. You bring me this? These visions? Why?"

TohPeht turned and started away. He started toward BehLahk. He said nothing.

"And the future?" Joseph called after.

"Choices, Joseph Britton. There is more than one path."

Chapter Fourteen

Jenny waited at the foot of the porch steps as Carolyn crossed the dusty yard and approached the cabin. Monroe hovered protectively at the top of the steps.

There had to have been several hundred men, women and a few children, probably the entire population of Carolyn's keep. Many began settling in just inside the clearing, separating into smaller groups. Others started across toward the barn, and a few followed Carolyn toward Jenny.

"Aunt Carolyn," said Jenny. "What brings you my way?"

"Jenny," nodded Carolyn, a bit on the cool side. She stopped within arm's distance of Jenny. "I hope you don't mind if we spend the night?"

"Not at all," said Jenny. She silently noted that Carolyn's people had already begun moving into the barn.

"Thanks," said Carolyn. "We'll be out of your hair before dawn."

"Take whatever time you need. It's what the station is for, after all." Jenny put on her most genuine smile, absently scratched behind her ear. "I must say though; I never thought I'd see the day... a Britton coming through here taking a group back *into* the province." She gave her aunt a thoughtful look. "I saw a couple of flyers passing over the other day, heading east; early next morning, came back heading west. Those were yours?"

"Your uncle Kenneth's," said Carolyn. Her own flyer had been with those flying back to Seattle. She looked back to her team. "See to the perimeter guard; command post in the barn."

"Yes, Ma'am," said one. All but one of the team set off. Steven remained, standing silently beside Carolyn.

Carolyn turned back to Jenny. "I appreciate the use of your space."

"You are moving into the province then?"

"That's the plan." Carolyn wasn't one to give anything away.

"You joining Kenneth? Seattle?"

"Seattle."

Carolyn's companion now considered it appropriate to speak up. "We'll be neighbors of your uncle," said Steven.

"Ah," said Jenny. Her Aunt Carolyn had been living in one isolated keep or another for most of Jenny's life. She was a tough, smart woman and had always been a bit of a mystery. Her actions were calculated, well thought-out, though on rare occasion she could act rash when provoked.

If she was giving up the life of the keep and moving into the big city, and into a Shillie province at that, Carolyn had good reason. Jenny hesitated asking what that reason might be, as her manner and posture suggested it wasn't a subject she wanted to get into.

Leaving the keep may have been forced on her, and if so it had almost certainly been due to the Veltahk or some other of Joseph's endeavors. Jenny was inextricably tied to her father and his activities, and that would explain Carolyn's coolness toward her; even more cool than had become her normal with Jenny.

Better to let the whole matter go unspoken.

"Monroe and I usually spend some time on the porch in the evening... hot tea, cold tea, whatever. Be great if you could join us later, if you have time."

"Of course," said Carolyn, though with little emotion. "If I have time."

"Of course."

Carolyn turned decisively to Steven. "Work to do, we should be about it."

Steven looked to Jenny before leaving. "Nice to see you again, Jenny."

"Yes," said Carolyn, and she turned to follow.

Once she was well away, Monroe took the steps down from the porch and stood beside Jenny. His attention was on Carolyn.

"A woman of few words," he said.

"Not like you at all."

Monroe actually managed a smile. "Yes, well... I suppose we both say as much as needs saying."

Jenny watched as her aunt reached the barn and went inside. She glanced up at Monroe.

"I may have missed a few syllables. Just what was said just now?"

"That there are changes coming, and she's not fully comfortable with 'em."

Joseph finished washing up at the bathroom sink. He dried his face and hands, carefully folded the towel and hung it back on the bar that was set beneath the shelf above the toilet. He took his shirt from the hook on the back of the door and put it on as he returned to the main room.

His was a corner room on the third floor of the old hotel; high-ceilinged, with a single, wood-framed window in each of the two exterior walls. It was furnished with a queen-sized bed, chest-of-drawers, desk and chair. A large over-stuffed chair with a musty smell sat in the corner.

A number of thick vines had made it into the room. These ran along the base of the walls and had sent clinging tendrils up the walls and along the ceiling and floor, had begun to spread over the furniture; hundreds of broad green leaves of varying sizes.

Joseph crossed the room, seeking out open spots on the floor as he worked his way to the door.

The hallway was a tunnel of vines and leaves, dark and gloomy, the only light streaming in through a window at the end of the hall. He reached the stairwell and worked his way down to the first floor, clambering over vines and leaves all the way down.

Miriam was waiting for him in the lobby, just inside the front door.

"They're at the community hall," she said, and led the way outside.

There was a clear path down the center of the main street, but even this was being threatened by the encroaching vine that covered most of the walls lining the avenue. The alleyways between the buildings were now mostly leafy tunnels lost in dark shadows.

Two men stood outside the community hall.

Joseph reached out and shook hands with Eddie Blythe.

"Eddie. Good to see you again."

"Joseph." Eddie nodded.

Joseph reached a hand then to Eddie's companion.

"Miguel, isn't it? You were one of Jason's people."

"That's right," said Miguel, nodding. "A very good man, was your brother."

"That he was." Joseph hadn't seen Miguel in a long time. He knew that Eddie and Miguel had grown to be good friends, so he wasn't surprised to see the two of them together.

He had seen Eddie a few months earlier. He turned back to him.

"What brings you two this way?" he asked. "It couldn't have been an easy trip, so I'm guessing it's important."

"You're guessing right. We got trouble."

"What kind of trouble?" asked Miriam.

"The human kind."

Miriam growled. "Shit."

"How so?" asked Joseph.

"A scouting party came through Franklin; a gang really; making demands, threats, told us that change was coming."

"What'd they mean by *change*?"

"They said they were the vanguard of an approaching army... *a revolution sweeping across the land,* they said."

"A bunch of thugs," grumbled Miguel.

"We are now under the protection of President Marlow. I figure that's their leader."

"They demanded tribute," said Miguel. "Food, supplies, and company, if you get my meaning."

"You told 'em to go to hell, right?" asked Miriam.

"Our mayor politely asked them to leave," said Eddie. "They shot him dead. No discussion. Things didn't go so well after that. There was only about thirty of 'em, but we weren't ready for something like that. We're not much, as villages go. Some of us fought, Miguel and I fought, but in the end, we had to ditch."

"We knew you were here," said Miguel. "You can get word out, do something about these bastards."

"This army," Joseph wondered. "You think it's real?"

Eddie nodded. "It's real. We've seen it. They're just a few miles east of Franklin, heading north. Gotta be a couple of thousand of 'em; and lots of tents and equipment, vehicles. Looks like a frickin' Roman legion."

Miguel nodded at this. "We figure the main force isn't caring much about the smaller villages like ours; leave 'em to these scouting parties to have fun with."

"You're probably right," agreed Joseph. "If they're heading north—"

"Garden City, Metcalf, and Freetown," said Eddie.

Hundreds of acres outside Freetown were in orchard. It had gone wild for some time after the invasion, but in recent years had been reclaimed by the town. Many of the original trees had been replaced and entire sections had been converted to new varieties of fruit or nut.

And for the moment there was little sign of the approaching Veltahk.

Michael felt a strange sense of nostalgia as he moved through the trees. He had made the trip quite a few times years earlier as part of the underground railroad, bringing refugees safely out of the province. But never with so many people, the group never so noisy, and the orchards never so ordered.

Sight and sound was all a bit off. The nostalgia wasn't quite right.

He called for a halt. They would establish camp within the orchard while he and a few representatives met with the leaders of Freetown and made arrangements to enter the community.

He led the small delegation of council members out of the orchard and onto an open meadow. Across the meadow was the high timber wall that ran along the base of the low mountain. Hidden just beyond the wall, set between wall and mountain, was the Outer Village. Within the mountain itself was the Inner Village, the heart of Freetown.

The double gate opened as Michael was starting across the meadow. A group of men and women met him halfway.

Michael held out his hand. "Craig. Just the man I wanted to see. You look well."

"Hello, Michael." Craig shook hands with Michael. "You look like you've been on quite a journey. Don't tell me you walked all the way from Garden City."

Michael noted the apprehension in Craig's voice and on his face. The others in the mayor's group looked either nervous or standoffish or a bit of both.

"Yes we did," he said. "And I'm afraid I have a favor to ask of you."

"From what I'm told, it appears you brought just about the entire population of Garden City." Craig's dodge of the upcoming favor request was obvious.

"More than just about. We're all here, my friend."

"Wow." Craig's smile was forced. "I see."

"Craig?"

"Michael... I hope you're not going to ask what I think you're going to ask."

Michael looked from Craig to those beside and behind his long-time friend. Body posture didn't bode well. He looked again directly at Craig.

"Is there a problem, Craig?"

"We're really crowded, Michael. I mean, we are busting at the seams."

One of those standing behind Michael took a step forward. "You can't just turn us away. Where do you expect us to go?"

"I'm very sorry," said Craig. He only briefly glanced to the councilman, spoke again to Michael. "We've taken in all we can and then some. Inner Village, Outer Village... we're absolutely packed."

One of Craig Warren's associates moved up beside the mayor. Michael recognized the middle-aged woman, but couldn't recall her name.

"We're doing all we can, Michael," she said. "We've been taking in folks for weeks, everyone who's come and asked for help. We just can't take in any more people. We can't. Not one more person."

"I understand." Michael should have anticipated this. He had expected there would have been some influx from some of the smaller nearby communities, but not to this level.

No... he really should have expected this. The world was getting scary, and when things got scary, Freetown had always been the focal point of safety, stability and support. Of course everyone would come here. He had come here. People had probably been streaming in since the first early signs of the Veltahk.

Michael knew Craig Warren well. He knew what it must have taken for the man to come out here and turn them away.

"It's all right, Craig. I imagine things are getting pretty tough in there."

"If you need anything..."

"Quite all right. No doubt you're running low as it is."

"We'll share what we have."

Michael held out his hand. Craig hesitated, then reached out and they shook hands.

Michael gave a smile.

"You take care, my friend."

Craig could only nod in response. He turned about then and led his group back toward the gate. Once out of earshot, several of the council closed in on Michael.

"You turned down supplies?" one asked heatedly. "Are you crazy?"

"Shut up."

"Really?" asked another. "Is that what you're going to say when we start going hungry?"

Michael turned about and started back toward the orchard. "Just shut the hell up."

NehLoc spooned the last of the soup from his bowl and lifted the spoon to his mouth. He slurped politely and swallowed, set the spoon and bowl aside and took a drink from his cup. He glanced around the cafeteria without making eye contact with any of the others in the room.

He didn't like interacting with subordinates during lunch.

He was sitting at the small corner table, his back to the wall. This afforded him minimal opportunity for inadvertent contact, while providing the earliest warning of a possible impending exchange. Everyone knew of his need to be left alone while eating, yet understood that should a time-sensitive issue arise, he wanted to be notified as soon as possible.

This satellite facility was smaller than NehLoc's main security head-quarters, but he rather enjoyed his time here. It was much less hectic here, the atmosphere tending to be less stressful. It was certainly quieter.

He set the empty cup down, used the back of his hand to slide it next to the empty bowl. He took a moment then to prepare for the afternoon. He closed his eyes, let both mind and body relax. He drifted. He felt warm and satisfied.

NehLoc opened his eyes then, took a quiet, calming breath and stood up from the table. He walked smoothly yet purposefully across the room, pushed through the door and entered the hall.

The main hallway ran the length of the facility's short east wing. The interrogation chamber was located at the far end of the wing. This gave NehLoc a few additional moments to prepare, with each casual step draw-ing him closer to the entertaining activity that lay ahead.

He stopped before the viewing window. The interrogation chamber lay beyond the one way glass panel. The Chehnon sat in the examination chair near the center of the room, cables running from sensor pads on his arms, scalp and forehead to the monitoring equipment on the counter behind him. A Shylmahn guard stood to one side, silent, eyes ahead but watchful. A guardian probe hovered beside and just behind the Chehnon.

Phillip Neville appeared to have lost some considerable weight since be-ing delivered from the Phoenix Labs facility. He was provided a diet suffi-cient to sustain him through the interrogation process, but nothing more. More would have been wasteful.

NehLoc stepped to the door, opened it and entered the interrogation chamber. He wore a cool, confident and quite genuine smile.

"Good afternoon, Phillip Neville. We shall continue, yes?"

Chapter Fifteen

The encampment was spread across five acres of orchard, tarps tied to trees and spanning the rows; tents of all sizes and types and condition. A hundred small campfires sent shadows dancing through the branches and pushed back the black, moonless evening.

Michael and Victoria sat side by side before their own small fire. Their little boy Nate lay asleep nearby beneath a blanket.

The meeting had finally ended an hour earlier. Michael, Victoria and six of the council had gathered 'round this very fire, with dozens of citizens pushing in around them from behind.

They had been unable to come to any resolution, and it had been decided they would get together again in the morning; everyone needed to come with reasoned comments and real, viable options.

Like that's going to happen...

Michael picked up the stick sitting beside him and stirred the fire.

The thing was, once you got past the blustering and the idiotic, there had been quite a number of very reasonable concerns raised, and Michael had agreed with many of their complaints.

There just weren't that many viable options.

A man in his sixties with graying hair came out of the shadows and stepped up beside their fire.

"Good evening, Doug," said Victoria. Doug was a member of the council, and one of the cooler heads.

Doug nodded greeting to Victoria, then to Michael.

"Mind if I sit down?"

Michael held a hand out, offering a spot near the fire. Doug settled onto the ground with a light groan. He grinned apologetically when Nate stirred under his blanket, fell silent.

"It could have gone worse, don't you think?" he asked, referring to the meeting. He tried to keep his voice soft, so as not to wake the child.

"I suppose that's true," said Victoria.

Michael said nothing for the moment. Doug glanced thoughtfully around them. Shadows and movement around the many campfires was lessening. Folks were finally settling down, falling into their own quiet conversations.

Doug turned again to Michael. "What are we going to do, Michael?"

"You know as much as I do, Doug. Nothing is decided."

"What I know doesn't really leave many options open to us. So what are you thinking we should do?"

Michael picked up his stick again and absently poked at the fire. "Any town we go to is likely to be in the same shape as Garden City. Overrun by the vine."

"And Freetown was unique; underground with limited access. Hell, even if there was another like her, there'd be no room at the inn."

Michael wasn't sure of the reference, but he got the gist of the comment. Any community with the qualities and strengths of Freetown would already be swamped with refugees.

"Which doesn't leave us with many choices," he said.

"Not once you throw out the crazy ones we heard earlier."

Victoria leaned forward and let out a soft sigh. "We head back home, we live in the bush, or... what else?"

"I'm not one for living in the vine," said Doug. "I'm too damned old for that sort of thing."

"Home, then? Back to Garden City?"

"Well..." Michael started. "Once they quit grumbling about our futile march through the wilderness to get here, that would probably be the option most accepted by everyone. But don't forget, we left for a reason. In another few months, Garden City won't be that different than living in the vine."

"But it is home," said Victoria.

"That it is," said Doug.

"That it *was*," said Michael.

There was a bit of a commotion down one of the orchard rows, movement in the shadows, exchanges of words that they couldn't quite make out. They saw then that someone was being escorted in their direction by two men.

Michael and Victoria stood up as soon as they recognized Craig Warren. Doug got to his feet much more slowly.

Victoria smiled and stepped forward. "Craig," she said warmly and gave him a hug. "It's been a long time."

"Much too long, Victoria. Much, much too long."

The two men who had brought Craig into the camp stepped back. "He said he needed to talk to you," said one of them.

"Thank you for showing him in," said Michael.

Craig was looking across the campfire at young Nate, who was slowly sitting up.

"Is that Nate?" he asked cheerily. "My, how he's grown."

Nate looked up, bleary-eyed, silent but smiling.

By now, some of the nearby Garden City citizens had started to drift nearer. The two men who had brought Craig in made no move to leave.

Michael noted Craig's glances about them. He gave Victoria a pat on the arm, a silent message, and then stepped away and looked to Craig. "What say we take a little walk?"

"Sounds good."

Michael gave the two escort a *wait here* look, then led Craig away.

They crossed through five rows of trees before they were far enough away that they felt they could talk with some semblance of privacy. There was still no moon in the black sky above the orchard canopy, and the encampment's hundred campfires were now but specks of flickering light in the dark.

"How many are you?" Craig asked conversationally. "Last I recall, Garden City was about three hundred."

"That's about right."

They walked then in an awkward silence, crossing several more rows of trees. Michael was content with that for now, but it made Craig uncomfortable.

"How's Jenny?" he asked at last.

"Well enough, I expect," said Michael. "She left a few days ahead of us; I figure she was heading for her cabin."

"That would be Jenny, all right."

"That it would."

"And Miriam?" asked Craig. "I've heard nothing of her since she left Freetown, heading your way."

"She left to meet up with my father further south, or so I understand." Michael decided not to get into a debate about Miriam's support of Joseph. Everyone knew of her loyalty to Joseph Britton.

Craig came to a slow stop, glancing around them. Michael turned about, waited for whatever it was that had brought Craig out.

"The council has some concerns," said Craig.

"Councils always have concerns," said Michael. *Mine is obsessed with them.*

"True enough," sighed Craig. He looked about them again. They were alone. "Some are afraid you may try to force your way into Freetown."

"That option did come up."

"I see." Craig felt a little numb. "And?"

"Not as long as I have any say. I expect that'll last a while longer; whether I want it to or not."

"We need you sitting right there at the head of the table, Michael."

Michael wondered what Craig meant by 'we'; *we need you right there.* How involved was he in what was happening?

Craig was one of the good ones; one of the best. He hoped the man hadn't been sucked too deeply into Joseph's schemes.

"I expect I'm still where I am because there's too much squabbling on how to replace me. However, the rumblings for my head are growing ever louder."

Craig started walking again, Michael following beside him. "What are your plans now? Where will you go?"

"No decision yet. I expect we'll end up back in Garden City."

"But didn't you leave because it was being overrun with the vine?"

"Yep."

They walked in silence for some time then, finally turning and starting slowly back in the direction of Victoria. They didn't speak again until they were near enough to see her sitting there beside the campfire, occasionally glancing in their direction.

"You still have many friends in Freetown, Michael," Craig said at last. "Should you need anything."

"I appreciate that," said Michael. "I'm sure we'll be fine."

Craig nodded casually. "Sure. Just let me know." They were now within two tree rows of Victoria.

"It's not right," he said. "The leader of humanity, a wandering refugee."

Michael snickered. "I'm just a figurehead, a representative to the Shillies. Besides, most of that humanity that you speak of has never heard of me."

Up ahead of them, Victoria stood and stepped around the fire. She smiled at Craig, who smiled back and held out his hand. Victoria took it and held it.

The two men who had escorted Craig into the camp came forward then. Michael noted that the crowd that had gathered earlier had returned to their fires. Nate had crawled back under his blanket and was asleep.

Craig turned to Michael. "I'd like to see you all again before you leave."

"I'll let you know our plans as soon as they're ironed out."

They said their goodbyes, and Craig was escorted out of the camp. Michael and Victoria held hands as they watched him leave.

"Okay... so?" Victoria asked quietly.

"Their council is as crazy as ours."

Carolyn and Kenneth walked down the center of the canyon-like downtown avenue, with Steven and several others of her staff following a few yards behind, the bulk of her people following well behind Steven.

Despite Kenneth's assurances, she had a team leading the way ahead and another trailing behind them, watching for threats.

Downtown hadn't changed much since Carolyn's earlier visit, after the crash when Jason had been killed, after her narrow escape from the Shylmahn. There was none of the Veltahk in the downtown area as yet, but it was only a matter of time. They had seen quite a bit of it in the outlying neighborhoods they had passed through on their way into the heart of the city. Kenneth had met Carolyn several miles outside the city and had guided her and her group in, pointing out some of the important or interesting details along the way.

The Shylmahn seemed to be okay with humans settling in the city. At the very least, they had left them alone. There was that one recent incident down around the airport, but that may have been due to the jet fighter the group of humans living down that way had been working on. Other than that, so long as they stayed close to the city, didn't try to spread out too far, the Shillies had kept a hands-off attitude to their being in Seattle.

There were now five groups of humans settled in the heart of the city, and at least a dozen other groups scattered about in the surrounding neighborhoods. Some were loosely affiliated, while others chose near total isolation. It was completely up to them.

The city and surrounding neighborhoods were divided into sectors, and those groups within each operated as independent cooperatives, this whether they chose isolation or not. A simple trade system had evolved. As some of the cooperatives were better at some activities than others, and by the luck of the draw as to the make-up of their sectors, each of the cooperatives offered its own unique goods for trade.

All had become adept at growing fruits and vegetables, but the selection varied from sector to sector. And one cooperative in particular had become quite expert at growing seeds.

The forward team crossed the next intersection and then stopped at a barricade that closed off the street ahead. They waited for Carolyn and Kenneth. Reaching them, Kenneth stepped through the barricade and they continued on, Kenneth now leading the way.

"Your sector runs from here three blocks down, includes this street and one street to either side."

Carolyn noted that this street alone had two hotels towering over a handful of smaller office buildings, as well as a separate stand-alone parking garage that took up half a city block. There were a lot of things one could do with a parking garage if you didn't need to use it for parking.

"Not bad," she said.

"I thought you'd like it," said Kenneth. He stepped around a pile of façade rubble that had come down from the nearby building and broken apart in the street. "It's been neglected for a couple of decades, so... it's a definite fixer upper."

It didn't take much effort for Carolyn to see that it was going to take a lot of work. But she had brought along a lot of good people. This was doable.

She slowed, considered her location. She finally indicated left. "You're that way?"

"One sector over."

"Still in the same hotel?"

"We like it," said Kenneth. "Big-time renovation project; the hotel and a lot of the other buildings in our sector. We're encouraging all the cooperatives to start projects of their own. Our goal is to eventually bring the entire downtown core and the rest of the city back to all its pre-invasion glory."

"That would be something." Carolyn didn't see how it was possible, but it was an admirable goal.

Kenneth could read the doubt on his sister's face.

"Well, it's something to shoot for," he shrugged. "And in the meantime, we make it as livable as possible."

"No, I get it. I like it."

"Great." Kenneth smiled. They stopped in front of the first hotel on this street. "This one's in better shape. The stairwells are solid, roof doesn't leak, and it still has a lot of its windows."

Carolyn glanced back at Steven. "What do you think?"

"Sure." All he could think was that this one building was bigger than their entire keep. At ten stories, it was less than half the size of many of the major downtown hotels, but it would suit them just fine.

"Good," said Kenneth. "And it's almost rodent free. When we laid out this sector a few months ago, we thought this hotel was the better choice, and so we set out traps."

"Rats?" asked Steven.

"Few months ago?" asked Carolyn.

"Not for you specifically. We thought it might be a good idea to establish sectors in the parts of the city that weren't yet occupied; so as to have things ready and minimize confusion." Kenneth grinned. "Just lucky, you deciding to move in now."

"Rats?" Steven asked again.

"Not many. Not anymore. I've had a couple of kids coming in every week emptying out the traps." Kenneth started up to the front doors of the hotel. "Come on. Let's check it out."

Carolyn and Steven followed him in, and then everyone else followed Carolyn. Some moved into the large commons off the main lobby, others worked their way further into the hotel, finding their way into several large conference halls with chairs and tables.

There were a number of these large halls on the ground floor, as well as admin offices, a gift shop, a restaurant and the main kitchen. There were several below-ground floors that held the utilities, laundries, janitorial facilities, workshops, as well as the hotel's underground garage.

Leaving the others to explore a bit on their own, Kenneth and Carolyn walked to the stairwell beside the elevators. There was a table beside the door with a number of flashlights. He handed her one, took one for himself.

"You'll have a generator, enough power to run lights and heat. I'd suggest you limit the hours. Fuel is at a premium."

They entered the stairwell. There was an old, musty smell, but it wasn't as bad as Carolyn expected. No hint of rodents.

The pair of flashlights sent spears of light dancing around the well.

"Have you thought about solar?" she asked. The keep had some solar capabilities, as well as hydro from an underground river.

"We're on that, actually," said Kenneth. "We've sufficient panels, it's the grid and solar batteries we're working on. If you have any brainiacs who might be able to help, the cooperatives have pooled their resources and we have a lab dedicated to establishing renewable energy in each sector."

"Yeah, a real bitch about losing almost everyone on the planet," said Carolyn. "All that knowledge they were carrying around in their heads suddenly becomes real hard to come by."

"Definitely harder to come by," agreed Kenneth. At one time, there may have been a million people who knew what they needed to know. Now? A hundred? Ten? And where were they? How could they find them?

When attempting to bring solar power to the keep all those years ago, Carolyn's engineer had brought up the issue of the grid. They had managed to scrounge up panels and some solar batteries, but Darren said their real obstacle was going to be distribution. He had been a college student at the time of the invasion, so he hadn't had much in the way of practical experience. In the end, it wasn't really a distribution grid they set up but rather a number of independent collection and storage stations throughout the keep. It may not have been very sophisticated, but Darren had done all right.

"I got someone," she said at last. "Just let me know where to send him."

"Excellent."

The hotel rooms themselves began on the floor above the ground floor. They took only a quick peek at a few rooms before continuing up to the tenth and top floor. Here were a number of business suites and the skyview restaurant and lounge.

Carolyn walked over to the restaurant's wall of glass panels. The windows were all intact. The view was partially blocked by several taller buildings a few streets to the west, but she was able to see the waters of Puget Sound beyond.

The city, the Sound, the sky... all was quiet and still.

"I still miss it," she said, so quietly she could have been speaking only to herself.

"Me too," said Kenneth. He knew exactly what she meant. "After all these years, you can still feel it; the hole where the old life should be; even with all its problems."

"I miss movies. I miss going to the store. I miss traffic lights."

"Thanksgiving at Bril's."

Carolyn grinned. "Well, if you're going to get nasty, I'll leave."

"Sorry."

They stood then, silent, side by side, and just took in the view.

"Kenneth," said Carolyn finally. Several minutes had passed.

"Yeah?"

Kenneth should know about the anticipated demise of the Veltahk. He was clearly the major decision maker here in Seattle and those decisions should take it into account.

"There's something you should know. Just between you and me. And one or two others I've already told."

Joseph moved cautiously out onto the outcropping of rock, found a spot and sat down, made himself comfortable. Eddie, Miguel and Mayor Tomlinson settled in around him.

From here they had a clear view of the wide, shallow basin below. A legion of men, women and assorted vehicles was working its way up the valley toward a narrow passage that spilled out onto the open plain to the north. The gently sloping hills on either side of the valley were blanketed in evergreen that was now being choked out by the Veltahk. The vine reached from the trees out across the once grassy basin floor. A wide swath had been cleared ahead of the main body of the massive caravan, allowing it to move forward unhindered. So there had to be a large group somewhere out ahead that was clearing the way. Joseph saw no sign of this advance party, so it was probably already out of the valley and in the plain.

"Check it out," said Eddie. He pointed to movement near the treeline at the edge of the valley floor a quarter mile south. A convoy of four vehicles had come out into the open. It made its way into the clear path and began to close in on the rear of the army.

"One of their scouting parties," said Miguel. He had brought a small pair of binoculars out from an inside pocket of his light jacket and was watching the line of 4x4 vehicles.

All the teams were rejoining the main body as Marlow's army worked its way north.

They would hit Garden City first, and then Freetown... at the pace the army was traveling...

The mayor looked over at Joseph.

"You'll be leaving us then, I expect."

"I'm afraid so," said Joseph. He didn't look or sound very happy about it.

"We'll need to start soon, to get ahead of them," said Eddie.

And then what? thought Joseph. What could a community of two or three hundred, or two or three thousand for that matter, do against an army like that?

And yet, they couldn't just abandon their towns. What would that accomplish?

They had to take a stand. They had to take a stand now. But they couldn't do it alone. All the northwest communities had to come together, create a coordinated defense and a counter-offense. And best they choose for themselves where and how to make this fight. And most importantly, for the civilization of humanity that Joseph still hoped for their future, they had to win this.

They had to crush this sonofabitch into dust now. Kill him, destroy his army, and let the world know that this was not an option.

Eddie shifted forward and got slowly to his feet. He took a step ahead, looked down on the mass of men, women and vehicles continue to work its way up the valley.

"I never thought I'd see the like again," he said. "An army of man, its only purpose to do harm to fellow man."

"There will always be bad," said Miguel. "Having a common enemy doesn't change that."

"I know." Eddie kept his eyes on Marlow's army. "It should."

Joseph saw a flash of light, a reflection, along on the ridgeline on the opposite side of the valley. He borrowed the binoculars from Miguel, focused in on the source.

Even with binoculars, he could see very little detail. There was a Shylmahn shuttle. There looked to be two figures standing beside the shuttle, and appeared to be observing the scene, just as they were. From their stature, they had to be Shillies.

One of them may have been looking in Joseph's direction, but he was too far away to be sure.

NehLoc stepped into the hall. He wasn't pleased. The interrogations of the Chehnon were giving him little. The creature clearly knew something of the device the Chehnon had been developing, but NehLoc had as yet been unable to extract this information.

Most disappointing.

He stood at the glass wall, looking back into the interrogation chamber. The Chehnon was being escorted from the chair to the small room at the back that had been the creature's cell since being brought to the facility.

He looked weak. NehLoc had a decision to make. Increase the Chehnon's rations and continue the interrogations, or put an end to this line of investigation.

NehLoc was fairly certain that whatever progress the Chehnon had made with the device, it had ended with the destruction of their Phoenix Labs facility.

Fairly certain, but not absolutely certain. He needed to be absolutely certain. What if they had smuggled the device out prior to the assault? He needed to know, one way or the other. EsJen needed to know.

EsJen required to know.

He frowned. He turned from the glass and was about to start to the mess hall when he heard footsteps. One of the staff was coming down the hall toward him. He appeared to have something in hand.

NehLoc recognized PhonToh as one of the team leaders searching the rubble that had been Phoenix Labs.

"Yes?" he asked.

"We found it," said PhonToh.

"It?"

"In the debris." PhonToh held up the box. He opened the lid.

NehLoc glanced inside. It was the energy pod component. "And the device?"

"There is no device," said PhonToh. The energy pod component had been found in the rubble of one of the laboratories, and there was no indication that there had ever been research on any doomsday device.

NehLoc held out a hand and took the box. He silently weighed the idea in his mind.

Could it be? Could it have all been--?

A slight smile then...

§

BehLahk stepped off the ramp and started towards the stark, low building. The shuttle behind him lifted off before he reached the steps.

TohPeht had stated simply that he had other activities to attend to. Though he had no specific reason to believe so, BehLahk suspected he didn't want to be around for this exchange with EsJen.

BehLahk took the long main passage that bisected the complex, turning once into a narrower, though just as long hall. Shylmahn nodded and offered polite greetings along the way. He offered little of his normal light-hearted banter in response, but he did at least manage to acknowledge each salutation.

Entering the audience chamber, a lone Shylmahn stood waiting.

"This way, please," he stated, turned about and started toward a rear door, not waiting to see if BehLahk would follow.

The escort led BehLahk down a dark hallway and out into an open courtyard. It was similar to the enclosed gardens that EsJen kept in other provincial headquarters, though this one was more sparse, the vegetation thinner and dryer.

EsJen and NehLoc stood at the center of the courtyard, at the hub of several gravel walkways. A small box, not quite the length of a Shylmahn arm, sat on a nearby bench.

ShahnTahr hovered some distance away, as if giving them their privacy.

BehLahk left the escort at the door and joined them. "EsJen, thank you very much for seeing me."

"But of course, BehLahk. It sounded important." She wasn't smiling, but sounded cordial nonetheless.

"I believe it is."

"And how is TohPeht?" she asked, putting off the important matter.

"He is doing quite well. He sends his regards."

"That is good. I do not see him nearly as much as I would like."

"He speaks of you often. I believe he is quite fond of you."

She did manage a smile, now. "And I him."

There was an awkward moment of silence. BehLahk glanced once to NehLoc, then back to EsJen. NehLoc had yet to speak a word.

ShahnTahr continued to hover at a distance. The illusion of privacy was just that. Illusion. BehLahk knew well the sensor capabilities of the Shahn-Tahr probe.

"And so, to the matter that brought me here," he stated.

"But of course."

BehLahk detailed then what he and TohPeht had observed. They had been tracking a large Chehnon force, thousands in number, that had been working its way west for several months, was now in the heart of the north-west. It was wreaking havoc wherever it went; murdering, raping, leaving absolute destruction in its wake.

EsJen was silent. NehLoc spoke up.

"We know of this army," he stated. Quite calm.

"Then you know its bloodthirsty nature. Do you know its purpose?"

"The stated purpose of its leader, and the witnessed actions of the body, are quite at odds with one another."

"They pillage for the sheer joy of it."

"Yes." NehLoc continued his calm demeanor.

EsJen listened attentively, but maintained her silence.

"And so?" BehLahk asked. "As you know about them, what is to be done?"

"Their violence has up to now been directed only to Chehnon."

BehLahk had sensed the conversation leading to this from the very start. He didn't like it, though BehLahk should have expected just such an attitude from NehLoc, as he knew very well NehLoc's feelings regarding the Chehnon.

It was EsJen's silence that truly made him uncomfortable.

"We have no choice," he said. "We must intervene."

"We most certainly do not," NehLoc said cavalierly.

"But of course we do." He turned to EsJen. "The army grows larger as many feel compelled to join them rather than be slaughtered."

EsJen at least appeared to think this through.

NehLoc appeared pleased.

But of course... the Chehnon that survive this self-imposed genocide, all gathered together in one grand mass. It wouldn't take much for NehLoc to have them labeled a threat; a few detonations and the Chehnon problem is solved.

BehLahk looked still to EsJen. "EsJen... we must stop this."

EsJen lifted her head, stiffened her neck. "For now, we continue to monitor."

"EsJen, I—"

"We observe only."

Outwardly, NehLoc showed nothing at this. Inside, he felt a sense of something akin to satisfaction. Perhaps EsJen was thinking along the same lines as himself. Perhaps she had finally come to the realization that the Chehnon were more trouble than they were worth.

Let them kill each other, then we'll clean up whatever is left.

It took much for BehLahk to maintain proper Shylmahn civility. He had never been in such a position before. Whatever his role in the past, whatever his position in the hierarchy, he had always believed himself in control of the situation. He had never entered into a circumstance without fully understanding every nuance of the situation and knowing exactly how it was all going to play out.

But this... this was wrong. This was all so very wrong.

He was at this moment completely out of his element.

Why was he not able to bring it all back into line?

TohPeht had known this would be the response. Better he take a step out so as to be in a better position later.

BehLahk was bewildered. He felt... lost.

How had he not seen this?

Chapter Sixteen

They were on their way back to Garden City.

The return trip wasn't going to be any easier than the trip out. They were following the same path they had trailblazed on their journey to Freetown, and were finding that only days later much of it had already overgrown. A small team worked ahead of the walking caravan, clearing the way, the duty rotating amongst the population.

Victoria walked beside Michael, who was carrying their son on his back. Nate walked when the terrain and vegetation allowed, but at the moment travel was difficult.

The decision to return to Garden City may have been inevitable, but it hadn't been painless. The meeting had been uncomfortable and sometimes heated. The council and a handful of others had met away from camp, near the edge of the orchard where it bordered a thick forest of the vine. Several of the council, led by Paulsen, had actually advocated forcing their way into Freetown. Paulsen seldom sided with Michael on anything, even if he actually agreed with him.

"Are you suggesting that we fight our way in?" asked Michael. Remaining calm hadn't been easy, but Michael had promised Victoria and himself that he wouldn't let those like Paulsen goad him into losing his temper.

Paulsen didn't back down, despite how the suggestion sounded.

"If it comes to that, yes."

"Are you really willing to kill those people?"

Paulsen did finally hesitate. "It won't come to that," he stated at last.

"Yes it would," said Doug evenly. Doug Bradford always spoke evenly. "And let's say we do get in. Do you really believe that those inside are going to welcome us after we've just finished murdering their friends and neighbors? Their husbands and wives and children?"

There was little to say to that, but Paulsen didn't look at all pleased. And coming from Doug Bradford didn't make it any easier. It was difficult to argue with Doug. The man was composed, quiet and kind to just about everyone. He was the least polarizing member on the council.

Michael had let the silence hang there for a while.

"Let's go home," he said.

"I'm not going all the way back there," said Paulsen. "Back to what?"

But what other options were there? A few ideas were tossed around, the names of a few other towns were brought up, but in the end most of the council chose to return to Garden City. Only Paulsen and one other chose to go out on their own. A few of the city's population would choose to follow them. Most would make the return journey home.

Several days from the orchards of Freetown and most everyone marched in silence. Thoughts had shifted from the legendary village in the cavern behind them once again to their home, to Garden City. They had given up much to leave it, and the reasons for leaving it still existed. What must they do to address those reasons?

The trail ahead leveled off and opened out. Michael brought Nate down and let him walk. The boy immediately ran ahead, quickly rushing past others in the line of travelers. Michael started to call after him when Victoria placed a hand on his arm.

Nate ran up to another boy, to his friend Mark, and the two walked together.

The future of humanity.

What would their world look like?

Joseph led the way through the south gate and into Garden City. Miriam walked beside him, Eddie and Miguel several steps behind. They each carried a small backpack; all had taken to using walking staffs, not just Miriam.

They had left Weston eleven days earlier, following the railroad tracks most of the way; first the sidetrack that ran from Weston west out to the mainline, passing the train Joseph had abandoned months before, and then the mainline itself, traveling north. It had taken as long as it had to reach Garden City due to the spread of the thick, twisting vines of Veltahk running along and over the track lines. Despite that, this route offered the easier and faster course.

Joseph and the others found the town empty. It appeared as though the population had left some time ago. Doors stood ajar, windows stood open. The streets were quickly being overwhelmed by the vine, but for the moment were still quite passable, somewhat easier in fact than what they had faced for most of their way here.

They worked their way to the main thoroughfare and then followed that into the heart of the town.

"Where do you think?" asked Eddie. "Freetown?"

"That would be my guess," said Joseph.

Miguel gave sharp, quick nods. "Good thing, you ask me. Bad guys can't be more than one or two days behind us."

Joseph figured Miguel's two day estimate was just about right. Since leaving the valley, Marlow's army had continued traveling north up the center of the open plain. That plain was forty miles due east and reached north for another couple of hundred miles.

They had probably already turned westward and had begun in their direction, would be at the gates of the city by sometime tomorrow at the latest.

Best not linger about. They still had half a day's light left, could get a few more miles closer to Freetown before stopping for the night. Miriam indicated a cross street, the quickest way to the north gate and out of town.

The pedestrian lane was narrow, with building fronts pushing up close from either side. The way was still mostly clear, with the vine only just beginning to creep in through breezeways and alleyways.

The group came up short at the sight of a figure standing in an open doorway on their left. He was leaning a shoulder against the jamb, arms folded, attention focused on those approaching. He was a tall man, with shoulder-length hair and a week's growth of beard. There was a large revolver on his right hip sitting loose in its leather holster.

Joseph wondered if the man wore the weapon all the time, what with the town seemingly empty. More likely, he had heard them coming, quickly strapped it on and then got into position to wait casually for their arrival.

Joseph took a last step and stood in the middle of the narrow lane. He leaned on his staff.

"Good afternoon," he said.

The man gave an easy nod, his shoulder continuing to rest against the jamb. "Hey."

Miriam moved to stand beside Joseph, the others stood beside Miriam.

"Are you alone here?" she asked.

The man unfolded his arms, let his right hand drift down and rest indifferently on his weapon. Not quite a threat, but it was enough to let them know that he was ready to defend himself.

"Expect so... pretty much."

"Where'd everybody go?" asked Eddie.

"North."

"Freetown?"

The man hesitated. "Suppose so."

Joseph took his weight off his staff, straightened. "Listen, friend. There are a couple of thousand very nasty characters headed this way. You're welcome to come with us."

"Yeah?" unenthusiastically. "And just where might you be headed?"

"North," said Miriam.

The man lifted his hand from the revolver, again folded his arms. "Expect I'll stay here."

Miriam started to stay something, stopped when Joseph lifted a hand. The man eyed them both, said nothing. He was done.

"Your choice," said Joseph. He started away without another word. It wasn't until they were well out of earshot that Miriam spoke, and even then she kept her voice low.

"The man's hiding something," she suggested.

"Likely," said Joseph.

Eddie cleared his throat. "What if he's part of Marlow's army? Like, the advance team coming in ahead of the main group."

"The advance team will be here soon enough," said Joseph. "I don't think he's part of it."

"You don't think so?" asked Miguel.

"He wouldn't have been alone, and we wouldn't have walked away from that conversation."

They came to an intersection and turned right when Miriam pointed her cane in that direction.

"So what's his deal then?" asked Eddie.

"I don't think he's from here," said Joseph. "He looked to me to have been out on the trail a while, and is only recently arrived."

Miriam thought about that. She considered the way the man looked, the way he dressed; his manner, his answers to their questions about the town's population.

"Maybe he saw the townsfolk on the march out in the wild, thought to come on in and rest a spell," she said, thinking aloud.

"Yes, a possible scenario indeed," said Eddie.

"Ah," wondered Miguel. "What does he do when the army comes to town?"

"One man alone; he could easily hide for a few days, wait them out, wait for them to move on."

Miriam frowned. "Or perhaps he will like their company better than ours."

Carolyn sat on the top step outside her building, elbows on knees, hands clasped. Her mind wandered as she glanced up and down the street, not really looking at anything in particular yet always aware of what was around her.

Dusk settled in over the neighborhood as she waited. The two lamps hanging on the wall behind her came on; more light spilled out through the windows from the lights in the lobby. Carolyn was bathed in a faint yellowish glow.

Restrictions on power use were continuing to lessen as improvements were made to the solar power structure and the expansion of the local grid.

Carolyn heard voices coming from up the street. She saw a team of men and women coming out of the three-storey building on the corner. It was the current target in the revitalization project of their sector.

Her team was finished for the day. They would be getting cleaned up and then likely meeting again in the hotel commons.

She heard the door behind her open and close.

"Sorry I'm late," said Steven. He stood beside her, apparently eager to be off.

Carolyn, on the other hand, was perfectly happy right where she was. She was slow to stand.

"All right," she grumbled. "Guess we ought to do this."

They took the steps down to the sidewalk and started up the street.

The meeting was being held in a restored office building in Kenneth's district. Past meetings had taken place in a meeting hall in one of his hotels, but they had put a lot into the restoration of the two-storey building, and Kenneth reckoned that holding meetings there would lend them greater status than a meeting hall in a hotel.

Carolyn didn't see it, but then she had never been one for this sort of thing.

They reached the street that defined the boundary between the two districts and passed under a tall wooden arch that someone had erected. They had attached a sign overhead that read "Sector 0-0-1".

While the sector concept had been Kenneth's idea, or at least he had fostered the concept, he did have some concern that this might create a fiefdom atmosphere throughout the city. To try and counter this, he had concurrently attempted to foster a citywide inclusiveness and strong common community.

Kenneth would have preferred the individual districts go unnamed altogether, but doing so would have been unwieldy. By default, each was initially identified by its primary street, and would remain so unless the residents chose to give their sectors a new name.

Kenneth had waited too long in coming up with a name for his own district. One day someone referred to it as "zero-zero-one". Others started calling it zero-zero-one and the name stuck. While it may not have been the official designation, the name wasn't going anywhere.

Kenneth's district was, for all anyone knew and would ever know, Sector 0-0-1.

Carolyn and Steven turned up the street that ran parallel to 0-0-1's primary avenue and walked the three blocks in silence to the newly renovated, brick façade office building.

The Brown Building maintained its pre-invasion name, the title emblazoned above the double-door at the top of the brick-covered front steps.

They were met inside by a young woman who led them across the lobby and down a wide hallway to the west end of the building.

The meeting chamber was airy without being overly large. Three walls were brightly paneled, the fourth wall windowed from floor to ceiling. A long conference table took up the center of the room without seeming to dominate it.

Most of the comfortable chairs were occupied. All but one of the districts had two or three representatives, all having arrived ahead of Carolyn. The non-represented Crawford District chose to maintain an isolationist stance, an option that was open to all districts.

There were a number of conversations going on in the room, most of them cordial, one a bit loud. There were a number of coffee cups and water glasses on the table. A side buffet held carafes and pitchers.

Kenneth was standing at the far end of the table in conversation with someone Carolyn had seen once or twice, but didn't know. On seeing her enter the room, Kenneth broke off his discussion and faced the table.

"I think we're ready to get started," he said, sitting in his chair. At that, other conversations came to a slow close and everyone settled in, brought their chairs up close to the table. Carolyn and Steven took their seats.

"I apologize for being late," said Steven. "My fault."

"You're right on time, Steven," said Kenneth. He looked then to the entire group. "It is I who must apologize. Something has come up, and I'm afraid we will need to set aside today's agenda."

Everyone in the room turned instinctively to the young man sitting at the table beside Kenneth.

"As you all know," Kenneth began, "we keep generally keep several teams in the field, primarily resource expeditions but also monitoring our friends the Shylmahn, as well any other potential threats."

"As do we," said a representative of Sharon Street District. Several others nodded as well.

"What's the bad news, Kenneth?" asked the woman sitting to Carolyn's left. Theresa Tanner ran one of the north districts.

"Bad news to be sure," he started, then hesitated. "An army of marauders has come into the northwest. They're plundering every town and village they come to."

"You mean humans?" asked someone.

"Figures," said another, dourly.

"I'm afraid so," said Kenneth. "All under the guise of bringing humanity together, but nothing more than organized slaughtering and raping and pillaging."

"How organized? How many?"

The man sitting beside Kenneth spoke up. "A highly structured army under the banner of Marlow, their leader. They number in the thousands."

"And right now they're closing in on Freetown," said Kenneth.

"And you want us to help?" asked Theresa.

"That's the idea."

"It would take us a week to get there, under the best of circumstances. And this isn't the best of circumstances."

"Then best we get started," said someone.

"And what about us?" asked another. "You think they'll stop at Freetown? Sounds to me like they're not one for settling down. They'll be coming here. We need to defend Seattle."

"We'll defend Seattle," said Kenneth. This quieted everyone down. "But we need to help Freetown. I suggest two forces. One goes to Freetown, one serves as the home guard. Each district provides as many as they can to both."

Most of those around the table were already in agreement. If they could defend their home, they were willing to provide help to Freetown.

Kenneth would organize the home guard. Each of the districts already had some local defenses in place. It was a matter of organizing them into a unified, citywide force.

"What about the Freetown team?" Theresa asked Kenneth. "You have anybody in mind to lead that?"

Some of those around the table looked expectantly at Kenneth; most looked at Carolyn.

Carolyn rubbed at her left temple. "Oh, crap."

Michael walked near the head of the caravan. They had been following the bank of a narrow river for several hours, the terrain here fairly level and this side of the river clear of the vine. The small team walking point a few hundred yards ahead could be seen just moving into a cluster of fir trees. Michael knew from their outward bound trip that the way through that band of forest was an easy march.

One of the point team came out of the forest and was quickly working her way back to the main body of the group. The caravan boss, walking just ahead of Michael, lifted a hand as a silent call to halt. He continued forward on his own as the rest of the group stopped, ready for a break.

Michael set his pack aside and followed John, who met the woman midway to the forest perimeter. He was talking with her when Michael reached them.

"What is it, Claire?" he asked.

It was John who answered. "Someone up there wants a word with you, Michael."

Michael looked curiously from John to Claire.

"First clearing," said Claire. "Couple of hundred feet into the woods. They were sitting there waiting for us."

"And they asked for me?"

"You'll see."

It took Michael another moment for it to fall into place. "Ah," he said. He looked to John. "Guess we break for lunch."

John gave a curt not and started back, leaving Michael to follow Claire to the woods and to the clearing within.

Joseph was waiting for him, Miriam standing to one side, Eddie and Miguel sitting a few yards away. At a sign from Claire, the others of the point team followed her out, leaving Michael alone with Joseph and his companions.

"Hello, Michael," said Joseph.

"Dad." Michael looked briefly at the others. "Hello, Miriam."

"Good to see you, Michael."

Michael turned back to his father. He wanted to cry out *what the hell have you done?* He decided to postpone that little conversation till later.

"Not a social call, I'm guessing... something important?"

"Very," said Miriam.

Joseph had kept a cool, unemotional expression. "You were heading back to Garden City?"

"Seems Freetown is all full up," said Michael.

"We'll have to go back."

"We? And like I said, full up."

"That doesn't matter now, Michael. And we don't have much time."

Now Michael couldn't help himself. "What have you done now, Dad?"

Eddie and Miguel were standing now.

"That is uncalled for, Michael," said Eddie.

"Oh, it's called for all right," said Michael. "That and more."

"You listen here, pup—" Miguel started.

Joseph slowly raised a hand for silence. Even Michael waited.

"Freetown is in danger," said Joseph. "If we don't work together, we're all done."

"What are you talking about?"

Miriam leaned forward on her walking staff. "We make our stand at Freetown."

EsJen had been back in the provincial capital for less than half a day. It had been an exhausting trip and she had insisted on a few hours rest before returning to business. Now, in her small office just off the meeting hall, she listened as ShahnTahr brought her up-to-date.

Everything else could be delegated out, but she had to make a decision regarding that marauding band of Chehnon that continued to ravage the northwest. They had just that morning swept into Garden City. They had found it empty, were apparently settling in for a brief respite from the trail.

This, at least, would give EsJen time to decide what to do on the matter.

To now she had been supportive of NehLoc's counsel. So long as they didn't present an immediate threat to the Shylmahn, let the animals slaughter each other. As a resource, the Chehnon just weren't worth the effort.

BehLahk, of course, had been of a very different mind. He had always considered the Chehnon a most valuable resource. Of late, it was becoming clear to EsJen that BehLahk had come to consider these creatures something more than resource, something akin to equals here on this world, contemporaries with whom the Shylmahn should share this world.

He would never say so outright, but the evidence was there.

His argument in this instance, however, continued to be that by intervening now the Shylmahn would be demonstrating its support for the Chehnon population in general and for Michael specifically. In both the short run and the long run, it was to the benefit of the Shylmahn.

And now ShahnTahr... his analyses suggested that the elimination of this band of Chehnon would provide increased stability throughout the region, while it saw no benefit to its continued existence.

EsJen got up from her chair, walked across the room and stood before the tall, narrow window. It looked out on her garden; this one private, much smaller than the public grounds on the other side of the complex.

She considered stepping outside, taking some time to let her mind clear. She was tired.

The cause of her weariness... the cause was obvious. The resolution? That too seemed obvious, but even here there were murky undercurrents.

Doing nothing and letting them kill each other, as they clearly wanted to do, wouldn't make the problem go away. But... in the short term, would it really make things worse?

So thought BehLahk, and perhaps ShahnTahr believed so as well.

Still, so easy... let it play itself out, for a while... see what happens.

Let me rest...

ShahnTahr broke the silence.

"EsJen... BehLahk wishes to speak with you."

"Of course he does," sighed EsJen.

Chapter Seventeen

Carolyn slowed the flyer and guided it out over the open field, leaving the landscape of forest and vine behind. Steven sat quietly in the copilot seat.

The field was butted up against a sloping hillside. It was more of a large meadow, and the camp took up most of the open space. There were only a few tents, interspersed with stations of stacked gear and weapons; the company was traveling light and fast. A few fire pits and a couple of latrine trenches had been dug, but little else. She could see guards posted along the encampment perimeter.

The force was small, considering the anticipated enemy. Each district had contributed as promised, but all had held back enough to defend their homes, should it come to that. Such was to be expected.

In the end, Carolyn had left Seattle with 180 troops and just the one flyer. She would make do. She didn't intend to take the invading army on all on her own, after all.

She landed the flyer near the command post, the largest of the tents in the camp. When camp broke in the morning, it and most of the heavier gear would be loaded into the small compartment of the flyer.

Jackson welcomed her as she and Steven stepped out of the flyer, walked with them back to the tent. She asked for the map, and Jackson unfolded it and laid it out on the folding table for her.

Carolyn absently patted at her pockets as she hovered over the map. Steven handed her a pair of reading glasses. She put them on and looked down at the map again. She looked askance, eyes squinting.

Steven tapped at her arm with a second pair. She took them, mumbled something under her breath. These did appear to work better though, and she tossed the first pair aside.

"They're long gone from Garden City." She pointed at a spot on the map. "The bulk of the army is here, with a smaller force ahead of them here. The forward group clears the way for the main force. They've got trucks, 4x4s, tankers, even some small artillery."

"How can they support that?" asked Jackson.

"They can't. Not indefinitely. For now though, they resupply by keeping on the move."

"Damn."

"Yeah. And right now, they're heading straight for Freetown."

"And the largest warehouse in the northwest."

She tapped her finger on the map, at Freetown. "And... right about now, the entire population of Garden City should be knocking at the gate. When we spotted them, they were no more than three miles out."

"Are they gonna let 'em in?"

"I would think so. They know what's coming. I imagine they'll take all the help they can get."

Jackson frowned and scratched at his scalp. "Speaking of which, we're still two days from providing any assistance."

Carolyn studied the map. She finally gave a hesitant, anxious grin. "Oh, I think that'll put us there just in time for the party."

She suddenly had an image of the Vikings sweeping across England.

Now that be a blast from the past...

Joseph stood at the railing beside Craig Warren. They were on the second terrace landing of Freetown's Inner Village. It was a large, open cavern within the mountain, sixty feet from floor to ceiling, and several hundred yards from the apartment terraces at the back of the cave to the front of the cave and the tall opening leading to the Outer Village.

It was hardly the same cave network that Joseph and Barbara had discovered decades earlier. The Inner Village had been greatly expanded, and had been made much more civilized. Back then, dark and dingy and smelling of damp earth, they had been little more than a warren of rabbits hiding in a hole in the ground.

Now... now it was a genuine town; graveled pedestrian streets, comfortable homes, running water and utilities. There were schools, markets, a hospital; playgrounds and parks and a community center.

Looking down on the floor of the community, Joseph could see hundreds of people going about their business. All the more so now that they had begun preparing for what they knew was to come.

The community had started with Joseph, had grown with Michael, and continued under the guiding hand of Craig.

What was to come of it?

"Freetown has taken on overwhelming odds before," he said, giving voice to the thoughts he had been weighing.

"The attack by the Shillies?" asked Craig. He shook his head. "No. What we did back then was hold 'em off till we could slip out the back."

"You don't give yourself enough credit, Craig. What happened that day has become legend. That was a helluva fight. And slipping out the back? A lot of people are alive today due to that little maneuver. Good stuff."

"Well... I don't think that's going to be an option this time."

Joseph considered that. If all appeared lost, sending the children and the wounded out the back might become necessary, while those who were able continued to fend off the attack. He suspected that Craig had already planned for this possibility, despite what he had just said. The mayor of Freetown was seldom given enough credit.

He had now managed to bring in the population of Garden City without too much fuss. There had been some rumblings of discontent among the locals, but most saw their arrival as a net positive. Folks were asked to double up where possible, and a small tent city had been created in the central plaza. Several even smaller tent clusters here on the terraces. So, yes, living space was tight.

But a major part of the incoming Garden City population was remaining outside in the Outer Village, forming their own military contingent within the larger Freetown force that would defend the wall. This, it could not be argued, was definitely a good thing.

A young man appeared at the far end of the terrace, coming up the stairs from the lower terrace, and approached Joseph and Craig. He looked directly at Craig.

"What is it, Will?" asked Craig.

"Sorry for the interruption, Mayor."

"Not at all. What is it?"

"There's some folks settin' up camp in the orchard, right across from the main gate."

"More refugees?"

"No sir. Don't think so. They don't look much like refugees."

"How many?" asked Joseph.

"Forty or fifty. Could be more. And they got vehicles."

Craig straightened, took a deep breath. Joseph gave a slow nod.

"That would be the advance party," he said calmly.

Will nodded agreement. "Yeah, that's what Michael said."

Joseph and Craig walked through the wide, high camouflaged opening, leaving the Inner Village and stepping out into the Outer Village. Heavy doors, made from narrow steel panel strips, hung on great hinges, ready to be closed, ready to seal off the Inner Village from the outside world.

It would be all that stood against the attacking marauders should the wall be breached.

The Outer Village looked to be in a state of barely controlled chaos. Some residents were quickly working to get moved inside, while the world between the wall and the hillside was as quickly evolving into a military encampment.

Joseph and Craig worked their way to the wall and then up the steep staircase to the observation platform set near the top of the timber wall beside the double gate.

Two armed guards stood watch on the platform. Beside them stood Michael, arms folded, looking intently toward the orchard on the other side of the clearing.

"Dad," he said flatly, then to the Mayor: "Craig, you have company."

"So I was told," said Craig.

"Have they made any demands?" asked Joseph. He and Michael had decided to set aside their differences until after this threat was dealt with.

"Not a one." Michael and his father may have been on speaking terms, but the sentences were brief.

"The silent treatment," said Craig.

"They know that we know," said Joseph. "Let the games begin."

"I'm sick of games," said Michael. So the truce between father and son was on shaky ground.

There was movement deep in the orchard, well into the camp. A few moments later a hard-canopy Jeep came slowly into the clearing. Midway into the clearing, it turned and stopped, the passenger side of the vehicle facing the village gate. A middle-aged woman stepped out of the driver's seat and walked around to the passenger side. She faced the gate.

"Mr. Marlow would very much like to speak with Joseph Britton."

She waited then, hands clasped in front of her.

The two guards on the observation platform remained at the ready, watching for cause to open up on the woman and Jeep.

Michael and Craig looked curiously at Joseph.

"Well, well," said Joseph.

"You're not going down there?" asked Craig.

"I'm considering it."

"Why?"

"Why not?"

"Oh, I don't know... cause they might kill you?"

"That's a possibility whether I go down there or not." Joseph stepped off the platform and started down the staircase. "Wish me luck."

"Luck," said Michael.

Craig called down to Joseph, already halfway to the foot of the stairs. "How did he know you were here?"

Joseph walked toward the Jeep. He heard the gates closing behind him. As he approached the vehicle, the driver stepped to the rear passenger door and opened it, stepped aside.

A big, broad-shouldered man sitting in the backseat smiled as he looked out at Joseph. "Mr. Britton. Please, join me."

Joseph set one hand on the roof of the Jeep, hesitated climbing in.

"I promise to return you safe and sound," said Marlow. He looked to be in his early forties, was neat, clean, dressed in khaki slacks and a long-sleeved shirt, the sleeves rolled up one turn.

"How about we talk here?" suggested Joseph.

"I would prefer a less exposed location."

The man was definitely playing games. Why drive into the clearing at all? And why this faux-friendly exchange?

Joseph looked back over his shoulder. Figures stood partially protected behind the wall up on the observation platforms on both sides of the gate. They would certainly fire on the Jeep at the slightest sign from him.

He turned back and calmly slid into the back of the Jeep beside Marlow.

The driver closed the door, stepped around and climbed in behind the wheel. She started the vehicle and put it into gear. They travelled slow, ten or twelve miles per hour, driving parallel to the village wall. Reaching the end of the wall on the right, the orchards on the left, they continued out onto the open expanse for a few hundred yards. Cresting a slight rise, the driver stopped the Jeep and turned off the engine.

"Shall we?" Marlow asked Joseph as the driver opened the door. Marlow climbed out. Joseph slid across and followed him. They walked a short ways, out to where they could see the distant horizon.

Sunset was a few minutes away. Marlow appeared content to simply stand silent and watch the sun settle into the horizon.

Joseph took the opportunity to run the recent events in his mind.

Marlow hadn't asked to speak Craig Warren, nor the more generic 'leader of Freetown'. He had asked to speak to Joseph Britton. So, he had known that Joseph was there.

More games.

Joseph said nothing of this.

"Why did you ask to speak with me, Marlow?"

"Simple curiosity, Mr. Britton."

"How so?"

"I've always been impressed by the Britton Family reputation, sir. To be perfectly honest, I've always wondered how much was fantasy, how much was fact. Fabrication and truth."

"I am afraid you will be disappointed, Mr. Marlow."

Marlow took a moment to look side-glance at Joseph, returned his attention to the sunset.

"False modesty," said sighed. "It does not become you."

"There's really not that much to me," said Joseph. "I am a rather uncomplicated man; just a middle-aged millworker."

There was another long, peaceful pause before Marlow spoke again. Again he kept his eyes to the horizon.

"I am an extremely good judge of character, sir. I see much. I sense much. I do not overstate when I say that I read people very well." He waited for a comment from Joseph. None came. "With you..." he continued, "there is much under the surface, much unsaid. And you dance very well this life. You are a very dangerous person."

"You should meet my sister."

"I intend to."

Yet another long pause, then, as they watched the sunset. The sun touched the horizon, was quickly swallowed up by it.

"We will not surrender Freetown," Joseph stated.

"I know that."

"Then why ask to speak with me?"

"I told you. I was curious. Nothing more."

"And so we have met."

"Yes." Marlow hesitated. "I really should kill you. Here. Now."

Joseph managed to push down a sudden, brief moment of fear. He spoke in a soothing calm. "Bad form, breaking a promise."

"Yes... I despise bad form."

"I'm counting on that."

Michael watched from the observation platform as the Jeep returned. It stopped as before directly in front of the gate, midway between the village wall and the edge of the orchard. The driver got out, stepped around to the rear passenger door and opened it.

Joseph climbed out, moved back as the driver climbed in behind the wheel. The Jeep returned to the orchard, maneuvered its way through the trees and was lost in the shadows.

Michael and Craig were at the gate as it opened and Joseph slipped in. Michael held his silence, letting Craig ask the question.

"What did the man have to say?"

An odd, unsettled look passed across Joseph's face. Michael had never seen that look before.

"I don't really know," Joseph said quietly. "Strangest damn thing."

"What do you mean?"

"I, uh... he said he wanted to meet me."

"That's it?"

"I'm sure there was a lot more to it than that," said Joseph. "I'm just telling you what he said."

"If that's what he said, what was he thinking?" asked Michael.

"Exactly," said Joseph. "I'll tell you this. That guy is one very cool, calm and scary dude."

"That would explain how he got where he is," said Craig.

"The fact that he's an egomaniacal psychopath may have helped."

Michael slipped the rifle strap over his shoulder, turned up the wide path that led away from the cluster of small homes and outbuildings that had been assigned to the Garden City contingent of the Freetown defense force. The Outer Village was now fully militarized, each unit with its own quarter and assignments. Equipment stores, gear and weaponry were situated in strategic locations along the central path running through the Outer Village.

Michael stepped into the narrow plaza set between the large doors of the Inner Village on his left and the main gate on his right. He saw Don Townsend calmly taking the staircase up to the observation platform on the wall to the left of the gate. Townsend had been designated Freetown's military commander, and from what Michael could tell, he was doing the best he could with what he had. The problem was, he didn't have much.

Joseph was already standing on the platform. He shook hands with Townsend, and the two of them turned to look out beyond the wall.

All along the top of the wall, running left and right away from the observation platforms on either side of the gate, was a hastily constructed catwalk, little more than planks laid atop L-frame supports. Makeshift ladders were attached to the wall thirty feet apart, reaching up from the ground to the catwalk above.

Craig Warren came through the Inner Village doors and walked across the plaza toward Michael. Behind him, the doors began to close. There was finality to the sound of the great crossbar sliding into place. Somewhere behind those doors, behind that crossbar, was Michael's family. Victoria was assisting with the secondary defense line, and Michael suspected the last-ditch backdoor escape as well, should that become necessary.

Reaching Michael, Craig started to say something as he looked back in the direction of the closed doors; instead he said nothing and turned back. He shrugged.

There was another, smaller door set into the mountain about eighty feet to the west. That was now their only retreat, if they needed it. It opened to a long hallway and the inventory chambers.

If it came to that, Michael saw one hell of a nightmare in the making.

"Have you had dinner?" asked Craig, half joking, attempting to sound serious.

Michael grinned and shook his head. "Maybe later."

"You really should eat something." Craig looked questioningly around the plaza, then at the wall and those on the catwalks. "Maybe I should send someone around with sandwiches."

"Good idea," said Michael absently.

They again stood silent. Craig wondered about the logistics in preparing and distributing hundreds of sandwiches.

There came a sudden, deep, concussive boom... a powerful explosion on the other side of wall. A wide section of wall just to the right of the gate pushed in as if taking a deep breath. Timbers splintered, but for the moment the wall held.

A second blast then, this one thirty feet to the left of the gate. The timbered wall shuddered. Several of those standing on the catwalk were thrown the sixteen feet to the ground.

Craig took off at a run, hurrying to see if those not yet getting to their feet needed help. Michael was about to follow after him when a third explosion breached the wall, this blast at the same location as the first. Michael instead rushed toward the breach, joining a number of others preparing to make a stand. All around them came the sound of gunshots and more explosions. Smoke was already beginning to roll through the narrow streets of the Outer Village.

Up on the left observation platform, Townsend was shouting orders to those on the ground.

There was no sign of Joseph.

He had been standing beside Townsend only moments before.

Carolyn brought the flyer in from the south at about three hundred feet above the orchards' treetops, slowed and hovered then well back from the conflict. She was probably within rifle range, if the marksman was a good shot, so she was ready to pull back at the first sign that she had become a target.

The far edge of the orchard was a hundred yards or so further ahead; beyond that was the clearing and beyond that Freetown's timber wall.

There was definitely a fight going on down there in the open space between wall and orchard. The wall had been breached near the gate. People were rushing out through the opening to meet the marauders who were coming out of the orchard.

The wall looked to have been hit a number of times and was severely damaged in several locations. Carolyn finally located the two small artillery guns deep in the orchard that had been used to breach the wall. At the moment they were silent. She suspected they would be used again once the marauders were through the wall and ready to enter the Inner Village.

The Inner Village doors wouldn't last long against an artillery assault.

The two sides met now in the clearing. Even from this distance, Carolyn could hear gunfire and the screams of hand to hand fighting. The Freetown forces, as resolute as they appeared to be, wouldn't stand long against Marlow's army. Sharpshooters on the wall continued to fire down on the attackers, and this did help some, but there were those in the orchard taking aim at those on the wall, some with devastating accuracy.

Carolyn's own forces now approached from the west, following the line of the orchard perimeter. They would reach the conflict within minutes.

She pulled back the flyer, circled around and brought it down low. She would land it just ahead of her people and join them. She wanted to lead a team into the orchard and take out the artillery before they had a chance to use it on the Inner Village doors.

Joseph worked his way along the base of the wall, blood in his hair, some of it his own and some not, his shirt bloodied and torn. He reached the breach in the wall and hurried out into the clearing.

There was hand-to-hand fighting everywhere. Hundreds of people were rushing in all directions, slashing and lunging with bayoneted weapons, with knives and machetes; some looked to have lost their weapons and were fighting with their bare hands.

Joseph had spent most of his adult life at war with the Shillies, but unlike Carolyn he had seldom actually raised a physical hand against them. Now, well into his fifties, he found himself fighting hand to hand... not against the Shillies, but against humans.

As Carolyn would say... *it figures.*

One of the earlier artillery blasts on the wall had thrown Joseph from the platform and out into the open. He hadn't been seriously injured, but had found himself alone in no-man's land. He had gotten to his feet and hurried along the wall away from the gate. After what he thought a safe distance, he had run across the clearing and into the orchard, began to work his way back.

Once the hand-to-hand began in the clearing, Joseph rushed out and took on the attackers from behind. He managed to bring several down before they turned on him and he had to make a strategic, defensive withdrawal.

When he saw one of the bad guys reach the wall and start toward the breach, Joseph followed. The man made it inside, and Joseph hurried in after him.

The marauder wasn't much more than a boy, but he was mean and seemed to really enjoy what he was doing.

Joseph's age was beginning to tell on him. He was exhausted and about done in. He nonetheless was the one who walked away from the fight. The boy wouldn't be hurting anyone else.

Back in the clearing, Joseph worked his way to the right, walking cautiously between the wall and the heart of the fighting. He wanted a moment's rest but was also looking for an opportunity to get back into it.

He rushed in then when he saw Michael struggling to bring a wounded man out of the fray. The man was half again as big as Michael and appeared to be severely injured. Michael was doing his best to carry him out.

"Can you use a hand?" asked Joseph. He reached in and supported the man on one side. He and Michael then rush-walked him toward the wall. They eased him to the ground, resting his back against the timbers.

"Go," the man said. Blood trickled out of his mouth. "I'll be fine. Go."

Michael was looking anxiously back at the morass of men and women all doing their best to kill one another.

The attackers had to be stopped. That was true enough.

Joseph kneeled beside the man. "Give us a sec to try to stop the bleeding. We've time to get back into it."

"I'm done," said the man. "I know that. Better just me out of the fight than three of us."

True enough, thought Joseph. Looking up at Michael, he saw that his son was thinking the same thing.

He saw a bright flash then out of the corner of his eye. He turned and stood. He looked across the clearing, past the mass of bloodied and torn humanity, and into the orchard.

He knew that flash.

"Dad?" asked Michael. He was trying to see what his father was seeing.

There was another; a moment later, another.

The next one blossomed just inside the edge of the orchard. A large bubble of energy, larger than many he had seen in the past. It took out a number of trees and several of the attackers.

Each blast turned everything within the bubble into a powdery dust. *CEBs...*

Michael moved up beside Joseph, his attention still on the orchard. "D'you bring some secret weapons with you?"

"That's not us." Joseph looked up into the sky. "That's Shillie work."

More CEB blossoms then, some in the trees, some fully in the clearing. There were screams from those nearest the blossoms. The remnant dust of humans and trees and earth was rising up from half a dozen locations deeper in the orchard.

A CEB blossomed in the heart of the clearing, in the heart of the fighting.

"My god..." Michael mumbled. "Those are—"

"Sure are."

Eddie and Miguel came up to them, following the wall from the direction of the far end of the village. Miguel had blood in his hair and on his shirt, Eddie had a welt on his cheek from a rifle butt to the face.

"Joseph, you seeing what we're seein'?" asked Eddie.

"They here to help, ya' think?" asked Miguel.

"Only if it helps the Shillies."

"It won't be much of a rescue if the rescue kills us all," said Eddie.

"Rescue?" Joseph looked to Michael. "Get everybody behind the wall."

Michael looked over his shoulder to the wounded comrade sitting against the wall. "I'll be back for you."

At a sign from Joseph, Eddie and Miguel followed Michael into the battlefield. Joseph turned then and hurried toward the breach in the wall. There was some quick organizing to do. They had to get their people back inside the wall while somehow managing to keep the bad guys out. It was going to be a mess, but better a bottleneck at the hole in the wall than opening the gate and everyone stampedes through, good guys and bad guys.

§

The world was quiet and gray. Carolyn's flyer was covered in the same thin layer of debris that lay over the landscape. The surrounding orchard was an ashy landscape of scattered trees, the organized rows almost lost. Gray gritty dust drifted across the scene.

Carolyn had been surprised to find the flyer in one piece. Clean the windshield and check the oil, and she could fly out of here.

She finished her exterior inspection, came around from the back of the shuttle and was about to walk up into the shuttle when she saw Michael coming toward her.

She had talked with Michael and Craig earlier, immediately following the abrupt end of the battle, after which they had gone their separate ways. They had much to do. Craig had a wall to rebuild, Michael a caravan to put together for the journey home.

Both had wounded to take care of, dead to bury.

"I want to thank you again for coming to help," said Michael.

The way things turned out, they hadn't really needed her help. She sat on the ramp, elbows on her knees. "How many'd you lose?"

"Still counting. Twelve to fifteen, by human hands. Freetown lost more. CEBs, harder to tell. No bodies. We have to see who's missing."

Carolyn's people had already gotten a head count. They had lost six, most all by CEBs. It could have been worse. The team she had led in to take out the artillery had been twenty yards from the wheeled guns when the CEBs had done the work for them.

"That Shillie pop does have a way of making folks disappear," she said.

"Suppose it does." Michael looked around them, at the stark devastation around them. "As bad as it was, if the Shillies hadn't stepped in, I don't think any of us would have survived this."

Carolyn wasn't going to go there. Michael was way too close to EsJen.

She looked down at her clasped hands, frowning.

"Some may see us an on equal footing with the Shillies. This shows just how far down the food chain we are." She looked up at Michael. "And just how precarious our situation is."

"S'pose," Michael mumbled uncomfortably. He kept his focus outward, away from his aunt, the legendary Carolyn Britton.

He saw his father in the distance. Joseph was walking with Craig Warren and another man. It looked to Michael like Jackson, one of Carolyn's people.

Carolyn noticed them, too. She cleared her throat, let out a loud sigh.

"Your father's pulled a lot crap, and I wouldn't mind beating him into the ground with a heavy stick," she said. "But when it comes to the Shillies, he knows exactly where we stand. Whatever happens, I gotta give him that."

"If you say so."

"I do; not for the first time." She half smirked, looking to her brother in the distance. "The bastard."

TohPeht and BehLahk stepped away from the small shuttle, their protective escort walking out ahead of them. The landscape around them was a gray wasteland, with swirling clouds of ash rolling across the terrain. In the distance stood the timbered wall that ran along the base of the low mountain. Several hundred yards to their left was another shuttle, one of the hybrid flyers the Chehnon had designed.

That must be Carolyn Britton standing beside it.

Not far ahead of the escort walked a group of Chehnon; Joseph Britton and two companions had changed direction and were approaching. One of the protectors looked back. BehLahk gave a slight gesture of the head and the escort slowed and stepped aside, allowed TohPeht and BehLahk to continue past before falling in several paces behind.

"My friend Joseph," said BehLahk. "A surprise. I did not know you were here."

"Of course you didn't," Joseph said doubtfully.

BehLahk indicated Joseph's head wound, also noting the blood on his clothes. "I trust your injuries are minor."

"I'll survive."

"That is good."

BehLahk looked to the other Chehnon. Joseph introduced Craig Warren and Jackson. BehLahk appeared genuinely pleased at meeting Craig.

He had heard much of the mayor of Freetown and thought it a shame they hadn't met sooner.

TohPeht had said nothing as yet. He appeared somber, almost sad as he continued to study their surroundings.

"That it came to this is most regrettable," he said at last. He spoke to no one in particular.

"Most regrettable indeed," agreed BehLahk.

"We lost a lot of people today," said Craig.

Joseph was looking sharply at BehLahk. "Your CEBs don't discriminate, you know; between good guys and bad guys."

"Most unfortunate," said BehLahk. "However, the Shylmahn prevented your own losses from being so much worse this day. This we all know to be true."

Joseph's expression darkened. "I suppose we should thank you for that."

"It is EsJen you should thank."

"No arm twisting on your part?"

BehLahk gave a most human shrug. "She needed only to be provided with the facts and options."

"Uh, huh... and I'll bet NehLoc was pleased as punch."

"NehLoc serves," said TohPeht softly, absently. He had turned away, was looking in the direction of Carolyn Britton and her hybrid flyer.

BehLahk gave a gentle nod at that, continued to look to Joseph. "That he does," he said.

"Why are you here, BehLahk?" asked Joseph. "Another visit just to say hi?"

"As I said, I did not know you were here."

"That is so," agreed TohPeht. The TohPeht/ShahnTahr entity let his gaze drift to the timbered wall. There was much activity near the gate.

BehLahk looked from TohPeht back to Joseph.

"TohPeht expressed the need to come here," he said. "While he supported the action that was taken, he feels much regret at the loss of Chehnon life."

Jackson spoke up for the first time. "You mean those sons-of-bitches that attacked Freetown?"

"TohPeht continues to refine his understanding of our universe from the perspective of the entity that is both TohPeht and ShahnTahr, and neither." BehLahk smiled. "For one such as he... a life is a life... sons-of-bitches or not."

"Well, of course, but—"

"Logic and analysis advised that the action should be taken; this in contrast to the severity of a life ended, and our responsibility in the ending of that life; such is a concept that generates new and evocative emotions in the new being TohPeht."

"Really," Joseph said cynically. "That didn't seem to be a problem for either one of them before."

"Neither of them stands before you," BehLahk stated coolly.

TohPeht stepped away from the others, began a slow walk further into the devastated landscape. BehLahk gave an abbreviated bow to Joseph, then to the others, and followed after him.

TohPeht's mind was far away, even as he took in their surroundings. BehLahk knew from experience that when TohPeht was in such a state, it was best to simply wait.

And so they walked. They eventually reached the perimeter of the destruction. TohPeht stopped, his feet at the very edge of the yellow grass that lay beyond.

"Joseph and EsJen are very much alike," TohPeht wondered aloud. "Are they not?"

"A keen observation," said BehLahk. "They were born of very different worlds, and yet began from a very similar essence. Their... souls... are much the same."

"I understand," said TohPeht. "I have touched them."

BehLahk wasn't sure what TohPeht meant by that, but he had sensed that there was something about TohPeht, *this* TohPeht, that connected him to this new world. He was more of this world than either Chehnon or Shylmahn.

"Joseph and EsJen have followed very similar paths. Perhaps it was inevitable they would arrive as one." BehLahk saw them both as sincere, flawed and absolutely blind to all but their individual causes.

We of the past are quickly fading into that past.

The future was closing in on the present state of affairs. The face of that future may very well be TohPeht. TohPeht was more of this world than were either Joseph Britton or EsJen. TohPeht was brilliant, inspired, talented, terrifyingly analytical, and yet very childlike. The combined entities of TohPeht and ShahnTahr and all that they brought, and the life experiences of these past few years, had come together to create this incredible individual walking beside him.

TohPeht turned and looked calmly at BehLahk. The two had grown close over these past months. They saw things very differently, but they had similar goals, similar desires for the future of this planet.

For very different reasons; despite BehLahk's protestations to the contrary, TohPeht knew that the actions and beliefs of the doctor, him being a true Shylmahn, would always be colored with the inexorable duty to serve. And while BehLahk had developed a sincere fondness for the Chehnon, they were after all only Chehnon.

They weren't Shylmahn.

TohPeht was not encumbered by such things. He believed in the destiny of the Shylmahn, but was not blindly driven. Not all that existed, existed only as a resource for the Shylmahn.

There existed merit and meaning beyond the Shylmahn.

"I will be leaving soon," he stated.

"Leaving, TohPeht?" BehLahk had quite enjoyed TohPeht's company these past months.

"I am confident there is nothing further I can do. All that will be, will be. It is time I was on my way."

BehLahk wasn't quite as certain as TohPeht that all would play out as they hoped. There was a lot that could still go wrong. But then, he wasn't absolutely certain that what TohPeht wanted was exactly the same as what he wanted.

TohPeht saw things...

"Where will you go?" BehLahk asked.

TohPeht raised a hand and pointed east. "I have not been that way. Perhaps I shall go that way."

Chapter Eighteen

The city of Seattle was an island of humanity set deep in the heart of one of the Shylmahn's principal provinces. To maintain the peace with the Chehnon, the Shylmahn had given over the abandoned city for the Chehnon to occupy. The Shylmahn also established an airspace corridor through their province linking the Seattle reservation to the outside world beyond the Shylmahn province. This corridor was opened briefly on a weekly schedule.

The current Seattle skyline didn't look much like the pre-invasion skyline. The higher skyscrapers were gone, replaced with jagged shards of concrete and steel. Nearer street-level, the residents of half a dozen inner city sectors worked daily on projects to restore and renovate buildings that were deemed recoverable. Streets and homes of a handful of neighborhoods surrounding the heart of the city were also at varying stages of restoration.

Few if any of the several thousand residents had any illusions that the city would ever look anything like the Seattle of the past, but they worked to make it livable and life in the city did have a level of normalcy.

The Shylmahn very seldom entered the reservation, and then only to meet with Kenneth or the council. Within the borders of the Seattle reservation, the Chehnon were left alone.

Sentinel probes did closely monitor the invisible perimeter encircling the reservation. While they weren't programmed to prevent violations and had only defensive weapons, the probes did immediately report breaches and these were addressed quickly.

The more immediate threat to the Chehnon was the vine. It had found its way into the outer neighborhoods and was spreading. Each district was responsible for fighting back the vine within their individual neighborhoods, and a team comprised of citizens from all sectors worked the overall perimeter. This did slow the spread but it could never be stopped.

Carolyn stood at the far end of the three acre park, studied the thick growth of northwest vegetation threatening to push in on the recently mown lawn.

She saw no sign of the vine.

She turned around and looked back across the neighborhood park. There was a group gathered around the tables set under the picnic shelter. There was a light snow on the ground from the dusting of the day before, but the sun was bright and the air was warm for winter in the northwest.

She could see the bay in the distance to her left; no boats on the water. There were seldom boats on the water these days.

Kenneth and Michael stepped out from under the picnic shelter canopy and onto the lawn. They looked to be in a friendly conversation, Kenny more animated than the more reserved Michael.

Carolyn remembered the raucous Britton family gatherings back before the invasion, decades earlier; Bril, with his booming voice and his loud, commanding presence, seeming to dominate every get-together, or at least trying to.

Joey, trying his best to mediate, while Jason patiently tried to show Bril the error of his ways; Liz shaking her head at almost every pronouncement of their older brother.

Daryl, sitting quietly taking it all in.

And of course Carolyn's own role in the family composition... she smiled at the memory of a long-suffering Bril at a total loss as to how to deal with the wild little sister.

She looked across the park now at Kenneth. Bril had been quite a bit older than his brothers and sisters, and had taken care of them when their parents died, Kenny not much more than a baby. Bril had been so very protective of the boy.

Despite the harsh years between then and now, Carolyn could still see that little boy. Kenny had been in the army at the time of the invasion. He had grown up fast, or at least those first months and years had done much to wear at the edges. On his own, away from the family, he had finally grasped hold of life and then had taken control of it. And through the years of the occupation following the invasion Kenneth Britton had become a leader. Seattle may have been divided into half a dozen inner-city sectors and as many or more districts in the surrounding neighborhoods, but most everyone saw Kenneth as the man in charge of it all. He was the one everyone looked to.

Did Michael see his uncle that same way? He had never known the young Kenny, had never known the Britton family before the invasion. He had never known those Britton family gatherings.

Thanksgiving on Bril's island...

Michael had grown up in Freetown. He had seen his father, his aunt and uncles, only rarely, those who had survived the invasion; then it was usually resistance business. The Britton family get-togethers were of the before time.

Michael was living back in Garden City now. Some of the small town was lost to the vine, but the residents did what they could. They had adapted. Many of the buildings were covered in the Veltahk; narrow streets had become green, leafy tunnels, particular those nearest the perimeter wall surrounding the community.

After his return to Garden City following the battle at Freetown, Michael and his council had decided that they would do all they could to keep the town alive. Even now, with so many throughout the world moving into the long-dead cities of the past, including Seattle, Michael chose to remain in Garden City.

His presence here now was work related, a conference of sorts to exchange information. This afternoon was a chance to get reacquainted with family and friends; perhaps mend a few fences...

A flyer appeared overhead, crossed the narrow band of landscaped park and hovered above the parking area between lawn and the rough, wild vegetation that bordered a rocky beach. It settled slowly to the broken, cracked asphalt.

It was Jenny.

Jenny too had chosen not to move into the city. She had returned to her cabin in the mountains. There were frequent visits from Monroe, who lived nearby, but she spent most of her days alone, which was the way she wanted it. Her relationship with others in the family had remained awkward following the reaffirmation of the truce with the Shillies. The awkwardness only grew worse as the vine continued to take hold of the world.

Jenny started across the park toward the gathering at the picnic shelter. Seeing her, Michael stepped away and met her. Brother and sister held one another, clumsily pulled apart and held hands. They turned and joined the others. Theirs was probably the most awkward of relationships. They were both struggling to regain something of what they once had, but considering all that had happened, it was unlikely they would ever be again be close.

Carolyn steeled herself and began the long walk to the gathering.

It definitely wasn't the family Thanksgiving of old.

Early winter in the northern hemisphere. BehLahk worked his way uptrail through the thick forest of trees, shrubs and vine. There was a dusting of snow on the leaves and branches, and a chilly bite in the air.

The trail emptied into a large clearing surrounded by a tall wall of vegetation, the clearing open to a pale blue sky. BehLahk's private research complex stood in the center of the clearing; a solid, heavy, square building, alone, isolated in the thickly forested foothills just outside the perimeter of the Seattle Reservation.

From his original research facility, later to the post-migration village, then to the communities in the wild, and now this, BehLahk had been studying the natives since the day of their arrival on this world.

That research continued. He had strongly recommended the Chehnon be given access to this abandoned city, and others like it, citing the powerful draw these dead communities held for many of the elder Chehnon. He argued that giving them these cities, even those within the provinces, cost the Shylmahn nothing. The Chehnon had significantly shorter life spans that Shylmahn, and each year that passed saw fewer and fewer Chehnon who were around pre-migration.

These aging natives were the Chehnon potentially of greatest threat to the peace. Give them their cities and let them live out what few years they had left to them.

BehLahk of course appreciated the opportunity for yet another avenue of research.

He noticed then a second shuttle on the landing platform on the roof of the complex.

He had company.

The door at the front of the building opened and NehLoc came down the steps. He stopped at the foot of the steps and waited.

"NehLoc," called BehLahk as he came near. A Chehnon expression came to mind. "To what do I owe the pleasure?"

NehLoc was accustomed to BehLahk's peculiarities. He took BehLahk's meaning and responded. "Several items in your recent reports."

"You have concerns?"

"Questions that I thought best addressed in person."

BehLahk made to start up the steps, saw then that NehLoc had no desire to go inside. BehLahk turned about then and the two of them looked out beyond the clearing. The treeline was thick with the vine.

BehLahk's second line of research, and the more important to both Es-Jen and NehLoc, was the study of the Chehnon-developed Veltahk. His last report had been certain to generate interest.

"My observations regarding the Chehnon vine."

"I wish to hear directly regarding your belief that the Veltahk is dying off."

"The analyses are documented in my report."

"I want to hear your words."

"Of course." BehLahk wasn't sure just what NehLoc expected. "There are strong indications that the vine is beginning to die off in several ecosystems. Further research lends credence to my suspicion that the Chehnon have designed the eventual demise of the vine into its creation."

"The ability to propagate removed."

"And a shortened lifespan for the existing plants."

"Yes, yes..." sighed NehLoc. He stepped away from the building, moved slowly out into the clearing. He spoke without turning to look at BehLahk. "I have seen no indication that the Veltahk is dying."

"It is not widespread as yet. It is not evenly occurring."

"Your conclusion is certain... the Veltahk will die."

"It was designed so."

"That does not answer the question."

From what BehLahk had been able to ascertain, the designed die-off was not progressing as quickly as the Chehnon had intended. He did not as yet know what impact this might have on the numerous ecosystems.

BehLahk chose not to delve into this with NehLoc.

"The vine will die," he stated simply.

"Very well." NehLoc looked directly at BehLahk. "In your report, you denote concern as to the impact of a sudden die-off."

"Something we should study further," said BehLahk.

"I have a team performing calculations."

"That is good," said BehLahk. He was running calculations of his own. There was a lot of vine out there. Dying off all at once...

They were going to be buried in it.

"Do you have options?" asked NehLoc.

"Not as yet. But I will." Much depended on the numbers they came up with.

BehLahk realized then what had brought NehLoc out to meet with him face to face. He was looking for something more positive than what the report reflected. After all, BehLahk had written that the Veltahk was dying. That should have been nothing but good news. So why had BehLahk hedged his comments?

"Do not be overly concerned, NehLoc," said BehLahk. He smiled slyly. "Consider the abundance of nutrient-rich compost for our fields."

"Do not make light of this, BehLahk."

"Do not be so serious, NehLoc."

NehLoc gave a dark, dour look to BehLahk. "I do my job. I serve."

"Fine, fine," BehLahk droned. He had been right not to bring up his concern about potential impact to the ecosystem should the vine stretch out its death throes.

NehLoc was almost certain there was no doomsday device. Follow now the news that the vine would die out. From his perspective, Joseph Britton's schemes had failed utterly.

The Shylmahn were here to stay.

Why so glum?

True, the Shylmahn had changed much in their adaptation to this new world, but from what BehLahk knew of NehLoc, this had never been of real concern to him.

Ah... but of course.

If nothing else, Joseph's scheming had brought about a definite rethinking of the relationship between Shylmahn and Chehnon. BehLahk's own maneuverings had done much to help things along.

NehLoc had to be less than thrilled.

BehLahk on the other hand was quite pleased with the way things were going, all in all.

Joseph stepped out onto the front porch of his small, two bedroom house. The sky was clear and the sun was shining, but the early morning air had a definite winter chill. He zipped up his light jacket, then took the short walk down to the street and worked his way to Main Street.

The town of John's Park. The four lane bowling alley was gone. The cleared lot was being used to store materials recovered from a number of demolished buildings. The several dozen cars that had once been Tony's Used Cars had been towed away, the rusting hulks taken to the large, open field behind Fir Street, three blocks down the side street from the car lot. The field had become the town waste disposal site.

The restaurant had been the first of the Main Street buildings to be renovated. Many of the forty three residents of John's Park spent at least some of their morning there each day, sitting in one of the booths along the windowed wall or at the long counter, conversing about their plans for the day.

The sprawling building that had once held city hall, the police department and the town library had been restored. Next door, the variety store was now the community pantry.

The restoration of the movie house was progressing much more slowly. Most of the contents had been hauled away, a total loss. Work on the load-bearing walls was nearly complete, work on the roof and floors had just begun. Once finished, the old theater was to be the community meeting hall, but that was still a long ways off.

With Main Street cleaned up, the unrecoverable buildings demolished and those deemed salvageable at least in the first stages of restoration, there was an atmosphere of, if not normalcy, at least an appearance of comfort, even contentment.

Such appearance was misleading.

John's Park was not an open community. It wasn't even what the Shylmahn referred to as a reservation. The perimeter encircling the John's Park community was monitored by a network of guard probes. These probes were different than those monitoring the Seattle Reservation. These probes would respond with deadly force to any violation of the perimeter.

John's Park was a detention facility. Joseph Britton was its principal resident.

His presence here had been a condition of reestablishing the peace. It had been a difficult arrangement, the specific provisions hard-fought.

The choice of John's Park as the location of the community had been a negotiated compromise worked out between NehLoc and Joseph Britton himself.

Isolated, limited accessibility, and yet development potential.

The handful of survivors from Phoenix Labs, and a select few others from around the northwest, had been the only other Chehnon the Shylmahn insisted be brought to John's Park. It had come as a surprise to many that Carolyn Britton had not been among them.

She had certainly been on the original list for John's Park, second only to Joseph himself. It was only after several internal discussions among the Shylmahn leadership that it was decided Carolyn Britton would better serve the future by being allowed to reside in the closely monitored Seattle Reservation.

NehLoc had supported the concept of the Seattle Reservation and other similar large communities; further consolidation of the creatures into fewer and fewer centralized locations.

Joseph walked past the restaurant, giving only a casual wave to those inside, as he continued up the street. Passing the movie house, he could hear that someone was already hard at it. It would be at least another hour before work there began in earnest.

The door to the community pantry was standing open. Miriam was inside organizing stores, making preparations for the weekly arrival of supplies scheduled for delivery. The isolated community wasn't likely to be self-sufficient for a very long time, if ever.

A large parking lot at the far end of the town had become the shuttle landing pad. Reaching the lot, Joseph noted the two pallets of supplies, but the shuttle wasn't the one that made the weekly deliveries. EsJen stood at the foot of the ramp, hands clasped before her.

Joseph hesitated, then started across the lot. EsJen stepped away from the shuttle.

"EsJen," said Joseph tentatively. "This is a surprise."

"Hello, Joseph." EsJen's tone betrayed nothing. Her words were matter-of-fact. "It has been quite a long time."

Joseph indicated a row of benches bordering one side of the parking lot. They started toward them together. "To what do I owe this unexpected visit from my old friend?"

Friend, thought EsJen. That brought back memories in a flood.

That first meeting in the Chehnon neighborhood; their long conversations throughout their awkward, evolving relationship. That day she brought him out of that rundown campground only moments before his scheduled elimination.

The destruction of the island...

There was so very much history between her and this uniquely defiant Chehnon.

It took her a few moments to come back to the present. She turned about and sat down on one of the benches.

"Our world continues to change, Joseph."

Our world, Joseph thought bitterly. *Let it go.*

"I have a limited view of the world these days," said Joseph.

"You see more than most. You always have." EsJen shifted position on the bench, looked about them, glanced across the lot. Two Chehnon locals had arrived to load the delivered supplies onto a pull cart. They looked curiously in her direction as they worked.

She shifted again, looked straight ahead now as she spoke.

"You did not fail, Joseph Britton."

"Oh, I would argue otherwise."

EsJen chose her words carefully. It was difficult. She seldom spoke the Chehnon language these days. "The world is what it is, will be what it will become, because of you, and because of me. In the end, it may not be what either of us envisioned, but consider the evolution of the relationship between Shylmahn and Chehnon."

"Hard to see from my vantage point."

"I understand your bitterness," said EsJen, perhaps tiredly. She had a bit of that herself. "I have a few vision issues of my own."

Gee, that's tough, thought Joseph.

"What brings you here, EsJen?" he asked.

EsJen nodded thoughtfully. She again considered her words.

"We are here to stay, Joseph."

"Yeah. I get that. Hence the whole *failed* thing."

"No. That is not what I mean. What I'm trying to say... the new world, the world out there... it is of our making, yours and mine; born of choices yours and mine. It continues to change, to evolve. What it will eventually become, I cannot see. But do not doubt that our actions, the actions of Joseph Britton and EsJen, created it."

"I should think you would be happy with however it turns out," said Joseph. "The Shylmahn are here to stay. Isn't that what you wanted?"

"I do not believe the world we have created is a world for you or me."

"Why? Because you have to share the planet with Chehnon? It isn't like we're on equal footing."

"It is not that. It is not that at all. It is..." EsJen struggled again for the words. "Joseph... the world newly born has born its own children. The Chehnon to be are not Chehnon. The Shylmahn to be are not Shylmahn."

We are no longer Shylmahn...

"My friend Joseph," EsJen continued, her voice now soft. "The world of our creation is not for us. This new world does not need us. Our memories, our histories... they get in the way. Let the children of this new world follow the path to the future, wherever it may lead."

Joseph took a long, deep breath, giving himself a few seconds to process all that. He could see that EsJen had taken a difficult path of her own.

"There's not much choice, is there? Not really."

"There is always choice. You have taught me that."

"Ah." Joseph smiled. It was a rather sad smile. "So I did."

They sat quietly then, EsJen her back straight, hands in her lap; Joseph leaned forward, elbows on his knees, his hands clasped. They watched as this week's supplies were carted away.

The world grew very quiet.

end

Lightning Source UK Ltd.
Milton Keynes UK
UKHW041824040321
379813UK00001B/32